MA

The MAGI SAGA
Book 2

By
Andrew Dobell

The book is Copyright © to Andrew Dobell, Creative Edge Studios Ltd, 2019.
No part of this book may be reproduced without prior permission of the
copyright holder.

All locations, events, and characters within this book are either fictitious, or have
been fictionalised for the purposes of this book.

Welcome to the Magi Saga

This is book two of a long, sprawling adventure over several series of books.

This book has been through various editions, with this being the latest.

I hope you enjoy reading about the adventures of Amanda and the Magi, as much as I have enjoyed writing them.

Acknowledgements

For my Grandfather, who was a continual inspiration and support. I miss you, and this is for you.

Thank you to my wife and family for their love and tolerance and help. You make everything worthwhile.

Thank you to my old gaming friends, you guys have inspired this story more than you can know. I have some of the best memories from those hours sitting at the gaming table.

Thank you to my Editors Julie Hall, CP Bialois, and Hanna Elizabeth. Your input has been amazing, thank you.

Thank you to Vicki Blatchley for being my cover model.

Dedication
For my boys, my kids, I love you!

Language
I'm a British author living in Britain, and I write in British English with British spellings.   ;-)

Table of Contents

Welcome to the Magi Saga 2
Acknowledgements 2
Table of Contents 3
Booklist 4
Prologue 5
Chase 8
Arrival 19
Death Sentence 27
The Jade Palace 35
Reassigned 45
House Call 53
The Morning After 72
A New Player 85
Surveillance 92
Vendetta 101
Hostile Takeover 120
Bureaucracy 131
Antarctic Trek 142
Ritual 147
New Information 165
One Woman Army 177
Pit Fight 195
Taking stock 227
Epilogue 1 232
Epilogue 2 233
Author Note 235
Booklist 236

Booklist

For full list of Andrew Dobells Books, visit his website at;
www.andrewdobellauthor.co.uk/booklist

Prologue

Haiti

Dark stone walls echoed the chants sung by ten figures kneeling on the rough stone in the center of a cavern. They knelt around an elaborately drawn circle which consisted of three concentric rings marked by runes and symbols.

The ten males and females had their heads shaved, their exposed skin was covered in fresh scars, welts, and bruises. They wore only rags—the remnants of their clothes, ripped and ruined.

Held in a Magical embrace, helpless to resist, they sang in perfect unity, chanting their call into the void. They were merely puppets, controlled by Arch Master Nymira, the Voodoo Queen. Lucian's master and mentor.

Lucian and Nymira stood outside the circle in deep concentration, using their combined Magical strength to force their Magic into and through the Null Realm, pulling it, stretching it, and doing their best to weaken it between here and the Abyss.

They didn't do this very often, but Lucian always got a thrill from rituals such as these. He concentrated hard, using his power over Essentia to push at the powerful barrier.

All Magi knew it could never be broken. If Nymira couldn't pass through the Null Realm into the Abyss, then surely no one could.

Of course, there were rumours of Nomads who had made the Magnus Transitus, the Great Crossing, into the Abyss. Legends of skilled or powerful Magi who had found a way to pass into the Abyss and meet humanities once and future lords, but Lucian had never met any and frankly doubted the stories held any weight.

While it might be too strong to break, that didn't mean the Null Realm couldn't be thinned or weakened.

As Lucian and Nymira pushed and thinned the barrier, they could feel his approach. Lucian and Nymira opened their eyes at the same time, ready to receive him.

On the other side of the barrier, hidden from sight, but close and all about them, their ultimate master drew near. They could feel the massive power and weight of personality as something monstrous pushed back, forcing itself against the barrier that kept Archons from our world.

Lucian stared into the circle, watching intently as he felt the Archon's shadow pass over his mind. The power of this being felt immense, almost like he was being smothered by this vast but insubstantial thing.

Above the circle, floating in mid-air, appeared a speck of black mist. Slowly, it grew and stretched out, reaching for the floor, and up, filling the space inside the circle with a shape made from black smoke. Bigger than a man, it roiled about like some mad miniature storm.

Opposite him, Nymira gazed at the growing form of the Archon's Avatar with similar awe. As awesome as this was,

Lucian knew this wasn't actually the Archon they could see. It was merely an Avatar, a magical construct created by the Archon to communicate and interact with them.

Before him, the song of the kneeling supplicant changed pitch, becoming discordant and broken.

As they watched, out of the darkness at the centre of the amorphous form, a skull-like face appeared, glaring at them.

The heads of the ten kneeling supplicants burst, exploding like balloons under too much pressure, showering gore over Lucian and Nymira.

Lucian thought he might know a fraction of how these ten dead Riven might feel, as the weight of this Archon's presence settled about him.

"Speak", the thing said in a low, deep, rumbling voice like two huge boulders grinding together. The voice of the Archon felt like it penetrated everything. It felt like it went right into his brain, bypassing his ears entirely.

Lucian bowed his head to his ultimate master.

***

Later that night, Lucian sat outside on the roof of a building looking out over Haiti. He felt justified and righteous in his chosen path, knowing that powers such as the Archon Samael were behind them.

How the Arcadian Magi could ever hope to stand against them was beyond him. But they did, even in the face of such overwhelming odds.

Lucian was looking forward to getting back to New York City. He disliked leaving his Coven for too long, even to pay homage to his master Nymira. He knew some of those in his Coven were always looking for a weakness, something to use or take advantage of to wrest control away from him.

He would rather die than let that happen, but it was difficult to stop something when you weren't actually there to stop it.

Still, when Nymira called, he knew he had to answer. There was no way around it.

As part of the summons, Lucian had informed her of the various operations he had running, moving drugs from one place to another, often to well-connected dealers who could supply wide areas of the city. One such shipment happened to be travelling across France in the next few hours. With France being Legacy territory, he knew the risk of such an operation. The Legacy would be looking for Nomad activity, and if they had discovered Lucian's plan, it would put the operation in jeopardy.

Only time would tell.

Chase

The Legacy Mansion, France

"Let's burn some rubber!" whooped Xain.

Amanda twisted the handle of her modified Fire Blade motorbike, gunning the engine. She smiled at Xain's enthusiasm as the rear wheel on her bike spun, kicking up dust and smoke as it screamed for the open road.

"We're on the express elevator to Hell, going down," Amanda replied, quoting one of her favourite films as Xain's energy got her heart pumping. She let off the brake and the tyre gripped the concrete, shooting her forward towards the far wall of the underground garage only a few metres away. Pyrotechnics fizzled in her Aetheric sight, lighting up the room as Amanda barrelled through the Portal, followed closely by Xain.

After a second of dislocation and dizziness, Amanda shot out of the Portal, her bike bouncing and fishtailing as it hit the road on the other side. Holding on tight Amanda corrected the bike before giving it some power. They were heading toward a bridge on a slip road that passed over an elevated AutoRoute just ahead.

Taking a moment to absorb her surroundings, Amanda found herself under the open sky of western France near the Swiss border in an area surrounded by rocky hills and cliffs. The AutoRoute snaked through the landscape, alongside cliffs, through tunnels, and along elevated sections held high in the air by concrete pillars. The AutoRoute below wasn't too busy, but there were still enough people on the road that it could be a problem if things got really messy.

~The Nomads should be approaching your position now,~ Ekkehardt Möller informed them through the mental link that connected her and Xain to the others involved in the operation.

Amanda looked to her left at the oncoming traffic and spotted the Nomad coven right away. They were close and would pass under the road Amanda and Xain were on in the next few seconds.

~I see them,~ Amanda answered as they rode up onto the bridge.

The Nomad convoy consisted of several motorbikes that encircled a white van and a grey 4x4. Amanda thought she counted about five bikes of varying shapes and sizes. The whole group seemed to have little concern for the rules of the road, and as she watched, the bikes bullied a car out of the way, narrowly avoiding a crash before racing under the bridge.

~Moving to engage,~ Amanda stated, looking over at Xain. Although his face was hidden under the matte-black motorbike helmet, through her Aetheric Sight, she could see he was looking at her. She nodded. He nodded back, and they both headed for the side of the bridge. A swift working of Magic and the barrier on the right-hand side of the road became liquid. It splashed to the tarmac, where it fused solid, creating a small ramp in the gap big enough for a bike to fit through. Taking the lead, Amanda launched her bike through the opening, dropping from one elevated highway to the one below.

Amanda's bike bounced as it landed and settled onto the road. Xain landed right behind her.

"Whoop!" Xain yelled as he gunned his engine. ~Come on, Red, let's go to work.~

Moments later, they were gaining on the backmarkers of the Nomad coven.

~We're dealing with the civilian traffic. We'll try to make the road as clear as possible for you,~ Möller informed them.

Amanda glanced behind her and saw the civilian cars had started to back off as the Legacy Magi back in Paris began working their Magic. As she passed under an electronic sign, she noticed it had changed to a warning about a crash up ahead. Amanda smiled to herself and returned her focus to the Nomads in front of them.

~Incoming,~ called Möller over the link.

That's when Balor struck. Magically hidden from view, Amanda watched as an amorphous shape swooped down from above and slammed into the side of the rear-most biker. Balor, bike, and rider all disappeared over the side of the highway with a bang.

~That'll sting in the morning,~ Xain commented as he pulled his sword from its scabbard on his back.

As they approached the two rearmost bikers Amanda checked her Aegis and the other Magical effects she held ready for the fight. Amanda flipped up her visor as she came alongside her chosen target and smiled sweetly at him.

"Hi," she greeted him.

Confused, the biker glanced back to where his teammate had been moments before. Amanda swerved towards him and landed a sudden and fearsome punch across his face. Her Essentia-laced fist manifested as a web of golden fire that, for a second, passed through the head of the man. His bike wobbled as he tried to hold on, the front wheel weaving dangerously.

Closing the gap again, Amanda kicked out, her foot striking the front fork of the bike. Her enhanced kick was strong enough to buckle metal, and the bike went down, the front wheel bent sideways.

She watched as Xain's target tumbled from his bike seconds after hers.

Their attack had alerted the convoy to their presence. A man in the leading 4x4 barked orders from his window to the remaining two bikers who slowed and dropped back to Amanda and Xain.

~Orion is inbound,~ Möller said over the link.

Up ahead, in front of the convoy, a red 4x4 swerved wildly onto the road from an adjoining track before it righted itself. Amanda saw Orion lean out of the passenger window with a semi-automatic and open fire on the Nomad's off-road vehicle. The men in the Nomad's grey 4x4 leant out of their windows and returned fire.

Ahead, the last two bikers braked, brandishing guns.

Amanda re-checked her Aegis and dumped a little more Essentia into the shield. Better safe than sorry, she thought. She didn't fancy getting shot.

The biker closest to her fired while Amanda weaved her bike, doing her best to dodge the gunfire. Several hit home. They had been Magically enhanced, but they still ricocheted off her shield. Beside her, Xain used his sword, swiping it before him at blinding speed to knock the bullets from the air.

~Show off,~ she called to him through their link.

~Jealous, Red?~ he asked.

~Maybe. But I have a few tricks of my own," she laughed.

Amanda lifted her arm and lightning arced from her hand to the biker in front of her in a flash. The Magic crashed over his Aegis, not reaching her intended target, although, the force of the attack nearly threw him from his bike.

In front of them, the rear doors of the van flew open. Several men stood inside, holding semi-automatic machine guns.

~Heads up,~ Amanda called. The Nomad biker swerved sideways towards the central reservation, moving out of the firing line. Amanda followed as the shooters in the van opened fire, peppering the road around her with bullets.

Up ahead, a connecting service road joined the two sides of the carriageway. Smashing through the free-standing barriers, the Nomad biker swerved into oncoming traffic and into a tunnel with Amanda close behind him.

Three metres separated her from her target as she followed his weaving path through the traffic. Gunfire sprayed wildly from his weapon as he tried to shoot her. Bullets slammed into the nearby cars and ricocheted off of her Magical Force Shield.

Laughing as he accelerated, the Nomad barrelled through traffic that swerved erratically out of his way. As he went, he opened fire on the innocent drivers he passed.

Amanda knew she had to stop him before more people were hurt. She opened up the throttle and closed the distance between them. Concentrating hard, she summoned a knockout punch of Essentia into herself to destroy the Nomad's Aegis.

~How you doing, Red?~ Xain asked. ~Where are you?~

~I'm fine. I'm in the tunnel on the opposite side of the road. You'll see me shortly,~ she replied.

Seconds passed as she closed the gap on her target. The Nomad glanced back as Amanda blasted Essentia at his Aegis. It may have been a well-made shield, but he wasn't a powerful Magi, and the Aegis failed under the onslaught of Amanda's Magic.

The Nomad somehow managed to stay on his bike, bouncing off the side of a passing bus as he fought to stay on two wheels. Regaining control, he moved into a gap in the traffic. Raising his weapon, he tried to get a bead on her.

Wanting to end it before any more bystanders got hurt, Amanda conjured a solid metal bar in the spokes of his front wheel.

The bike flipped violently and slammed into the tunnel's ceiling, before crashing back down again. It came to rest a short distance ahead of Amanda, well away from other cars. Within seconds, she'd passed it on her way to the end of the tunnel.

As she emerged into the daylight, she crossed over another service ramp back onto the right side of the road just behind the convoy. Ahead of her, Xain approached the back of the van, standing on his bike's seat, using his sword to deflect the bullets the Nomads were shooting at him.

"Show off," she whispered to herself with a shake of her head.

Ahead of the van, the Nomads in the 4x4 were still in a firefight with Orion.

She glanced back into the tunnel they'd just come out of and saw a fire burning in the darkness on this side of the road, no doubt the other biker that had gone for Xain.

Looking ahead again, Amanda watched as Xain jumped from his bike to the van. He cut down one of the men with his sword as he landed. Instantly, he was up and fighting with the other two men in the back of the van as it weaved about.

~Balor inbound,~ Möller warned them, and Orion braked his 4x4, dropping back.

Balor dropped in from above like a rocket, hitting the Nomad's 4x4 from the top. It was instantly crushed as it exploded in a fireball. Metal and concrete flew in all directions as the elevated highway beneath them cracked from the force of the attack.

Balor stood up amidst the burning debris, spreading his bat wings like a ten-foot-tall stone-skinned demon rising from Hell, as the Nomad's van swerved violently to avoid the crash.

Its wheels caught. Xain jumped out, landing deftly on his feet as the van flipped sideways and then tumbled, rolling along the road. As it came to a rest, Xain moved around it to find the driver, the last man alive in the convoy.

Amanda braked hard and skidded sideways to a stop, breathing hard as she looked upon the wreckage.

Xain hauled the van driver out of the front of the vehicle and subdued him for later questioning with a burst of Magic. Just beyond them, Balor stepped out from the flames that had consumed the destroyed 4x4, his grey stone-like skin untouched by the raging fire. Orion stepped out of his 4x4, guns in both hands. He smiled and nodded. They'd won this one.

She registered a familiar Magical signature snap into existence a short distance away from her. Royston Kendrick, the current head of the Legacy Coven appeared nearby. He immediately started working his Magic to create a mirage around the scene that would hide its true nature from passing cars.

Amanda pulled her helmet off and shook her long, bright red hair free, letting it catch in the wind as she ran her fingers through it, rubbing her scalp. It always felt good to remove her lid after a bike ride. Kicking her bike-stand down and turning off the ignition, she dismounted the Fire Blade, her red custom leathers creaking as she moved. She hung her helmet on the handlebar of her bike and approached Royston, who had finished with his Magic and was looking over the spilt contents of the van. Kilos worth of cocaine and other drugs in tightly-wrapped clear plastic covered the ground.

These Nomads had been running drugs. Last week's target had been a lone serial killer. Next week's mission could be anything, but they were never very pleasant people.

"Congratulations. You did well today. You should be pleased," Royston began.

"A few more Nomads out of the picture is always worth it. Do ye know who they were?" Amanda asked as her breathing slowed.

"Drug runners with connections to Haitian Nomads. They won't be pleased about this."

"Will they know who did it?"

"I'm sure they'll take a wild guess. This is Legacy territory, and they should expect us to protect it." Royston turned to Amanda. "So, is it back to Gentle Water and Elizabeth for you now?"

"To be sure, once this is all cleared up."

"The clean-up crew will be here momentarily, head back with Xain and the others, we'll deal with this."

"Are ye sure? I don't mind mucking in."

"No, please, go ahead. You've got a lot on your plate right now. I'm surprised you joined in on this mission."

Amanda smiled. "The boys asked, and I agreed. I couldn't say no to them."

"Well, we're grateful."

"Thanks, Roy."

"Good luck with your move. Let us know if you need anything, won't you?"

"I will, and thanks. I'll see you around," she answered.

***

Royston watched her walk away towards Xain, Orion, Balor, and the waiting Portal. She had come a long way these past few months. Her Magical ability was advancing at an alarming rate, and Amanda was now a very active member of the Legacy Coven. This was only the latest of a string of missions she had taken on with the boys.

She'd proven herself to be a very competent Magus.

The naïve young girl that Gentle Water had taken on in Ireland was now a much more confident young woman, and Royston felt somewhat proud of her. He'd never had children of his own. Instead, he considered these young Magi to be his children, and he wondered if this might be how fatherhood felt. He took a deep breath and turned back to the mess awaiting him. There was a lot to clean up, and he knew the authorities would be on their way. But they'd done this a thousand times before, and no one would be the wiser.

***

In a darkened room of a Haitian garrison, the dreadlocked Nomad sank to one knee before his master. She turned slightly to look upon him, the bones draped about her ebony skin rattled as she moved.

Lucian did not relish reporting the loss of such a big shipment of drugs, but it had to be done. He would suffer the pain of her displeasure for it, but pain was fleeting and unimportant. What was important was that once it was over, he would find those responsible and flay the flesh from their bones.

"My Master, Baal Nymira, I have news for you…"

***

Amanda snapped into existence outside the gates to the Himalayan monastery that had been her home for the past several months. Gentle Water had brought her and Liz here to help with Liz's recovery after the events on the train.

Liz was doing well and seemed much better these days. She'd been enjoying learning Magic and could now talk about the events that had changed her life. She cried when she thought about it too much, but then, who wouldn't? That scar would be with her for the rest of her days.

The snow fell and the bitterly cold air pulled at Amanda's hair as she walked up to the gates that were guarded by two deceptively still stone temple dogs that sat on either side of the entrance to this hidden place. She stepped up to the door, took hold of the enormous metal ring that hung in the centre of it, and slammed it home. The boom of it echoed off the valley behind her as she waited for the doors to open. Even though it felt cold out here, Amanda's Magic kept her toasty and warm, immune to the effects of the biting wind.

Seconds later, the locks unbolted and the door swung wide to reveal a short, arched passageway and a square courtyard beyond where the snow fell lazily to the ground and blanketed the trees in the centre. On the opposite side of the courtyard, standing on the second-floor balcony, a monk looked down at Amanda as she entered. As Amanda stepped into the open, she felt the monk's gaze and looked up.

"Good morning, Little Phoenix," he said. "Welcome back."

"To be sure, it's good to be back," she answered.

"Go on through," he said gesturing to the door below, which also opened of its own accord like the main gates had.

She nodded and passed through the door he'd indicated and into another short passage, then on into the temple proper, where the scene changed dramatically.

The air here felt warmer and more comfortable, and no snow lay on the floor.

A coven of Magi-monks lived within the walls of this monastery and were supported by many mortals The residents lived a frugal life up here, away from the chaos of the modern world. In many ways, it was an idyllic life.

Gentle Water had been an apprentice here, and as she understood it, his master had been a Western woman called

Graceful Phoenix. So, as Gentle Water's new apprentice, the link as to why they called her Little Phoenix seemed clear.

The Red Temple sat high up on the slope of the mountain above the snow line, allowing the clouds to drift in below. Amanda often sat here and stared out at the view, taking in the vast awesomeness of the whole thing. But Amanda couldn't spend too much time on it today. They had a lot to do to be ready for their trip in a few days. Along with the ongoing mentoring that Gentle Water gave to Amanda, and Amanda, in turn, gave to Liz, Amanda never felt bored.

After spending a few hours with Liz training her in the Magical arts, Amanda sat with her apprentice on the edge of the communal area, their legs dangling over the side of the sheer drop.

Amanda leant back on her hands and closed her eyes, enjoying the warmth of the temple grounds, while Liz sat forward, her hands in her lap. They both wore casual clothing from their training session. Amanda's red hair fell loosely about her shoulders, while Liz kept her blonde tresses tied up in a ponytail.

Liz had suffered more than her fair share at the hands of the Nomads and Inquisition already, having lost her family and friends to them. Amanda hadn't known her before the events on the train over a year and a half ago, but these days, she seemed quiet and shy. Amanda had grown very fond of Liz. She thought of her like a little sister.

"So, the coven we'll be visiting in the States, they're called *Liberty's Children*?" Liz asked.

"To be sure, they're probably the most influential of the US covens."

"Are they on the Magi Council?"

"Victoria, the current leader of the Liberty's Children is, yes. Ye seem to be getting your head around the complexities of Magi society. Well done."

Liz smiled and nodded. "Getting there, I think. So, we're visiting the Liberty's Children House in a few days, right?" Liz asked.

"That's right. I'm looking forward to it. You?" Amanda smiled.

"Of course."

- The Red Monastery, Tibet.

Chodak smiled but kept his eyes shut and waited as he listened to the footsteps that approached and then stopped a few feet away from him. He heard the rustle of her clothes as she sat down next to him.

Confident she was settled, he opened his eyes and looked over at Graceful Phoenix.

"Welcome, it's been a long time."

"Too long," the woman answered.

"To what do I owe this visit?" he asked, although he thought he already knew the answer to that question.

"Amanda, she's gone?"

"She has."

"Then my memories were right. Tell me, how was she?"

The monk smiled. He'd expected Graceful Phoenix to visit now that Amanda had left the monastery.

"She's on the next leg of her journey. She's moving to New York."

Arrival

Washington DC

Amanda, Gentle Water, and Liz popped into existence inside a well-appointed room with plush, red carpet, wood panelling on the walls, and potted plants sitting in the corner. Amanda's immediate thought was that this room's express purpose was for anyone Porting in from outside. Her Magical senses lit up with powerful and extensive weavings of Essentia all around her. The building was well protected.

The double doors opened and a woman walked in. She had short hair and wore a business suit. She smiled at Amanda and her friends.

"Welcome, you must be Amanda-Jane Page," said the dark-haired lady.

"That I am, and this is Gentle Water and Elizabeth Fox." She shook the hand of the woman as she spoke, noticing that she didn't glow in her Aetheric Sight. So, she wasn't a Magus, just an Initiated Riven.

They'd all dressed up for this visit, wanting to make a good impression on the Americans. Amanda wore a pantsuit with a jacket, white blouse, and slacks over strappy heels. Gentle Water sported chino's and a white shirt, while Liz opted for a long dark skirt and grey jumper.

"Hi," Liz greeted the woman, giving her a quick wave. Gentle Water nodded in his typically stoic way.

"You may call me Miss Evans. I am to take you straight through to Victoria. She's expecting you".

"Of course, lead the way."

They walked briskly from the room, crossing through a powerful Aegis as they did so, and down a corridor, passing offices and meeting rooms as they went. All around them people were going about their business. It looked like a government building, but Amanda could feel the Magic here.

The Liberty's Children Coven was one of the three biggest covens in America, and the only one that had a seat on the Magi Council. Their status was clearly on show within the confines of this building which sat in the heart of Washington DC.

After a short walk, they turned through another set of double doors into a waiting room. A secretary sat behind a desk, while comfortable-looking chairs waited on either side of the room. Their guide motioned for them to wait while she approached the secretary, allowing Amanda to get a look around.

The only other people in the room were three young women, all of them Magi, judging from their glow in her Aetheric Sight. Surprisingly, Amanda recognised one of them as a Hollywood celebrity named Melissa Gemelle-Rowe, who she'd seen in several films over the years. Amanda was shocked that someone with such a high profile could be a Magi and couldn't help but stare for a moment.

Melissa sat with another blonde, both of them comforting a dark-haired girl who seemed upset over something. Melissa looked up, her face blank as she gazed at Amanda and her companions before returning her attention to her friends.

"She's ready to see you. Come with me," Miss Evans said, returning from the secretary's desk.

She led Amanda and her friends through the waiting room towards the large double doors at the far end of the room.

As they walked, Liz moved closer to Amanda and whispered, "Was that?"

"I think so," Amanda whispered back.

"Wow, a movie star and a Magus?"

"I know, it seems like it could never work, but, maybe it does."

"I'd love to get her autograph, but I don't think now is a good time."

"I'm sure you'll get to meet her. Here we go…"

The group followed Miss Evans into a large, plush office where a confident-looking woman with long dark hair sat at an oak desk. She stood and smiled, straightening her tailored jacket and smoothing her skirt as she did so.

"Amanda, so nice to meet you finally. I'm Victoria." She stepped out from behind her desk and shook Amanda's hand warmly. "And this must be Elizabeth. Welcome to DC."

"Call me, Liz." She smiled.

"Of course, welcome. And Gentle Water, so nice to see you again. It's been a while. How's Legacy these days?"

"We are well, thank you. Royston sends his regards."

"And I send him mine. Come in, come in, take a seat, please." She guided them to the chairs in front of her desk before returning to hers on the other side. "I must say, although I admire what you're doing, I do think it's folly. New York is not a place for Arcadians like us. It's dangerous. Lucian rules it with an iron fist."

"That may be so," Amanda answered, having expected this, "but it's my home and I simply could not live with myself if I didn't at least try to make a life there. Besides, I have a good feeling about it."

Amanda had quickly come to the conclusion that she wanted to live in Manhattan after the events on the train. She loved Paris, and Tibet was beautiful, but none of them really felt like home. She loved Ireland as well, and would always have a strong connection to Donegal, but after growing up there, she needed to be somewhere else, and only one place felt right.

New York.

There was just something about it. She just knew she needed to be there, that it was home. Maria had told her about Lucian months ago, and when she'd told Gentle Water, she'd expected resistance. She'd expected him to say it was suicide, but he hadn't.

He warned her. He made sure she was in no doubt of the risks of trying to set up a coven in a Nomad city, but he didn't try to stop her. In fact, he supported her from day one, as did Royston. They seemed to just accept that this was where she needed to be.

Amanda wasn't stupid, nor was she suicidal. So, there had been a lot of preparation in regards to security and secrecy, but she was under no illusions when it came to that. She knew that Lucian probably had spies and informants in the ranks of the Arcadians. He might already know of her plans and come knocking on her door one day. But Amanda hated bullies and had a healthy disrespect for authority figures. Lucian seemed very much like a bully to her, which made her all the more determined.

Besides, she'd fought and bested a couple of Nomads on her missions with Xain and Orion. True, none of them were of Lucian's skill when it came to Magic, but then, life in general could be dangerous, and you never got anywhere without taking a few risks.

"Good feeling or not, he won't hesitate to kill you. All of you." Victoria looked pointedly at all three of them. "But we've been through this before, haven't we? And I know there's no dissuading you."

Amanda nodded. They had spoken many times leading up to this day, with Victoria always trying to persuade Amanda to change her mind. But Amanda was certain that this was what she wanted to do.

"Has no one else objected to me moving to New York?" Amanda asked.

"Yes. They all think you're a dead woman walking. Sure, if you were setting up a Legacy outpost in Texas or somewhere in the Midwest, they might put up a fight, but not New York. They don't think you'll last a week."

Amanda half-smiled. Maybe they were right. Maybe she would be dead in a few days, but deep down, she knew this was the right thing to do.

"If you need anything, you can call me anytime," Victoria offered. "I'm not sure how much I can do for you in New York, and you know how slow things move when Magi politics comes into play, but I will do whatever I can."

"Why haven't you ever tried to take New York back?"

"Oh, we have, but Lucian has the backing of the Arch Magus, Nymira in Haiti. So whenever we've tried, I mean seriously tried, things have always turned ugly when Nymira arrives."

"I see, no bother then."

"Look, I can give you some help. I've mentioned before, that there's an Arcadian Magi that has lived in New York beneath Lucian's radar for several years now."

"Yeah?"

"Well, he's waiting at your house in Manhattan as we speak. He'll be able to help you settle in."

"That's awfully generous, thank you."

"No problem. My pleasure. So you're heading straight there?"

"That's the plan."

"Okay, very well. Miss Evans will take you to the Portal." Victoria stood and smiled warmly, although Amanda detected a hint of sadness in her eyes, as though she were saying goodbye forever. She offered her hand. "Good luck."

Amanda took the proffered hand in both of hers. "I'll be fine, trust me."

***

The air snapped and the trio appeared in a partially furnished room. The mid-sized room had been carpeted and decorated, and the power was on judging from the light just above them, but other than that, the room sat empty.

"We're here, in *my* house!" Amanda said, excitement making her voice squeak as she smiled from ear to ear.

"*Hai*. Yes, you are," said a male voice with a Japanese accent that she didn't recognise. A well-built, broad-shouldered, tall Japanese man walked into the room. "I'm Yoh, welcome to New York."

Liz ran to the window and looked out into the street. "Wow!" she gasped as she took in the view before charging off through the house.

Amanda walked over to Yoh and offered her hand. "I'm Amanda, lovely to meet you. Victoria told me all about you."

"Not everything, I hope. Your things have arrived from Paris, by the way. They're in the other room." Yoh shook her hand and gave her a quick, shallow bow in return.

"That's great, thank you." She smiled at Yoh, warmth spreading down her temples and a sense of shyness passing over her. He was handsome and tall. She quite liked the look of him.

"May I have my hand back, please?" he said.

"Ah, sorry," she answered, letting go of his large hand. He had a good firm grip.

"Nice to meet you," said Gentle Water, stepping forward and bowing. Yoh answered in kind, before Gentle Water excused himself, smiling at Amanda as he left the room.

Amanda caught the smile and opened the Link between them. ~Don't give me that look.~ Gentle Water didn't answer as he walked out of sight, still smiling.

"I'll be in the kitchen," Yoh said. "Have a look around and see what you think of the place. I know you haven't actually seen it in person before. We'll head out soon."

"No bother, I've been looking forward to this."

Amanda practically bounced out of the room to explore her new home. The place was a large Brownstone on the corner of an intersection. It had a basement and three floors above that, plus a roof terrace. The place was big, and Amanda knew she had to have it the moment she saw it for sale. And now that she was here, she loved it. She'd already chosen her bedroom on the first floor and was looking forward to her first night in her new home.

Gentle Water had retreated to the roof terrace, where Amanda eventually found him meditating.

She left him be and walked to the railing and looked out over the city. That familiar skyline sang to her heart and filled her with a sense of belonging. Yes, she was home. Finally.

***

Gentle Water opened one eye and looked over at Amanda. She stood at the railing, drinking in the view and taking in a deep breath of New York's air. She seemed happy—very happy—and that made this risky move feel just a touch easier. New York, for Arcadian Magi, was dangerous. This, to his mind, was a slightly foolish move, but according to those in the coven who knew better, it was the right move. He trusted their council and reluctantly agreed to support Amanda in this.

Only time would tell, he supposed.

***

Two floors below, Liz sat on her bed and looked at her newly rearranged room. She felt happy with it, for now at least. Her gaze returned to the large window that looked out onto New York's awe-inspiring streets, and as she watched the hustle and bustle, her mind wandered. She wondered what Fran, Ben, and Stephan would have thought about all this. She thought about them often and missed her family and friends dearly. It got easier every day, and Mandy helped as much as she could, but she knew it was something, that ultimately, she had to get through herself.

If only they could see me now. See how far I've come.

They would be amazed at what she could do now and where she'd been. She wiped a single tear from her cheek, took a deep breath, and turned her attention to the suitcase on the floor beside her bed. She had a lot of unpacking to do.

- Columbia.

Diego Alverez passed the envelope to the man standing on the other side of his ornate oak desk with its gold-plated pens and priceless ornaments. The paper envelope bulged with cash that threatened the seams.

"Make sure this reaches Governor Diaz tonight. The address is on the letter. Go."

The man left the room as quick as he could, no doubt thankful to be out of Diego's presence. The last man to skim off the top of a bribe was dead, his head sitting on Diego's desk as a reminder of who was in charge.

"Clean that up," he said to the two other men in the room, pointing to the head and then the corpse on the floor.

A short time later, Diego entered his private office and froze upon seeing the figure standing on the other side of the room.

The man wore combat trousers and looked like a scruffy Jamaican, but Diego knew him to be a Voodoo Priest. He'd seen the curses this man could cast. Immediately on recognising him, Diego dropped to his knees.

"Master Deon, I had no idea you were here, had I known…"

"Quiet. Tell me, has the bribe been made? What about the sacrifices?"

***

Deon stood before Marcus, head bowed in deference to his superior. A short distance away, Nymira was talking with other members of Marcus' coven, one of Nymira's inner circle of covens in central America.

"Speak, Deon mon, we don't have all day," Marcus snapped.

"Baal Marcus, of course. The sacrifices are being made ready. They will be delivered in a few days. The bribe is on its way to the Governor, we have some new FBI agents under our control, and the assassins are in place and ready to take out the cartel leaders if needed. The drug war will continue unabated, you have my word."

Death Sentence

The Pit Club, Manhattan

"What you plan on doing now, mon?" Ekua asked, the contempt clear in his Jamaican-accented voice.

Lucian sat at the head of the large, wooden, oval table, the padded office chair he sat in creaking slightly as he shifted his position. He leant back, feigning a relaxed attitude as he eyed his coven mate through the haze of cannabis smoke that hung in the air. Ekua leant forward, arms on the table, hands clasped as he stared at Lucian. Ekua's bright eyes bore into him, waiting for his answer, and for a sign of weakness.

No love was lost between them, and it had been that way since Lucian had taken control of this coven many years ago.

Lucian's gaze passed over the faces of the other members of the Harbingers of Darkness Coven as they waited for his answer.

"If you're thinkin' I'm gonna just roll over for these Legacy fucks, Ekua, you couldn't be more wrong. We're following up on some leads to get some local help. The delivery will happen, don't you worry." Lucian added some sarcasm into those last few words, annoyed at Ekua's latest barb. "So, any other business?"

The dimly lit room had only one light right above the table that seeped through the mist and haze, lighting the seven other people with an ominous glow.

Next to him on either side sat his two most loyal supporters, Raal and Lex. Raal sat to his right, his black robes almost disappearing in the gloom, his arms crossed, his tattooed face neutral. He rarely spoke at these meetings, preferring to listen and watch.

Lex, to his left, sat forward, listening intently to everything that happened. As usual, her large leather-bound journal sat open in front of her, its pages covered in her handwriting. She often took notes or referred back to it during these meetings. Whereas Raal played the role of the strong silent type, Lex took a far more active part, speaking often and making sure the meeting didn't move off-topic.

Tattooed from head to toe in runic script, even over her face, Lex certainly made an impression. She lifted her head to look over the faces of the other coven members who sat at the table, waiting to see if anyone would speak. Beyond Ekua, sat Bull, Noah, and Shaun, all of whom shook their heads or made gestures to indicate they had nothing further to say.

Bull wasn't terribly bright anyway and rarely said much at their meetings unless it related to his pack of rabid Scion dogs down in the basement. Shaun and Noah, both of whom were Scions, also preferred to remain silent.

Sitting between Lex and Shaun, Aneurin seemed to be ignoring Lucian's question and was reading something on the glowing screen of his tablet. Lucian looked at him for a moment, waiting to see if he had anything to add.

Aneurin couldn't have been more different to Raal or Ekua, being relatively small and thin-looking, but Aneurin's strengths lay in other areas, rather than in his fighting ability.

Lucian waited a few more seconds, but with no motion from Aneurin, he took a breath and went to speak.

Only to be silenced by a raised finger from Aneurin. Lucian paused and waited until his coven mate looked up, a look of slight concern on his face.

Lucian scowled at Aneurin. He did not like being silenced like that, and the moment Aneurin looked up, he knew he'd made an error.

"Apologies, Baal Lucian," he said meekly, "but I believe you will be interested in this."

"Go on," Lucian urged, withholding judgement until he knew why Aneurin had been so presumptuous.

"I've just had word from Washington, it seems that we have Arcadian visitors in Manhattan. Three Magi have moved from Europe to New York, intending to settle here in the city."

Lucian raised his eyebrows and promptly forgot the momentary loss of respect that Aneurin had displayed a few seconds before.

It had been a while since the last Arcadian had tried to move into the city, and after he and Nymira had made an example of the previous lot, he had hoped that there would be no further attempts for a while.

New York had been Nomad territory since he'd been an apprentice, and now that he had risen to the head of the Nomad coven in this city, he had worked hard to solidify that position.

Arcadians, he thought with disgust, it made him sick to think of their sentimental love for the Riven masses of the world. One day, the Archons would teach them the true meaning of their birthright as Magi, the ultimate masters of humanity.

In the meantime, though, he would need to bring that lesson to them himself, and it sounded like his latest students had just arrived in New York.

"And who are the lucky Magi this time?" he asked.

"Their names are Amanda-Jane Page," Aneurin began.

"Hah, sounds like some hippy *bouzen obeah* girl to me, mon." Lucian scoffed.

"Indeed, Baal. Then there's Elizabeth Fox and Gentle Water," Aneurin finished.

"Gentle Water? I've heard of that fuck. He's a Legacy Magus, right?"

"I believe so, yes," Aneurin replied.

"Fuck. They think they can walk in here, into my city like I'm some kind of *qwenga*? Find out where they are. It's time I teach them a lesson."

"Like you have with Yoh?" Ekua asked.

"Fuck you," said Lucian as he stood up, not even looking at his coven mate.

Ekua knew that Yoh had been a constant source of frustration for him, as the one Arcadian Magi that had evaded

Lucian's justice in New York. But he had grown used to Ekua's snide remarks about Yoh. Ekua couldn't find Yoh, either, so he no room to talk.

"I'll be in my quarters contacting our master. As soon as you know more about them and where they are, I want to know."

Lucian watched Ekua sit back in his chair and smile to himself. Lucian didn't need to read his mind to know what his coven mate must be thinking. Lucian knew that if Ekua ran this coven, he would be contacting their master, Nymira, with this news as well. Ekua no doubt believed that Lucian was about to run crying to his mommy, but the fact that Ekua never voiced this opinion spoke volumes. Ekua knew that was very thin ice.

Lucian ignored the hidden criticism from Ekua. One day, the time would come, and he would get his just deserts as well.

In the meantime, he knew what he needed to do and left the room as the meeting broke up. Striding along the dim corridor, he passed through a set of double doors and into his apartment.

Lucian preferred a minimalist, open-plan look to his private quarters, with modern furniture and muted colours, something that people found strange in a man like him.

Standing over six feet tall, Lucian had dark Jamaican skin with strongly defined features. His complexion had a slightly worn feel to it that spoke to the years of experience he had. Lucian appeared to be in his mid-thirties, wore his black hair in long dreads that spilled over his shoulders and down his back. Jewellery and trinkets attached to his dreads caught the light as he moved while his dark sleeveless coat and trousers stood in stark contrast to the décor of his home. He also wore a pair of black wraparound shades that he never seemed to be without, even in the dark.

Closing the door behind him, he took one step into the room before realising he wasn't alone.

He froze, keeping still and silent, weighing up the feeling and what he should do, while at the same time fuelling his Aegis with power.

"Don't bother," said a feminine voice from his seating area. "I came to talk, not to fight."

Lucian knew that voice anywhere. He relaxed slightly, but not too much. The last time they'd met, she'd ripped through his mind to find God knows what and caused all sorts of trouble in the process.

Stepping forward, he moved into view of the intruder.

If he survived this little meeting, then he'd count himself very lucky.

***

The entirety of The Pit Club had been built underground, even the top floor sat in the basement of a fairly empty and rundown tenement block, accessed from a door on street level.

Each public level beyond that had been named after one of the seven deadly sins. Starting with Sloth, as the first level under the tenement block, it held the entrance kiosk, security, and coat check before you descended into the club proper.

Then came Gluttony, where you found the club's first bar area, as well as the club's kitchens and dining area. Below that came Greed, where a small casino could be found. Next came Lust, where visitors could relax in one of the chill-out zones, get intimate in a private, cushioned alcove, or get a lap dance from one of the resident dancers. These first three main floors in the club had a rectangular shape, and at one end of this rectangle floor, a gallery surrounded a square opening of maybe fifteen meters across, where one could look out over the balcony and see down to the main dance floor, known as Wrath.

VIP visitors could then descend once more to Pride, where the small VIP dancefloor could be found, or go one more floor down to Envy, the VIP lounge and bar.

Wide, easy stairs linked all of the floors, and those who walked on them found they didn't tire as much as they might otherwise have done elsewhere while walking up seven flights of stairs. For the lazy, however, there were three pairs of lifts between Wrath and Gluttony.

Beneath the VIP lounge were the private areas used by the Harbingers Coven, including meeting rooms and private quarters for Lucian and each coven member. Passageways, staircases, and ladders led off deeper and wider into the network of hidden tunnels and spaces deep beneath New York from the coven's living area. Since the earliest settlers on Manhattan Island dark and dangerous things had made their homes here, deep underground. Scions and Magi and worse always followed the crowds, and Manhattan had been no different. As the city expanded and the subways were built, the hidden city beneath the streets grew.

Below the coven's main living areas, two individuals made their home. Bull lived inside the main complex of the club in dark rooms and passageways with his Scion dogs. Shaun, a coven member and Scion, kept his lair away from the club's main structure, preferring to have some separation from the coven he did a lot of work for. You could still walk between the club and Shaun's lair using access passages and subway tunnels, though.

Lucian only came down here occasionally, usually preferring to send Lex, unless the matter required his personal attention. Shaun had proved himself to be trustworthy so far and also very useful. Like Aneurin, Shaun had an affinity for technology, but Shaun's skills were far and above Aneurin's.

Shaun had always been a hacker, a malcontent who hated authority and government, but also something of a conspiracy theorist, and through his investigations into the shadows of the world, he came to the attention of his creator who turned him into the Scion he is today.

Lucian passed through a series of dark corridors barely lit in places. Water dripped and pooled on the floor. While rats and insects skittered and crawled in the dark silence of this subterranean world.

But Lucian didn't need eyes to see down here, his Magic showed him everything he needed to see, even through the ever-present shades that he wore everywhere.

After a few minutes, he reached a thick iron door, pitted and rusted like something from a World War II submarine.

Lucian's Magic turned the wheel in the centre of the door and it spun easily and clanged as the bolts slid home. With a metallic squeal, the door swung open, spilling light into the darkness of the corridor Lucian stood in.

Warm electric bulbs glowed inside, throwing splashes of orange light and cooler shadows all around the large room.

Shaun lived in a forgotten subway access platform, complete with a section of curved track opposite the door where Lucian stood, with an old, rusted train car sitting next to the platform, ready to disappear into the darkness of the tunnel ahead.

Between the train and Lucian, on the platform itself, sat Shaun's living area. To Lucian's left were tables and notice boards pinned to the walls where monitors and computer towers sat amongst snaking cables humming away to themselves.

To the right were three beds, a kitchenette, and other detritus of life. Shaun lived here with two initiated humans, Gary and Vanessa, who helped Shaun with his work for Lucian.

All three of the occupants sat in front of the computers on the left. Gary and Vanessa were both tapping and clicking away on their respective workstations, while Shaun sat back in his chair, deep in thought, his eyes on the door to see who would be coming to visit.

Shaun had been one of the less lucky Scions. The change into a creature of the night had deformed him, giving him a waxy pallor, warts, and a ridge of bone that started in the middle of his forehead and passed over the top of his head all the way down his back. He also didn't have any hair whatsoever.

On seeing Lucian, Shaun raised his eyebrow ridges a fraction then quickly recovered. Lucian caught the tiny movement, giving away Shaun's surprise at his visit.

Lucian stepped through the doorway into the room and moved across the platform towards the front of the train car, beckoning Shaun to follow with a slight movement of his head.

"Hey, back to work," Shaun told his assistants who had stopped working and were staring at their visitor. They both quickly returned to their computers as Shaun stood and moved to follow Lucian, eventually, coming to a stop next to him at the platform's edge.

"What can I do for you, sir?" asked Shaun.

In hushed tones Lucian said, "I have a job for you, Shaun. Something you need to keep between you, me, and your assistants. No one else is to know for now. You feel me?"

"Of course, sir, what can I do for you?" Shaun asked, curiosity narrowing his gaze.

"It's a surveillance job, nothing too strenuous." Lucian passed Shaun a manila folder. "Everything you need is in there. You need to find them, inform me the moment you discover where they are, and monitor them; that's all. I'll give you further instructions later."

Shaun nodded at Lucian.

"Thank you. I'll get right on it."

- Chat between Blind Eagle and Chronos on the DWeb Message Boards.

Chronos: Thanks for responding. You have access to the Liberty's Children Mainframe?

Blind Eagle: I do. What's the pay?

Chronos: Cash or info, your choice.

Blind Eagle: Cash, $10,000, upfront.

Chronos: No deal. $2,000 upfront, balance on delivery.

Blind Eagle: Deal.

Chronos: Payment details?

…

- Redacted –

…

Blind Eagle: Got it, thanks. What do you want to know?

Chronos: You had a visitor to the coven house recently. Goes by the name of Amanda-Jane Page. We need anything the Liberty's Children have on her.

Blind Eagle: I'll see what I can find. I'll message you later.

The Jade Palace

New York

Amanda bounced down the stairs to where Yoh waited for her near the front door. She pulled on a light jacket over her strappy white vest top as she descended, pulling her hair out from the back of the jacket so that it spilled over her shoulders.

"So, we're ready, then?" she asked, smiling.

"Just about." He smiled back. She liked his smile. His whole face lit up when he smiled, which he didn't seem to do a lot of, but she loved it when he did. She thought he looked really rather handsome, especially when he was happy.

"What about GW and Liz?" she asked.

"We're here," said Gentle Water from behind her. She turned to see him and Liz walking into the hallway, both wearing coats, ready for the outside air of New York in May.

It wasn't usually freezing in May, but there had been a bit of a turn in the weather these past few days. Not that the cold really bothered any of them, their Magic took care of that, but it would look odd for them to walk about in summer clothes when everyone else was dressed for the weather.

"Excellent. So, we're ready? Let's head on out!" Amanda said.

"Are we walking all the way there?" asked Liz.

"Just so you can start to get your bearings, yes," Yoh replied. "But we won't walk out your front door. We'll Port to the other side of the junction, just as a precaution."

"Do you think someone's watching this place?" Liz asked, concerned.

"I'd say that's unlikely, but when it comes to the Nomads, and Lucian-kun in particular, it pays to be careful," Yoh replied.

"To be sure. Where were you thinking?" Amanda asked.

Amanda could feel the small working of Magic that stirred from Yoh and reached out to her and the others.

"Would you be happy to link with me?" Yoh asked.

They all answered in the affirmative and a couple of seconds later, they had a real-time view of an alleyway on the other side of the junction in their mind's eye that Yoh had shared with them. He'd been psychically checking the area out to make sure it remained empty.

"Shall we?" Yoh asked.

Liz had not yet reached a level of Magical ability that allowed her to teleport, so it would be down to Gentle Water to take her, as he was currently the only one of them that could Port other people, as well as himself.

Amanda often marvelled at the things she could do now, from throwing lightning bolts or fireballs, to teleportation, mind reading, and conjuration. All things that seemed relatively normal to her now, but just a year or two ago would have seemed really freaky. The world was a strange place and appeared to be getting weirder every day.

Amanda nodded, Gentle Water took Liz's hand, and all four of them disappeared from the hallway.

At the same instant, they appeared in the alleyway on the other side of the four-way junction. The sounds and smells of the city filled their senses and the noise felt overwhelming for a moment, compared to the silence of the house.

Amanda looked about her. They had all Ported safely over and stood in a passageway between two buildings with refuse bags and huge bins on casters.

They were a short walk from the street where people went about their business, but no one had noticed them.

"This way," Yoh directed them, leading them out.

At the end of the alleyway, Amanda spied her house on the other side of the street, a short distance up the road and felt a swelling of pride for her new home.

Soon, they were on their way and following Yoh along the sidewalk, walking the handful of blocks to Yoh's place, which she knew he called The Jade Palace. This, according to Yoh, functioned as a restaurant, spa, and gym, as well as a living space for Yoh and another Magi, named Stella.

Yoh walked beside Gentle Water, talking casually, with Yoh doing most of the speaking

Behind the two men, Amanda walked beside Liz, who had taken hold of Amanda's arm and stayed close. She looked around, her eyes as big as saucers, her jaw slack in apparent awe of the city, something Amanda could relate to from the time she lived here before becoming a Magus. New York always left an impression on new visitors.

While Liz took in the sights of the city all around her, Amanda admired a different view, and despite trying to look elsewhere, she just couldn't help but enjoy the shape and form of Yoh's bum.

She couldn't see much of it beneath the suit he wore, but she could see just enough to hold her interest.

In the middle of wondering what Yoh might look like without his suit on, she realised that Liz had been speaking to her.

She tore her gaze away and looked over to the other side of the street, past the traffic, and gazed at nothing, anything, something. She didn't care what it was, she just didn't want to get caught staring at Yoh's arse.

But what an arse it was!

No, not again, she thought. This was scandalous. She needed to think of something other than having a firm hold of that rear with both hands while she lay beneath him …

"When do you think Lucian might turn up?"

Liz's question broke through her daydream, snapping her back to reality and away from the fantasy she'd been indulging in.

"Sorry, what?" she asked.

"Lucian, he's not appeared yet, but he must know we're here, surely."

Amanda furrowed her brow in response, glad for the distraction.

"I'd ideally like to think that he has no idea we're here, but I think realistically, he must know. He's a competent Nomad from everything I've heard. So, I would suspect there must be at least one informant within the Liberty's Coven House, probably more. We've been here, what? A few hours? I'd expect he'd know we were here by now."

"I don't feel very safe on these streets. I keep expecting to be jumped at any moment."

Amanda looked around at the people going about their daily lives, ignoring the Magi in their midst. Might there be an Initiated amongst them, secretly watching them, monitoring their movements, and reporting back to Lucian about where they were headed?

It was certainly possible, and the thought of that possibility darkened her mood a touch as they walked.

After a couple more blocks of uneventful walking, Yoh came to a stop beside a magazine kiosk on the sidewalk. He picked up a newspaper and pretended to look in it as he turned to his companions.

"The Jade Palace is on the other side of the street a short distance up, can you see it?" Yoh asked.

Amanda, Liz, and Gentle Water looked up the street to see the square-fronted, two-story, beige building with a sign out front proclaiming it The Jade Palace.

It looked big from what she could see and busy from the number of people sitting out front at the tables and chairs.

"Lovely," said Amanda. "Are we not walking in the front door?"

"No, too risky. We'll Port to the side entrance and go in that way," Yoh answered.

"Sure," Amanda replied and looked at her two companions who also agreed.

"*Hai*, when I say, follow me, don't hesitate."

Moments passed, and Amanda could sense the small working of Magic coming from Yoh, but only because he happened to be standing right next to her. She knew that he had shielded the Magic from casual detection, and anyone not right next to him wouldn't notice it.

Seconds passed, and after a moment more, he put down the magazine and set off.

"Follow me," he said as he turned.

Amanda followed Yoh into a nearby coffee shop and walked with him towards the back. The ambient Magic of the group worked in their favour, allowing them to slip sight-unseen through the shop and a door marked Staff Only at the back. A short walk along a corridor, past a breakroom where someone sat watching television, they finally passed through a rear door into another alley.

"More alleyways?" Amanda asked.

"Occupational hazard." Yoh shrugged and then sent the group details of the location of their next Port. "We'll be Porting here."

"Let's go, then. I'm not a massive fan of alleyways," Amanda said. New York alleyways reminded her of the attack a couple of years ago by the Scion, Horlack that had turned her into a Magus and killed her good friend Stuart, so the less time she spent in them, the better.

That said, she knew one day soon she would want to return to the site of the attack and try to make some kind of peace with it.

Seconds later, they stood close to the side entrance of what Amanda presumed to be The Jade Palace. Concentrating on her location, she knew exactly where she was in the city in relation to where she now stood and her house.

Looking about her, she couldn't sense any Magic at all. Yoh had done a great job of hiding the magical signature on the building that would give away his location to Lucian's coven.

"In we go," he urged as he opened the side door of The Jade Palace and ushered them in, a tiny flare of Magic the only sign that he'd passed through the building's hidden Aegis.

They all walked into a small entryway as Yoh closed the door behind them.

"Welcome to The Jade Palace. I'll give you the dime tour and introduce you to a couple of people as we go. Follow me."

Yoh proceeded to show the trio around the ground floor of the building, walking them through the softly lit corridors and showing them the spa area with its treatment rooms, small pool, jacuzzi, sauna, and more. Amanda loved the idea of spending a day here, making use of the facilities, something that Yoh made clear would always be open and free to them whenever they needed it.

After that, he walked them through the restaurant at the front of the building that seemed to be gearing up for the midday rush. The smells of cooking food made Amanda's tummy grumble. She would need to get something to eat soon.

Next, on the opposite side of a sparring area, he showed them the private members-only gym where several people were working out.

The building itself had a square footprint, with an open-air Japanese rock garden in the centre.

Yoh led them out through a glass door into the Zen garden with its winding paths, raked gravel areas, carefully arranged rocks, and pruned plants.

The whole building had an air of calm, relaxation about it, especially the garden, which seemed very serene.

Small water features burbled away as they admired the space around them.

Amanda noticed a beautiful, young, black woman with long silver hair stand up from a bench on the other side of the garden. She smiled at Yoh and approached the group carrying a leather folder in one hand. As she drew level with Yoh, they stopped and bowed to each other.

"I'd like you to meet Stella, my business partner and apprentice," he said. "To the best of my knowledge, we're the only two Magi who have ever managed to live here under Lucian's nose for so long."

"It's lovely to meet you all," Stella greeted them. "Yoh has told me all about you. You're very brave choosing to set up here in New York. I wish you all the luck in the world, but don't underestimate Lucian, he's a tricky character."

"Oh, to be sure, we won't, and thank you."

"A pleasure. I'll catch up with you soon, I have some work to do. Enjoy the tour."

With that, she walked away.

Yoh proceeded to show them the offices at the back of the building on the ground floor, before showing them through a locked door and up a staircase.

Upstairs, the Japanese style intensified, with dark lacquered woods and a minimalist look. Everything was in its place, clean and orderly.

Yoh showed them through a few rooms before leading them into a large library where the walls were lined with hundreds of books with a small seating area in the centre.

"Aah, Maya, there you are," he said walking over to a woman sitting in one of the chairs. She turned to greet him, and Amanda smiled, recognising the Vampire Scion from the Legacy House in Paris. She was a little surprised to see a familiar face here, but it had been a few weeks since Maya had last been in Paris.

Maya stood an inch or so shorter than Amanda. She had a slim build and ashen skin. Her long, dark hair fell in lustrous waves around her head, framing a distinguished face with dark eyes and ruby lips. She wore a long black figure-hugging dress and had the languid movements of someone supremely confident in herself. Amanda's Magical senses picked up on the lack of life signs within Maya's body. Her heart didn't beat, and she didn't seem to breathe other than to speak.

Yoh and Maya bowed to each other and then kissed cheeks with a smile. They were friends, but nothing more, Amanda guessed.

"Good morning. I see you've brought some friends with you," she said in her cultured accent with French undertones.

"*Hai*, this is..." Yoh began.

"...Amanda." Maya finished the sentence for him, smiling mischievously. "We've met."

"Oh," Yoh answered, surprised.

"I'm pleased you finally made it to New York. It's good to see you again."

"And you," Amanda replied. She liked Maya, even though their contact up to this point had been limited. But there was something else about her that she couldn't quite put her finger on. There was a feeling of familiarity with Maya. She felt comfortable around her, almost like she knew her from years ago somehow.

It was strange, but she didn't dwell on it.

"When did you arrive?" Maya asked.

"Today. We've only just got here, really. It's good. Feels like coming home."

"I'm glad," Maya replied.

"So, you know Yoh?"

Maya nodded. "I do. In fact, I live here, on Long Island."

"Oh, that's grand, so it is."

Maya smiled, enjoying the conversation. "Thanks. You'll have to visit me, sometime."

"We will."

"Excellent. Go on, I think Yoh wants to show you around the rest of the building. I'll see you soon."

"To be sure," Amanda answered, and followed Yoh and the others from the room, leaving Maya to her book.

The next room was huge, but warm and inviting and was clearly for one purpose only—training. It was Yoh's dojo. There were mats covered the floor, weapon racks where Japanese swords and other martial arts implements hung on the walls, and not too much else.

Amanda smiled, she liked this room.

Yoh walked over to a set of windows that overlooked the garden below. Sunlight streamed through them bathing Yoh in a golden light. Amanda couldn't help but stare, he just looked so handsome in that light.

She breathed in and sighed to herself, she liked him, a lot. But she also liked Raven. She liked them both, and then there was Maria.

She found her thoughts returning to the brunette more and more recently, after her advances at the museum. She couldn't help but notice Maria's glances at her when she visited Legacy House, and the knowing smiles.

There was something about her that she really quite liked, and yet, her interest in men hadn't diminished either.

She closed her eyes, not quite sure what she should do. She needed to think about it, but not right now.

"I respect your bravery in coming to New York, Amanda-san," Yoh said, without looking at them. "I'm not sure how wise it is, a move like this. As you know, this is Nomad territory, and Lucian has always been ruthless toward any Arcadian Magi who've come here. Few have lasted very long. I'll help you, support you, but ultimately it's up to you. If you want to remain here, you really only have two choices. You hide like I do, taking precautions and assuming that the slightest fuck up means you're dead or on the run, at least. Or you face him and try to stand up to him." Yoh turned to look at Amanda. "No one has succeeded at the second of those two choices yet."

Amanda nodded. "I understand. And for the time being, I'm happy to be careful and stay out of his way."

"I'm happy to hide, too," Liz said, nodding enthusiastically at Amanda.

Amanda smiled at her apprentice. "Don't worry, I have no intentions of looking for a fight."

Liz stepped closer and gave Amanda a hug.

Amanda looked at Gentle Water, who just nodded back at her.

"*Hai*, that's great!" Yoh said. "So, two things. Firstly," he looked at Liz, "I understand you're looking for a job, maybe?"

Liz looked at Amanda. "Um," Liz began. Amanda nodded to Liz, who then looked back at Yoh. "I am, yes," she answered.

"Great. Amanda told me, so I wondered if you might want to work here?"

"Really?" Liz asked, her whole expression changing from slightly confused, to elated and surprised.

"Really! There are a few things you could do. You can try everything from bartending to being Stella's assistant. See what fits. Sound good?" Yoh said.

"Yeah! That sounds great. Thank you."

"*Dō itashimashite*, my pleasure," said Yoh, before looking back at Amanda. "Secondly, I wondered if you might be up for a quick sparring match, *kohai*?" he asked indicating the floor mats in the room with an almost cheeky smile on his lips.

Amanda raised her eyebrows, surprised by his request.

"Don't worry, though, we can do this another time, doesn't need to be today," he said before Amanda could answer.

Amanda smiled, sensing the friendly challenge in his tone. "Oh, but it does, *senpai*," she quipped with an equally cheeky smile, and removed her jacket, shoes, and socks.

Yoh threw her some padded gloves. "Let's keep this friendly, shall we?"

"Not afraid of a few bruises, are ye?" she answered, backhanding them out of the air and onto the floor beside her.

"Not at all," he said with a smile as he removed his shoes and suit jacket.

"Good, then let's do this," she said, raising her fists.

- Online chat between Seraphim and Edge dated April 1st.

Seraphim: Interesting blog you have there. I think you're on to something.

Edge: Thanks.

Seraphim: I might be able to help you out if you're interested.

Edge: Sure. What do you have?

Seraphim: I know of a secret organisation that's linked to some of the events on your blog.

Edge: Which events?

Seraphim: The unexplained deaths of those people with no official records in South America. The Missing Boat in the Indian Ocean. The Artifact that was stolen from the museum in Dubai.

Edge: Really?

Seraphim: The organisation is known as the Syndicate. It's run by a man who doesn't exist and is known only as Mr Black, and I know why those events I just mentioned happened.

Reassigned

Syndicate Island

It felt like an age had passed since Angel had walked down these polished wood and marble corridors; a lifetime ago almost. And in some ways, it had been. The place seemed different, and yet the same. She knew the hallways and rooms well, and the majority of the same people were here. She nodded and said hello to those she knew as she passed them, feigning interest in their lives and work.

But things were indeed different now. That difference, though, she knew, was internal, not external.

The reasons for her to be here were now somewhat different. Before the events on the train, she had been investigating the Syndicate for her own ends. Becoming one of the Syndicate's trusted employees to get to the information that she wanted. But now... now, Angel reported to Yasmin. She was here at her behest, but for much the same reasons.

The Syndicate was hunting down artifacts, Magical artifacts, and so was Angel.

Before, Angel had her eye on one artifact that she knew they were looking for—the Lazarus Scroll. But now, under Yasmin's orders, her remit had widened to any artifact of significance.

She'd been away for a while now. As far as the Syndicate knew, she'd been following up leads and having a vacation, but this was far from the truth.

In reality, she had been on the trail of a book, an artifact of Magical power that would have been a useful thing for her to have, to say the least. It was a mission that culminated in a confrontation on a high-speed train through France with the Legacy Coven and members of the Inquisition.

Things had been going her way, as well. She outclassed the Magi who had been there, nearly killing the redhead. That was, until Yasmin showed up and showed her the error of her ways.

She had tried to escape from Yasmin, but her new mistress had made it clear on so many levels that she would not stand for any insubordination. The choice was simple. She either served Yasmin, and worked as a subordinate of hers, or she died.

Angel liked life. As much as it pained her to work for Yasmin, she knew she didn't have a choice.

She, of course, had gone back to Nephilim Industries, first. She had been away from her business for far too long, and she needed to make sure everything continued to run smoothly and that her coven continued their work.

She also needed to make sure none of them were making power plays to take over. Something that was always a very real risk within the ranks of the Nomads.

Her coven was ambitious and competent, but luckily for her, they were also incredibly busy running the business. Meaning, there had been little time for internal politics within the ranks of the coven itself.

So, on Angel's return to the head office, things were not too much different from when she'd last left them. Still, she made sure to make an impression on them, taking a few days to make her presence felt and ensure they each knew their place within the coven. She also made sure they had enough projects to keep them busy over the coming months.

Once she felt happy with things, only then did she leave her Milan office and contact the Syndicate, asking to be brought back in.

And here she was, in the air-conditioned halls of power within the Syndicate. After a few more steps, she reached her office and stepped inside. She reached over and placed her bag on the desk in front of her chair as she sensed and then heard someone approaching the office door behind her.

She adjusted her pose for maximum effect as her Magical senses looked behind her and saw Ian, one of the aids to the board step into the doorway, only to be greeted with a view of her rear as she bent over the desk. Her pert bum pointed right at him, her skirt riding up and showing almost too much.

It brought him up short and made her laugh inside to watch his reaction. He didn't know where to look. Well, he knew what he wanted to look at, but he also knew that he shouldn't.

He did look though, for a second or two, admiring the view before he coughed to announce his presence.

Angel looked over her shoulder at him in mock surprise. "Oh, hi, Ian. I didn't hear you come in," she said as she straightened up slowly, letting the moment last a little longer.

"Sorry for the intrusion, Angel. I heard you were back and needed to come see you. The Director wants to have a meeting with you."

Angel raised her eyebrows ever so slightly. That was quick, she thought, and unusual. She knew she would be assigned to something, and that meant a meeting, usually with the board though, rather than the Director himself.

She wondered if she should be concerned.

She'd spent a long time building trust within the Syndicate, however. They knew she had some Magical talent. Sure, she could hide it, cover her tracks and seem to be nothing more than a regular Riven human, but that would be hard work and would likely backfire at some point with all the Magi here. Instead, she downplayed her power, convincing everyone that she was little more than a mere apprentice, new to the Magical Arts, and in no way a threat.

Her Magical talent meant she climbed the ranks a little more quickly than she would have been able to otherwise, as well.

Ian Hammond was not a Magus, but like nearly everyone within the Syndicate, he was an Initiated. Although he had no magical power of his own, he knew it existed and knew of the shadow world all around him.

He also happened to be close to the inner circle of Mr Black's organisation, so she had seduced him with barely any Magic and brought him "on side", along with some other staff in the building. She needed leverage, and she needed to get it without arousing the suspicions of the Syndicate Magi.

She already had more than enough material to blackmail Ian and the others, but they always needed a reminder of just where they stood with her.

Angel turned and perched her bum on the edge of the desk.

"Come in, Ian. How have you been? Busy, I take it?"

Ian stepped inside and smiled at her.

"Yeah, I have, thanks. It's been fairly manic here…"

The door shut by itself behind him, startling him slightly. Angel just smiled at him. He knew she could use Magic, so he quickly recovered.

"The new mission has been taking up a lot of my time. The logistics of it are a nightmare."

"New mission?" Angel asked quizzically.

"Down at the South Pole, it's the Director's new project. Not sure of the exact details; it's on a need to know basis, of course."

"Of course," she purred. "Have you missed me, Ian?"

Ian nodded, flushing slightly as he did so.

Angel smiled and raised one leg up and placed her foot on the chair to her right, spreading her legs. Ian looked, he couldn't help it. She could sense his heart rate quicken. She could read his thoughts and knew what he wanted to do.

"Want a taste?" she asked. "I did promise you, and it's been a while, hasn't it?"

Ian nodded. "It has," he croaked, his mouth dry with anticipation.

Angel placed her hands on the desk behind her and closed her eyes.

"Don't keep me waiting then," she said.

Seconds later, she let out a moan of pleasure as he knelt down before her, his head between her legs.

***

It didn't take long.

Standing to one side of the room, she checked her makeup in the mirror as he sat on her sofa where she had left him, trousers round his ankles, head back, relaxed in satisfaction as his arousal dwindled.

"Wow," he said under his breath.

"I think you missed that, didn't you?" she teased.

"Did I ever."

"How's the wife?"

Ian raised his head and eyed her. The mention of his partner subtly changed the mood and reminded him of the hold she had over him.

"Fine," he answered shortly.

In the mirror she saw him stand, pull up his pants and straighten himself out.

"Um, okay, so you have your meeting scheduled for 11 am," he said, checking his watch.

She turned and pulled her blonde hair back into a bun as she approached him.

"I'm sorry I mentioned her."

He smiled back at her, but there was no humour there.

"Don't worry, it's fine."

She stepped in closer, put her hands on his hips, and looked at him over her glasses.

"Play your cards right, young man, and you'll get a lot more than a blow job from me soon." She reached around, grabbed a bum cheek in each hand and pulled him in. She leaned in, her lips close to his. Slowly, she licked his lips with her tongue, her eyes looking deep into his as she did it. She could feel him harden against her lower stomach as she teased him. She smiled and let go.

"Now, back to work, you," she said, opening the door to her office and guiding him out.

She shut the door and turned back to her office, feeling pleased with herself.

Ian was useful. He knew a lot of what happened at the highest levels and was trusted by the board. She had already used him to gently sway the policies and direction of the Syndicate to her favour, and no doubt she would do it again sometime. The secret recordings of their sexual encounters were useful insurance against him, as well.

She reached out then with her Magic and stopped the hidden camera from recording. Another session to add to the archive.

***

Angel knocked on the black lacquered door that led to one of the more secure meeting rooms in the building. She could see her reflection in the high polish of the wood.

She carried some files and her organiser, ready to take notes. She didn't need it, but it was a useful prop.

The door opened and a large Security Officer looked down at her.

"Yes?" he said.

"Angel, sir, reporting for the scheduled meeting."

"Let her in," said a female voice from inside. The man opened the door wider and let Angel pass.

In front of her stood a long table, one end of it pointed at the door she had just entered through. A laptop sat in front of the nearest empty chair. The screen was black with a small white stylised *S* in the centre.

One of the board members stood beside the table. Angel knew her as Roxane Carter, and slightly behind her stood Ian.

Ian smiled warmly just for a second as Angel entered. Roxane did not smile.

"Thank you for coming, Angel. Mr Black wishes to speak with you. Please, take a seat and when you're ready hit any key.

Angel nodded and sat in the chair that Roxane indicated in front of the laptop. She glanced up at Roxane, who watched her carefully. Angel didn't know much about her, beyond that she was an Initiated. Angel also knew she had some kind of artifact on her, something that hid her thoughts. She'd seen these before, most of the Initiated board members seemed to have access to them. Most carried them around at all times. It was a precaution against the Magi and Scions that worked within the Syndicate, and something Angel had come up against a few times now. It was another reason why she concentrated on the board's aids, such as Ian, who didn't have access to items like that.

She could overload the item, destroying its effect. It didn't seem all that powerful from what she could tell, but that was a risky thing to do and would likely be traced back to her eventually.

There was no need for such actions at this time anyway.

So, Angel settled herself into her seat and tapped one of the keys on the laptop.

The screen sprang into life and the face of an old man filled it.

"Aaah, Angel. Good to see you. I trust your sabbatical was a restful one?"

It was Mr Black. She'd never met him, but knew his face from photos. He lived on a large, custom, private jet that he rarely left, and which hardly ever landed. An old man of about ninety years, he apparently walked with a stick, but where his body might be weak, his mind was sharp and quick.

"It was, thank you, sir. I'm feeling refreshed and ready for work."

"Excellent. Then I have a job for you."

"It would be a pleasure, sir," Angel replied, her voice pleasant and calm, while her thoughts railed against working for these mortals.

"Great, good to hear it, Ms Alergeri. You will need to wrap up warm. You will be joining us on our latest project in Antarctica. We have found something in the ice and we need all our talented individuals down here to help us. Roxane has the details of your flight. We look forward to your company soon."

Angel looked up at Roxane and Ian. Ian looked unhappy at the turn of events, no doubt wondering when his next blow job would be. Roxane, however, seemed to take pleasure in the idea of Angel not being here for a while.

Although extreme temperatures were not much of an issue for Magi, Angel didn't really relish the idea of spending time at the South Pole, but maybe it would be worth it. If they were bringing all the Magi with them, maybe there would be something worthwhile down there.

She made a mental note to contact Yasmin about this latest turn of events.

- Greenwich Village

Ben opened the door to the apartment and looked inside.

"Clear," he said and waited for Shaun to walk in, followed by Vanessa. He couldn't resist a quick glance at her perfectly shaped behind in that tiny skirt. He sighed quietly to himself and closed the door behind him. He'd worked for Shaun for years now, and it had just been the pair of them for a long time. Shaun had brought Vanessa in months ago, and they chatted like friends, but secretly, he really fancied her. He'd never had much experience with women. He never felt that confident around them, preferring his online life and interacting with people on there as Chronos, his online name.

Blind Eagle, his contact within the Liberty's Children Coven had come through in fine form, giving them a time frame of when Amanda had bought her house. They then hacked the MLS database and narrowed the choices down to the most likely houses that suited the profile of Amanda and her two friends.

Then they hacked the security cameras around the properties and went through hours of footage until they had finally recognised someone.

Ben walked over to the windows and stood beside Shaun and Vanessa. From here, they looked over the top of several buildings towards a large brownstone on the far corner of a crossroads.

"That's it," said Ben. "That's her house."

House Call

New York

These first few days in New York had been great. Being back in the city that, in all honesty, she most associated with being her home gave her a feeling of peace and belonging that she had missed since she'd moved back to Ireland.

Even though Amanda had spent her earliest years in Ireland and she considered herself Irish in nationality, it never really seemed like home. The closest she got to that was the cottage in Donegal, which she still used. That little house and the area around it would always be special to her and carried with it a lot of memories, but it was always New York where she felt most at home

Over the past few days, she had been both sightseeing and unpacking. She saw no reason to really rush things. She planned to stay here for a long time. She would make this her home, Lucian be damned!

So far, at least, there had been no confrontation, no major drama. But she had been careful and believed she'd covered her tracks and remained hidden from casual investigation.

In short, she felt very confident here in her new home.

Anyway, it wasn't as if she was alone. Gentle Water and Liz lived with her full-time, and Yoh kept stopping by and checking on them, all of which helped to keep her feeling confident and safe.

Also, for the moment at least, she had another houseguest. Raven had come to see them and agreed to stay a few days to help with the unpacking and settling in.

It felt great to see him again, but it also made her feel a little confused. She liked both Raven and Yoh. She felt attracted to each of them and really didn't know for sure which one she liked the most.

Yoh was a beautiful man, tall and muscular, powerfully built, always well turned out with his styled hair and strong jawline. His kindness shone through everything he did, and he really couldn't do enough to help.

Raven had a very different feel and look to him. Raven had a thinner frame, wiry and tall, but very fit. He felt very rough and ready, an outdoorsman, practical and self-sufficient, and he didn't seem to care so much about his appearance. Raven had an equally kind temperament to Yoh, but with less of the ritual and social graces.

Both men appealed to her, but making a choice between the two of them would no doubt prove to be a very tough to do, and that was not even taking into account her confused feelings towards Maria, whom she'd spoken to on the phone and through their Mental Link several times already since arriving here.

For now, she just enjoyed the sight of the guys lifting boxes and furniture in her lounge and fantasising about which one she'd like to take to bed that night as she rummaged through the next box of ornaments at her feet.

They had been unpacking for a couple of hours, preferring to do it, for the most part, manually and refrain from using Magic to move the furniture about the room. The house had been full of laughter and good feeling the whole morning as they indulged in some light-hearted sarcasm and humour.

Amanda felt relaxed and utterly at home as they worked. Her cheeks had even started to ache from all the smiling. When the doorbell rang, she went immediately to answer it, just as she'd done several times already for visitors and deliveries.

She opened the door still with a smile on her face from the last silly joke, and as she looked over the three faces on her doorstep, she had a moment of disconnect between the house and her friends, and what she saw before her.

A stocky, powerful-looking black man with impressive dreadlocks, Caribbean style clothes, and black sunglasses stood there staring at her, not looking at all happy.

She knew immediately who this was. She had seen enough photos of him to recognise Lucian. To Lucian's right stood a swarthy bald man with tribalistic tattoos covering his whole head. He wore black robes that had an almost ninja-like feel to them. On Lucian's other side stood a pale woman with thick, voluminous robes of tan and terracotta that fell to the porch all about her. She also had tattoos, but in contrast to the bald man's bold, sweeping designs, hers were made from delicate script that covered every inch of her visible skin, even her face, and seemed to extend under her long, dark hair.

All three of them stood there in silence for a moment, looking at Amanda and past her into the house, having a good look at the parts of it they could see.

For what seemed like an age, Amanda just stood there and stared in shock.

Amanda knew they could have had spies in Liberty's Children Coven, but she still wondered how they could have found her.

She had been careful, not leaving through the front door and doing her best to cover her tracks. But in a matter of days, here stood Lucian, and judging from the Magical glow coming from inside all of them, two of his coven mates. They all sported personal Aegises and seemed ready for action.

Amanda took a slow step back and balled the fist of her free hand as she came to her senses and realised this could get messy very quickly. The house had defences, powerful Aegis effects that still seemed functional and would hinder their progress inside, but nothing cast on this house could hold off a powerful and determined Magus for long. Had they studied the house's defences? Did they know how powerful its Aegis was?

She suddenly had flashbacks to the train in France and the fight she had with the Nomad, Angel. Amanda had been outclassed and soundly beaten by her. That fight had scared Amanda and had been one of the reasons why they'd lived at the monastery in Tibet for a while, giving her a quiet place to concentrate on her fighting abilities and to learn more Magic.

She did not want to be outclassed again. But now she stood here, not three feet from another Nomad, someone who would likely be as powerful as Angel. Suddenly, the confidence she had in her skill with Magic diminished. Quite abruptly, she felt incredibly vulnerable as she realised Lucian would probably be able to overpower her and take what he wanted.

With the four of them stood in a silent standoff, Amanda took the time to pull in as much Essentia as she could. She channelled that energy into her Aegis, storing it for later use.

Studying the brightness of the glow from inside each of them, and the way they moved Essentia around themselves, Amanda tried to get an idea of their Magical skill. Unsurprisingly, Lucian looked to have the most ability with shaping Essentia, and would likely be the most potent Magi out of the three.

Only a few seconds had passed, but already she heard the sounds in the next room change and then stop, followed by a subtle stirring of Essentia. The silence stretched out as the seconds passed.

Confusion blossomed in Amanda's mind. She'd been preparing herself for a fight which she assumed would be inevitable and that she would likely lose. All the stories about Lucian and how he dealt with Arcadians on his patch agreed that he was ruthless, with no quarter given. You either left before he found you or you died.

But this felt different.

He seemed to be holding himself back. She got the feeling that he wanted to attack and kill her where she stood, but for whatever reason, something stopped him. Could it be the Aegis on the house that gave him pause? Possibly, but she doubted it.

Cocking her head slightly at this strange turn of events, she relaxed her stance, growing more curious.

"So... um, Lucian, I presume?" she asked, keeping her tone light.

Lucian took a deep breath and blew it out through his nose.

"*Bouzin*, you gonna leave New York now, *irie*? This be your only warning. New York is mine!"

"Whoa, hold on a moment. Don't get me wrong, it's awfully nice of you to stop by and say hi, but I've just moved here. What makes you think I'm just going to up and leave?" she asked, putting on some false bravado.

"Cos, *bouzin*, if you don't do this ting, me posse gonna fuck up all your friends. That little blonde friend of yours, she'll do nicely as a plaything for da boys."

Inside, Amanda's heart raced, her thoughts were a mess as they sped through her mind like lightning as he threatened her and her friends. She still felt scared and vulnerable standing there, and the talk of him raping Liz started to make her blood boil.

But she had to try and remain calm, at least outwardly. He said those things to scare her, and in fact, that must be the reason for the visit. He wanted to terrorise her. It seemed like he wouldn't attack her, at least for now, for some reason that currently escaped her. So, if he wanted her to leave, but wouldn't resort to violence right now, terrorism would be his next best weapon.

She could feel the other Magi in her house, her friends, taking a keen interest in the events happening at Amanda's front door. They remained hidden, the less Lucian saw, the better, but she knew they were mere feet away from her and ready to spring into action should the situation call for it.

As if to confirm it, she suddenly felt the presence of Gentle Water, in her mind.

~We're here Amanda. We're watching and ready.~ His tone calm and reassuring.

Amanda gulped as she forced her focus back on the Nomads, her confidence bolstered slightly knowing her friends had her back.

"Really? Well, that's just grand. I'll be sure to pass that message on." She just couldn't help herself, sarcasm came naturally to her and had always been her way of dealing with confrontations.

She couldn't see Lucian's eyes, hidden as they were behind his shades, but the rest of him clearly displayed that he didn't like being disrespected. His friends didn't seem too happy, either.

Amanda continued. "Are you going to introduce me to your two lovely looking friends here? Those are some awful mighty tattoos you have there."

Lucian visibly trembled with anger and took a step towards the house—as far as the building's Aegis would allow, and pointed at her. "Fuck you, *bouzin*, you will watch your tongue when you speak to me, bitch! You think you some big *mambo* in your house, hidden behind dis Aegis? I will rip you a new batty hole. You got one day, den it be open season on you."

And with that, he turned and walked down the stoop to the sidewalk, his two companions following close behind, looking back at Amanda as they left with nothing but hate.

A few seconds later, they were gone.

Amanda closed the door and leant her back against the doorframe. She took a few deep breaths as she tried to calm herself. Her heart beat like a jackhammer in her chest as it pumped adrenalin through her bloodstream. She realised she'd tensed up and as her body relaxed, she felt exhausted by the whole meeting as if she'd just run a marathon.

Her four friends appeared round the corner. Raven and Yoh looked all business, their faces like thunder as they scanned the entrance area. Gentle Water held Liz as they walked into view. Liz ran forward and hugged her, Gentle Water close behind.

"Wow, Mandy, that was amazing. You were great! I can't believe you stood up to them like that," Liz said

"Thank you, I was as terrified as you, though, I think."

"You were so brave," Liz answered.

"Heh, thanks." Amanda took the compliment, feeling anything but brave. She felt sick to her stomach as her adrenalin started to ebb.

Yoh stepped up next to her and placed a hand on her shoulder. "Well done, Amanda-san, that took some guts."

"I thought, from everything you had said, I thought he would just attack me. Why didn't he try to come at me? If all three of them had attacked at once…"

"*Hai*, you are right. That would have been challenging."

"Deadly, more like it," Amanda countered.

"Well, they didn't, but you're right, that was very out of character. Everything I know about Lucian would suggest that he never does this. Usually, he attacks without warning and without mercy. You were off your guard. He could have punched a hole through the Aegis and killed you. But instead, he basically said, 'Get off my property.'"

"But why?" Gentle Water asked as he stood next to Amanda, a hand on her back to comfort her.

Yoh thought for a moment. "I admit, I am at a loss. Do you have any ideas?"

Gentle Water, Liz, and Raven all shook their heads.

Raven came forward and gave Amanda a hug. "*Howah*! Are you okay, Mandy?"

"Grand, I'm grand."

"What do you think? Do you have any idea why he didn't attack?" Raven asked.

"No."

***

Amanda stood on the flat roof of her house, three stories up and looking out over the city. Night had fallen and the glow of a thousand windows lit up the town around her. She could hear the rumble of the twenty-four-hour traffic drifting up from the street below, punctuated with the occasional car horn or the distant echo of a siren as it threaded through the city streets.

They had eventually returned to their unpacking, but the conversation never ventured far from the subject of Lucian's visit. Yoh and Raven were almost spoiling for a fight but kept their tempers in check. As ever, Gentle Water kept his own counsel, offering few opinions on the matter, but Liz had been scared by their appearance on their doorstep. She talked the most of everyone there, a product of her nervousness and fear, and needed the most reassurance that everything would be fine.

Amanda had talked, joined in with the conjecture, and as the afternoon wore on, the relaxed atmosphere started to return to the house. One thing that resulted from the day's events being that they all took a couple of hours to strengthen and add to the protective shields around the house, and they also took a closer look at the house's defences.

Dinner had been brief, everyone separating off to do their own thing, so Amanda headed up here and took a couple of hours to run through her fight training in the night air. She felt tired and even now, despite everything they had discussed and done to make the house safer, she couldn't help but feel scared. Deep down in the pit of her stomach, she felt unsure about her whole plan to come here and set up a life in a Nomad's backyard.

Had it been the best idea? Should she have returned to Ireland and stayed there? Would that have been better? Maybe. But she loved New York. She felt a burning need to be here, just like she had back in the orphanage.

As she looked out over the city below, she knew she had done the right thing. It had its dangers, she had come face to face with one today, but she couldn't leave now.

She might have walked into the crosshairs of the city's resident Nomad, so maybe it hadn't been the most sensible idea, but there was one thing she knew for sure. It had been the right choice for her.

That thought didn't help with her fear of Lucian, though. She still felt that sinking feeling in the pit of her stomach.

She hugged herself against the cold of the night as the wind pulled her crimson hair across her face.

She needed a hug.

She turned away from the city and walking back towards the door that led into the house. She needed someone. Someone to hold and to tell her everything would be okay. She might be a Magus, she might have some incredible and awe-inspiring powers, but she still needed love and support just like everyone else.

Without really thinking about it, she soon found herself approaching Raven's door. He'd been staying with them for a few nights now, and they had chatted, but she hadn't really spent much quality time with him yet.

She paused.

Was it Raven she wanted to talk to? What about Gentle Water, or Liz? But she dismissed them quickly. They weren't what she needed, and she began to wonder if she wanted something more than just a chat.

What about Maria? Amanda frowned at the idea, not sure if that was a good idea. Maria could certainly provide some comfort, and would be good to talk to, but what if things went too far? Did she want to go down that path? Maria had been a good friend to her, and she didn't want to lose that, despite the temptation.

She considered Porting to The Jade Palace and visiting Yoh. But why, when Raven's door was right here? Doubt bubbled up inside her at the thought of going to any of them for comfort, and maybe something more, and then getting rejected.

No, that was silly. She'd seen their admiring glances, their lingering gazes. They were interested in her just as much as she was in them, surely.

As her mind flicked from Raven to Yoh, and then to Maria, she walked up the corridor, only to find herself right outside Raven's bedroom.

She knocked on the door gently, hesitantly, still wondering if taking this step was the right thing to do.

The door opened. Raven stood there smiling back into the room as if from a joke he had just heard. She couldn't help but notice that he lacked a shirt and glanced admiringly at how toned he was. Yep, the fire she felt deep within her and the need to hold him grew. She knew this was the right choice.

A giggle sounded from inside the room.

Raven grinned at… someone, before turning to look at Amanda for the first time, a look of guilt and surprise on his face.

The giggle had been female, and Amanda realised that Raven wasn't alone tonight. He held a sheet around his waist, covering himself up. "Aaah, no bother, I'm sorry. I thought, I mean, I didn't mean to interrupt," she stammered. Amanda's smile had long since fled as she started to move away from the door.

Raven looked at her, his own smile also fading.

"No, no, you're okay. It's not a problem, but I'm sorry I can't invite you in. I have…"

"Company." Amanda finished. "I understand."

She offered a consolatory smile and walked away, her ego deflated. She could feel Raven's gaze on her back as he watched her go before she heard the door to his room softly click closed.

***

Raven shut the door behind him and looked back at the figure in his bed. She held her hand over her mouth, clearly smiling, her eyebrows raised.

"That was close," he said.

The woman nodded and widened her eyes for a moment before dropping her hand from her mouth.

"Certainly was." She smiled knowingly.

"You weren't worried she might see you?"

"Nope," she said, calmly and cryptically.

"No, I guess not." He smiled at her. He put his hands on his hips and dropped the towel.

"Well, Monsieur Raven, where were we?" she asked enticingly, flinging the bedsheet that had been covering her away, revealing her beautiful body to him.

Aroused, he climbed onto the bed and descended into her embrace once more, her arms and legs wrapping around him as she pulled him into her, moaning in delight.

***

Amanda sat herself down on her bed with an annoyed scowl on her face. She hadn't expected to be jilted by Raven. She felt sure that he was single, never having mentioned any kind of relationship in the past year, and now here he was with some girl, in her house no less.

"Feck," she said to no one at all. That had been an embarrassing and awkward few moments. She didn't relish the thought of breakfast the next day, seeing Raven and the awkwardness that would no doubt surround them.

She fell backwards onto her bed, her arms out to either side of her and sighed. She didn't feel like going to bed. Quite the opposite. She wanted to be out of the house, away from the situation. She wanted to go somewhere she knew, somewhere she might meet someone and have a fun night.

She considered visiting Yoh or calling Maria, but her encounter at Raven's door had killed the need to jump into their arms. She wanted to be out, away from these Magi, and spending some time with someone who didn't know Magic.

A thought occurred to her then. She had been meaning to visit Howie at his club since getting back, but the moment hadn't seemed right so far.

It seemed right, now, though.

She sat up and thought about it. She could shower, find an outfit, and get over there pretty quickly. Hell, Lucian knew where she lived now, there was no need to hide it anymore, she should just get out there and enjoy herself.

The idea really appealed to her, so she jumped up and hopped into the bathroom to freshen up.

***

Half an hour later, she Ported to the other side of town. She stepped to the edge of the alleyway she'd appeared in and looked at the Dark Side of the Moon Nightclub on the other side of the street. It hadn't changed at all.

The converted church looked the same as it had just a couple of years ago. The building looming over her like a black monster in the darkness. Multi-coloured lights danced on the inside, visible through the darkened windows as they pulsed and moved to the deep bass that she could feel even here, across the street. Wondering if Howie still worked there, she stepped out and made her way across the road, dodging around taxi cabs to approach the main entrance with its purple neon sign over the doorway. Other revellers and clubbers hung about outside the club chatting, drinking, smoking, and copulating in the shadows.

Amanda wore her bright red hair loose, cascading down over a fitted, green-sequinned, mini-dress with long sleeves. It was an outfit she'd bought a while back, but she hadn't until now found the right moment to wear it. She strode over the road in her black high heels that clicked-clacked on the asphalt as she walked.

A few semi-drunk guys catcalled her as she approached the club. She ignored them. She wasn't interested in their drunken attentions.

She needed to know if there might be any threats to her in the club, so she shifted her perception into the Magical spectrum. The world around her burst into golden light as the Essentia all around her suddenly became visible. She scanned the building and the bouncers with her Aetheric Sight, but everything seemed clean, no residual Magic here at all. So far, so good.

The club had been open a while, and the queue had dwindled somewhat, but she didn't feel like standing in line. Ignoring the queue, she walked up to the doorway and reached out with her Magic into the minds of the two bouncers who stood to either side of the door.

With a little Magical suggestion, they stepped aside and let her in. She also pushed a little deeper into the mind of one of them and within moments confirmed that Howie did still work here. In fact, he was now the head bouncer for the entire club. She smiled as she walked past the people in the queue, a couple of whom mouthed off about the skinny redhead who was too good to queue with the rest of them.

Amanda ignored the comments and stepped inside.

Colour and sound exploded around her as she entered the club. The whole room seemed to move and undulate as the vast throng of people danced to the music that reverberated through her chest.

She scanned the room and saw a few other members of the security team scattered about. Her enhanced vision soon picked out Howie, standing towards the back of the room next to the VIP lounge with two other security guys. She started to walk around the room, making her way towards him, watching him the whole time. He seemed happy, laughing and talking animatedly to his colleagues about something.

She stopped and leant against a pillar where she had a good view of him. She just wanted to watch him for a while, without him knowing she was here.

Seeing him happy and enjoying his work, melted her heart and gave her a lovely warm feeling inside. Howie had been kind to her when no one else had. He had taken her in and got her off the streets, which in turn, led to everything else and brought her here, today.

A true friend and a gentleman, he didn't like it when Amanda took to the streets with Georgina, prostituting herself. She understood why he didn't like it, but at the time, it had been the right choice for her, something she had to do. Her options had always been limited back then. As an illegal immigrant, she would have been deported had she come to the attention of the authorities.

She smiled to herself. She was still trying to justify her actions to Howie, even in her head.

Well, it didn't do her any good waiting here, she thought, so she walked around the dancefloor. She stopped a few meters from him and took a moment to admire him. He was still as handsome as ever with his hair shaved short against his dark skin and nicely tailored suit. He looked good, she thought as she watched him watch the crowd dance in time with the music.

It took a minute or so for him to see her, and he did a double-take when he finally did. A look of surprise and disbelief crossed his face. He waved hesitantly at her. She smiled back and motioned her head for him to come over.

Howie excused himself from the conversation he'd been part of and walked over, dodging drunk dancers as he approached.

"Amanda, wow! It's great to see you! How are you?" he asked with enthusiasm, but Amanda didn't miss the wary look in his eyes and nervous twitch at the corner of his mouth as he spoke.

"Hiya, I'm grand thanks. It's great to see you! One of the guys said you'd been promoted, is that right?"

"Yeah," he said, rubbing the back of his neck, embarrassed about his success. "I run security for this whole place now. I'm not just on the doors these days. Seems, they like what I do here."

"That's excellent, Howie! I'm pleased for you."

"How about you? How have you been? It's been ages."

"I know."

"You're looking great, by the way."

"Thank you."

"Are you still with Georgina?"

He didn't know what had happened, but he saw right away the way her face fell and her eyes took on a sad, faraway look.

"Oh, I'm sorry, I didn't mean to intrude…"

Amanda smiled and put her hand up to stop him mid-flow.

"It's fine, don't worry," she said and took a deep breath. "Georgina passed away."

"Oh. I'm so sorry. I didn't know."

"No, of course you didn't. It's no bother. It was a few years back, now. I'm over it, mostly. Took some time out, went back to Ireland, made some new friends who helped me get through it, so I did."

"So, are you just visiting New York?"

Amanda smiled more fully again, looking back up at Howie's soulful eyes.

"No, I've moved back, so I'm here permanently." It felt good to say that. To hear it out loud that she wouldn't be leaving the city any time soon. Not of her own choice, anyway.

"That's great, Amanda. Are you working, then? What are you doing?"

Amanda was sure Howie was fishing to find out if she was back working streets, but she chose to put him out of his misery.

"No job at the moment. I came into some money a little while back so I'm just enjoying life. I have no desire, or need, to go back to the streets, either."

Howie flushed slightly, realising that she knew what he'd been wanting to know and feeling embarrassed that she'd seen through his question.

"I know you didn't like me working the streets, Howie. So, here's me saying sorry. Alright? I'm sorry. Are we grand?"

She could see him relax as she spoke.

"We are. I'm just happy to see that you're alright and doing well."

"Thank you. Would you like to get a drink?" she asked.

"I can't, I'm afraid. Work stuff. We have a busy night tonight, so I'm going to be run off my feet. Can I have a rain check?"

"Of course, Howie, anything for you. Another time, maybe." Amanda felt disappointed, but it wasn't surprising. She had just waltzed in here and kind of expected him to drop everything for her. But he had responsibilities now that he couldn't just walk away from. They hugged and said goodbye before she made her way through the crowds of people to the exit, the music becoming muffled as she stepped outside into the cool night air.

Nearby, she found a low wall and sat down on it. It didn't seem to be her night at all. It had been great to see Howie, and they had swapped numbers so they could arrange to meet up again. Something she felt keen to do soon. But that didn't help her tonight.

Seeing Howie brought back the feeling she'd had earlier in the night, before she'd knocked on Raven's door. She wanted to be with someone. Someone who knew what she was going through. Someone she could just be with.

She thought about calling Maria, but it seemed like a lot of hassle when The Jade Palace was just a few blocks away.

So, she jumped up from the stone wall, brushed the debris off her rear, and left the club behind.

***

A short while later, after a much-needed walk that helped clear her mind, she stood outside the back door to The Jade Palace and reached out to Yoh's mind. The link she had previously created with Yoh let her presence be felt by him, even though he was inside his Aegis-protected building. She felt the link open up right away and could feel Yoh's presence.

~I'm outside, can you let me in?~ she asked.

~Sure, Amanda-san. Are you okay?~ Yoh's voice sounded in her mind.

~Grand, just grand.~

It didn't take long. Within a few short moments, she sat in his living room, upstairs at the back of the building. She relaxed into her chair across from Yoh, holding a drink in her lap.

"Thanks for coming over. You certainly dressed up for me," he observed.

Amanda laughed, looking down at the shimmering green dress she had on.

"Yeah," she said, drawing out the word in a sarcastic tone.

"I take it you've been out tonight?"

"Visited an old friend at a club not too far from here."

"Aaah, I see. You don't seem too happy about it."

"No, I am. It was great to see him. He was busy, though, so…"

"You came here."

Amanda nodded, looking down at her drink. She wasn't entirely sure if she should be here. Sure, it felt like a great idea back at the club. But she really wasn't sure what she wanted from Yoh, now that he sat not six feet from her.

She'd gone to see Raven, if she was brutally honest with herself, for some affection and maybe some sex. When she found out he had been getting that elsewhere tonight, she'd gone to the club to see Howie—on the rebound. Seeing him had been great, but their lives were so far apart now. She wouldn't have been able to talk to him. Also, he'd never been interested in her in that way, as far as she knew, and she didn't want to ruin things before she got to know him again.

Then she came here, still on the hunt for something that, maybe, she just didn't need. She barely knew Yoh, really, and here she was, alone with him in his apartment, wearing a sexy little dress that barely covered her ass.

She felt cheap, like she'd been out for one thing and one thing only. But now, having given herself some distance from it, some perspective, she felt like she could see herself from the outside and wondered if her desperation for some affection would be as obvious to others.

"Forgive me for saying so, Amanda-san, but you seem a little… off balance, if you don't mind me saying so."

Her eyes flicked up and she looked at him from under her scarlet eyebrows.

"That's probably accurate. With everything that happened today, with Lucian turning up like that, it's thrown me into a bit of a tailspin, I think."

"*Hai*. He can do that to you."

"I don't understand how he found us, though. We were so careful."

"He has his resources. I suppose it was inevitable. I'm surprised he has not found me yet, actually. Although my circumstances are somewhat different," he mused.

"Different?" Amanda asked, curious as to what he meant.

"Well, no one knew I had come here. I didn't announce it to the US covens. I just slipped in quietly and kept to myself for a long time. I, of course, soon found out about Lucian and even talked with Victoria."

"You were more careful, is what you're saying?"

"Maybe. I also keep to myself and don't interfere with Lucian or his plans."

"Fair play to yeh."

Yoh smiled. "You seem to have a period of grace with Lucian yourself, though. Something that's totally out of character, I must admit."

Amanda took a deep breath. She could feel the butterflies in her stomach return, the nerves of having to deal with another Nomad, someone who could likely kill her very easily. And then there was his sponsor, Nymira, the Haitian Arch Magus who regularly came to his aid. Someone else Amanda didn't feel like meeting any time soon.

Tonight's antics were almost certainly linked to the threat Lucian posed. The need for some affection and wanting to do something she felt confident doing. She'd spent two years on the streets of New York as a working girl. She was good at that. She felt confident when it came to sex.

She didn't feel anywhere near as confident when it came to her Magical abilities. But Lucian knew where she lived now, he would be after her and he wanted her dead.

Maybe he knew others had been in the house with her today. Maybe he knew that she had backup and that's why he didn't attack. He was assessing her strength, deciding whether he needed to ask his master, Nymira for assistance.

"Oh, shite, what have I gone n' got myself into this time?" she asked, lifting her head to the ceiling, talking to no one, really, other than herself. She buried her head in her hands as a sob racked her body.

Seconds later, Yoh squatted down in front of her and took her hands in his.

"Look at me," he said.

She looked up and gazed into Yoh's dark eyes.

"What you have done, by coming here to Manhattan, is incredibly brave. And it seems like 'the King of New York' has given you some space. Something I have never seen before. We're all here beside you on this, Amanda-san. We will help protect you if you let us. We're not out of options yet."

"You promise?" Amanda asked, feeling a bit pathetic.

Yoh shifted onto his knees, which raised his head up level with hers.

"Of course."

She looked back at him and smiled, and for a moment, they just stayed like that, looking into each other's eyes. As she looked at him, and he stayed right there, not moving but looking into her soul, holding her hands in her lap, the moment just seemed right.

It happened without her really thinking about it, she moved her head towards his, just a touch, parting her lips as she did so. He responded and leaned in, so she finished it and kissed him.

He felt soft and gentle to Amanda, hesitant almost as if Yoh, like Amanda, wanted to be sure this would be the right thing to do.

The kiss grew into more kisses and slowly he pulled her in, closer to him.

She liked it. It seemed right. Amanda reached over and put her drink on the coffee table, before reaching around his waist and pulling him closer, spreading her legs to pull him tight against her chest.

The movements grew more passionate as they both gave in to their desire.

"I've wanted you since I first saw you," she said as he kissed her neck, his hands moving over her back and along her thighs, pulling her dress up over her hips.

"I know," he replied. Looking meaningfully at her as he said it.

Amanda giggled at the *Star Wars* reference. Did he do that on purpose? She didn't care.

He pulled on her dress, pulling it up over her head. It had been far too long since she'd done this and having this powerful man hungrily kissing and touching her, made her feel so good.

"Let's take our time. We have all night, after all," she moaned. She wanted to enjoy this.

- The Purge of New York by Louisa Hunt, Magi Scholar of the Ordo Obscura Coven

Everything changed in New York after the fire at The Crystal Palace. The official story of events that night differs from what actually took place.

Details are sketchy, but the fire certainly seemed to be Magical in nature. Regardless, it's not the fire itself that we're concerned about here, but the events after it that led to the Nomad coven known as the Harbingers of Darkness taking control of New York.

At that time, there were several Arcadian Magi living in New York, but following that fire, all the Magi in the city were killed. We don't know who did it, but they were quick and left no trace of who they were.

The city had been left wide open, and Nymira saw an opportunity. The Harbingers arrived in New York, and with the help of Nymira, defended it from attack.

Lucian, the current leader of the coven, had been a young member of the Harbingers at the time. He soon rose through the ranks as he grew in power, until he came to lead the coven.

But let's go back and look at the events on the night of the fire before we examine the purge of New York…

The Morning After

Battery Park, New York

The waves in the Upper Bay, where the Hudson and East River met before heading out to sea, undulated gently. The waters were calm and today seemed to be turning into a fairly warm day for mid-May.

Amanda stood in front of the railings, leaning on them, her forearms holding her weight as she looked out over the bay towards Liberty Island. In the distance, the Verrazano Bridge, the gateway to the Atlantic Ocean, stretched across the narrows between Brooklyn and Staten Island.

A light wind whipped her hair around her shoulders in waves of red that stood out against the faded blue of her denim jacket. She sipped a coffee that she'd bought from a street vendor moments ago and listened to the water lapping against the side of the dock below her.

The morning sun felt warm against the left side of her face, while the sound of children playing in the park behind her lent a sense of normality to everything.

Everyday life continued all over the city, blissfully unaware of the things in the shadows.

Liz stood next to her leaning against the railing, but facing the city rather than the sea. She also sipped on a coffee, her demeanour introspective and thoughtful.

Amanda stood up straight and leaned her hip against the railing.

"How you holding up?" she asked her apprentice.

Liz blinked and looked up at Amanda. There wasn't too much difference in height between them, Liz stood just a couple of inches shorter than Amanda.

"I'm good, thanks."

"Even with everything that's been going on?"

"I'll cope," Liz answered.

Amanda smiled to herself. "I don't mind telling ye that I'd be lying if I said I was fine. I'm optimistic about the future, to be sure. I think we'll be okay in time, but right now, I'm scared. Lucian turning up on our doorstep? That scared the shite outta me, so it did."

Liz sighed. "Yeah, me, too. I mean, how the hell did he find us? That's what gets me. We were careful, Porting everywhere. We never left through the front door either."

"Never underestimate a Magi, let alone a Nomad," Amanda mused.

"Don't you worry about that. I won't."

The pair fell quiet again as Amanda eyed her surroundings, feeling just a little uneasy.

She put her bum to the railing, mimicking Liz, taking in the view of the tall buildings stretching up to the sky. Her apprentice had been through a lot the past couple of years. But she had come back from the brink, built herself back up, and Amanda thought she seemed to be stronger now than she had ever been.

Losing your family and friends in the space of a couple of days must be tough. Amanda felt she could relate to it a bit, having lost Stuart to violence and Georgina to illness.

In those early days, after the incident on the train, Amanda had stayed with Liz day and night. When she felt ready to talk, Amanda had been there and they'd talked for hours. Liz had shed many tears as they relived the emotions of the events. Liz swung from the deepest lows of despair to being relatively normal for a while as she tried to deal with the powerful emotions. Liz and her friends being the unwitting victims of horrific violence, her world had been shattered by the machinations of the Magi.

It took months, but slowly, Liz had crawled out of the darkness and eventually started to smile again.

Amanda knew she would never be the same. That grief would always be with her.

She felt immensely proud of Liz for everything she'd done. Liz could quite happily have taken the easy route and ended it all, but instead, with a little support from Amanda and Gentle Water, she had taken the difficult path.

Amanda took her on as her apprentice and had enjoyed the challenge of teaching her Magic. Amanda hadn't been sure she would be considered old enough to be a mentor, but Gentle Water had encouraged her to do it. Liz had latched onto her, and they were almost attached at the hip for a while. No one else could have gotten near her to even attempt to teach her, so Amanda seemed like the natural choice.

Gentle Water had coached her, taught her how to pass on her knowledge. Liz progressed a lot slower than Amanda had, something for which Amanda felt very grateful. It gave her time to learn the ropes and to see what worked.

Amanda had also been starting to teach Liz the same fighting style that Gentle Water had been teaching her, the Art of the Phoenix. Again, Liz wasn't quite the natural at it that Amanda appeared to be, but she worked hard and over time, improved greatly.

These days, Liz didn't talk about her family and friends much. They came up in conversation from time to time, but it didn't seem to bother her like it used to, providing the conversation didn't dwell on them too long.

Amanda wanted to change the subject. In fact, she had something she really wanted to talk to Liz about.

"Sooo, I slept with Yoh last night," Amanda said, having plucked up enough courage to say it out loud.

Liz froze partway through lifting her drink to her lips and stayed there for a moment. "Oh," Liz finally said.

Amanda waited, but Liz kept quiet, sipping her hot drink. Amanda couldn't just leave it at that though.

"Is that it? Just, 'oh'?"

"What do you want me to say, Mandy? You're a big girl, I'm sure you can make your own choices in life."

"Well, yes, I can. But what do ye think?"

"I'm not sure it was the best thing for you to do, sleep with our guide here. But I suppose I can see why you did it. He is a bit gorgeous, isn't he?" She smiled at Amanda.

"Yeah, he's grand."

"Go on, then, you can't leave me in the dark now. How did it happen? And anyway, I thought you liked Raven?"

"I did. I mean, I do. But, well, I went his room last night. I don't know. I suppose I needed some comfort, so I did. But he had someone in there with him. A girl. I didn't see her, but they were having a good giggle about something."

"Ah, okay, but I thought he was single?"

"Apparently not," Amanda said flatly. Her emotions on the subject showing through.

"He didn't bring her down with him this morning. She must have left early."

"Good thing, too," she answered with a little too much bite.

"Easy now. I'm sure she's lovely."

"I know. I'm just…"

"Jealous?" Liz asked, finishing Amanda sentence.

"Nice," Amanda commented, only for Liz to give her a look. "Okay, well, yes, I suppose a little bit."

"Thought so. Well, I think I can guess how you ended up bumping uglies with Yoh, then. Can you say rebound?" Liz commented, goading Amanda.

"Ye little gobshite. What's got into ye today, little miss feisty?" Amanda teased.

Liz laughed. "Come on, how did you end up in Yoh's bed?"

"I went into town, visited an old haunt of mine. But there wasn't much there for me, so I stopped in at The Jade Palace on the way back, and the rest is fairly obvious."

"The broad strokes, yes, but I want details. So, come on. How was it? Was he any good?"

Amanda looked up, smiled, and gave a mock sigh.

"Actually," she said, "it was awesome, just what I needed. He wasn't half bad either, there's a tiger in there, for sure."

The pair laughed and giggled as they chatted some more. Amanda enjoying this moment of just being normal girls talking about their lives. She seemed to do this so rarely now, there always seemed to be some crisis or other that needed their attention. But just for a short time, away from the house and the boys. Amanda loved this moment of just being girls talking about boys.

A short time later, the pair of them dropped their empty takeaway cups into the bin before they strolled back to Amanda's bike.

She'd parked it nearby, and with a small casting, no one noticed it parked illegally. She'd brought the bike over from Paris, where she had customised it after buying it last year. She'd never thought that she'd be able to afford one of these, but the ability to just conjure money from thin air whenever she needed it made life a hell of a lot easier.

She loved her bike. It was a corny thing to say, but it really was her pride and joy. The bike looked like a Honda Fireblade, for the most part, but she'd made a few Magical adjustments and given it a custom paint job of black with colourful red flames.

She straddled the bike and let Liz climb on behind her before she fired up the engine. The motorcycle roared into life as she revved the engine a couple of times, checking that her route looked clear. A moment later, she gunned the engine, and the bike wheelspun away, shooting over to the nearby road where she joined traffic.

She guided the bike around Battery Park before joining West Street and heading north along the west side of Manhattan Island.

The first part of this highway up through the city had buildings along both sides of the road, and they were soon approaching the World Trade Center and the 9/11 memorial.

The colossal building of One World Trade Center towered above them, along with the rest of the monoliths on the southern tip of the island with the highway creating a valley, a fissure between them with a river of cars running along it.

Amanda stayed with the flow of traffic, not speeding or dodging through lanes. Sure, it could be fun to do that, and with her Magic, it also meant it could be done safely and without anyone even noticing, but she didn't want to do that today.

This morning had been an enjoyable departure from the pressures of life as an Arcadian in a Nomad city, and a leisurely drive through the glass and chrome of the town she loved, felt great.

They soon passed the World Trade Center and a short time later rode beneath a footbridge. After that, the buildings on their left came to an end, and the view across the Hudson to New Jersey opened up.

The trees on the median were a bright green where the sun caught their leaves, while the rippling waves in the river glistened in the sunshine.

An engine rev to her right caught her attention. She looked inland, straight into the eyes of two other bikers on Harleys who were staring right back at her.

A movement behind her caught her eye. She twisted for a better view.

More bikes, making a group of seven in total, all with one or two people on them, and they all seemed to be focused on her.

Then she saw him.

Lucian sat on a huge Harley directly behind her, his eyes focused intently on her. She also saw the tattooed guy who had been with Lucian on her doorstep that morning riding alongside him. For a moment, all she could do was to stare at them.

The sight of Lucian and his gang made her heart race. What was he going to do? There was no Magical Aegis between them now, and she was outnumbered by over three to one.

Did he want to fight? Would she be able to stand against him? Would her Magic be enough to fight him off and protect her friends? She had no idea. She needed distance, she needed to try to get away.

Liz spotted them too and gripped Amanda tighter around the waist.

Amanda patted her hand. ~Don't worry, Liz, we'll be fine, let's get out of here,~ she sent through their Mental Link. As she reassured Liz, she funnelled power to her Aegis, strengthening it and also pushing it out to extend over Liz, as well. She felt Liz taking the opportunity to boost her own Aegis as well but to a lesser power level.

With that, she twisted the handle and accelerated away quickly, the magical enhancements on the bike coming into play.

The bike went off like a rocket, dodging between cars as it quickly picked up speed. Amanda concentrated on the road ahead, not wanting to crash her bike so early on after moving it to her new home. Amanda could Port out of there quickly, but she would be leaving Liz and the bike behind, which was out of the question.

But if she couldn't get away, maybe someone could come to them. With another working of Magic, she reached out, only for her attempted Link to be abruptly cut off the moment it left her Aegis. She felt Magic fade behind her and knew what it meant. Lucian was countering her Magic.

They were alone.

She held her breath for a moment as fear blossomed within her. For a few seconds, she couldn't breathe as the reality of the situation dawned on her. She had to deal with this herself, without any help.

But, did she really need help? She felt she like a competent Magi, and she'd been in a few fights now while on missions with Orion and Xain in Paris. Maybe she *could* stand against a Nomad like Lucian.

Maybe she *could* handle this.

She concentrated hard and used her Magic again, creating a common effect known as Multi-tasking, splitting her mind into two separate but linked parts that could work independently and also cooperatively.

Then, she placed her second set of senses behind her, allowing her to look both forwards and backwards. Her two minds enabled her to keep the two viewpoints separate meaning she didn't get confused as she dodged between cars.

Shifting all of her senses into the Magical spectrum, she focused on the gang of bikers, who had also sped up. Most of them were Riven, and the only Magical signatures on them were their bikes, and in a few cases, some weapons.

They were also gaining on her. These Magical bikes were apparently a match for her own. She wouldn't be able to simply outrun them.

She had guessed that it wouldn't be that simple but was worth a punt. You never knew your luck.

It appeared that only Lucian and his friend were Magi, judging from the way only those two were glowing.

That made things easier. Lucian would be powerful, though. You don't get to lead a Nomad coven if you can't defend yourself. His friend was another matter. She had no idea how powerful he might be.

Both the Nomads had Aegises in place. They were prepared for this.

But what were they going to do? Kill them? Make an example of them?

She didn't want to find out.

As she sped down the highway, the gang gained on her, dodging around cars who sounded their horns in anger at the crazy biker gang. Amanda tried to keep ahead of them, but the gang were more reckless.

She considered her options again. She couldn't be too obvious with her Magic in such a public place, and she had no desire to cause innocent civilians to die in a pile-up. So, she bided her time and waited to see what they would do, preparing herself for a fight.

She didn't have long to wait.

Moments later, one of the bikes to her right swerved in and slammed into the side of her bike. It wobbled but stayed upright as her Aegis took the brunt of the attack and fizzed.

The gang's bikes were filled with Essentia, and partially discharged when they hit her Aegis, but it had weakened her Aegis.

Then another biker hit from the other side. Liz yelped at each collision, holding Amanda tightly and jumping every time. They were unhurt, her Aegis holding for the time being, but this couldn't continue.

She focused on the bike to her right as it came back to hit her again. Amanda reached out with her Magic to pull on the attacker's brakes.

Essentia flared as Lucian reached out and blocked her Magic again. She caught him smiling to himself as he did it, and then the biker slammed into her again.

Damn it.

Amanda thought hard, going over her options. She could use all kinds of Magic, such as conjuring a stick in the spokes of a bike, making its petrol disappear, or shoving them off-balance with telekinesis. The list went on, but she knew that Lucian would be behind her on his bike, blocking her every move.

She needed to think of something.

"Get us out of here!" Liz bellowed, her voice muffled due to her face being buried in her back as another bike hit them again.

"I'm trying," Amanda yelled in frustration. She furrowed her brow and glanced to either side. Time to get physical, she thought.

As the next rider swerved, Amanda raised her leg and kicked out, releasing some Essentia as she did so. The kick connected, breaking through the temporary Aegis Lucian had erected around that rider and hitting the biker. He swerved away from her, barely missing the back of a car as he fought to stay upright.

Amanda smirked.

"Ha! If all else fails, kick it," she said to no one.

She looked to her left, and the biker there was hesitating after seeing what had just happened.

"Yeah, ye know what ye'll get," she growled. "My turn."

Amanda swerved towards him and kicked out again.

The biker hit the oversized central kerb, pitched over onto the road beyond and slammed into the side of a semi. The sound of squealing brakes and horns blaring made her wince.

Her second sight saw Lucian's eyes narrow and his jaw set in an angry grimace at the loss of one of his men.

Moments later, Lucian dodged round the same cars and accelerated towards her. She looked around, trying to find a way out of this. She wasn't sure where to go, or what Lucian might do.

As Lucian closed on her, she saw Essentia flare around him. A wave of force rushed out from him, kicking up dust from the road and slamming into the back of Amanda's bike, knocking it forward and causing her to wobble violently. With a Magical push in the right direction, she righted the bike and accelerated for all she was worth. Her concern for the innocent drivers on the road faded away as she realized she needed to end this now, before it got any worse.

She barely had a moment to think, though, before another wave of energy hit her. Amanda's Aegis flared and she had to use her own Magic to keep from becoming a smear on the asphalt.

Accelerating, she passed two more cars on her right. As the last one fell away, it revealed that Lucian's right-hand man, the other Magus, had drawn level with her. Leaning in, he glided towards her with nothing but hate in his eyes.

With only a moment to react, she turned away, pulling up her front wheel as she hit the central divider. She hit the kerbstone, and with a small Magical kick, launched herself into the air. Sailing over the stopped traffic on the other side, she landed on the far side of the road, hard.

The bike fishtailed beneath her as it bounced towards a gate of one of the abandoned piers. A Magical kick of force later and she swerved through the now open gates. Bringing the bike back under control she skidded to a stop halfway along the pier and looked behind her.

Lucian's fellow Magus had also made the jump and skidded to a stop a short distance from her. The man's dark eyes were glued to Amanda, his gaze not wavering as the other bikers joined him, having snaked their way through the stopped traffic.

Lucian arrived and pulled to a stop in front of his gang. Dismounting, he strode towards Amanda and Liz, his long coat flaring out behind him like a cape. He wore layers of dark clothing with baggy discoloured jeans, with little trinkets, like feathers, finger bones, bird skulls, and other items attached with twine or leather strips. They rattled as he walked.

Lucian's men stayed on their bikes and watched as their leader approached.

"Get off," Amanda hissed at Liz, who obediently climbed off the bike. Amanda followed suit and gathered what little confidence she had in her abilities, and faced the Nomad.

She refuelled her weakened Aegis as the Nomad came closer. Liz whimpered as Amanda stared down the approaching Nomad, the whole scene seeming to play out in slow motion.

Amanda's mind swam with fear and indecision as questions filled her mind. What would he do now? It wasn't like she had backup, only her and Liz's Magical abilities. Would he attack her here, in the middle of the day, in full view of the city? Would she be as outclassed as she had been by Angel? Or would he stay his hand and warn her off again? She waited, fists clenched and Magic at the ready, to see what he would do.

"I told you, mon. This ain't never gonna be over for you," he said, his voice angry, his arms gesticulating wildly as he spoke. "I will hound you. I will hunt you. You will never be safe. You know what me say to be true. Your life will be hell, mon. *Guete mambo,* bitch."

She frowned, her vision flitting from him to the gang behind him. Where was the attack? Why was he just yelling at her and not trying to kill her? She stood there and took the abuse, waiting for him to lash out at her and noting the man's cannabis-scented breath as drips of spittle landed on her face and top.

When he finally stopped raving and just stood there in front of her like an oversized jackal, Amanda realized he wasn't going to attack her.

Slowly, she wiped the spit from her face, the corner of her mouth twitching with a small smile. She needed to know what was going on, but a wave of bravado had swept over her.

"So kill me," she said, her voice even and calm.

Liz's grip on her arm tightened and she whispered Amanda's name under her breath, frightened.

Lucian lowered his chin, looking at her from behind his shades, his face framed by dreadlocks.

Lucian moved closer, his face mere inches from Amanda's.

"Me and ma' boys will make your life a living hell. Trust me little, *mambo*. If you don't leave, I will have to get... inventive. Understand? It's been a while since the boys have had a plaything."

Amanda felt a mixture of confidence and invulnerability straighten her spine as he said this, further cementing the idea that he either couldn't or wouldn't kill her. As she watched him, he very deliberately shifted his focus to Liz and then back to her. Then, he smiled.

It was such a cold, calculating smile, fear shot through her. His smile seemed to say that maybe he couldn't kill her, but her friends weren't off-limits.

Amanda stood tall, but fear for her friends nipped at her confidence. But just like when you're dealing with an aggressive dog, she knew she daren't let it show.

"Really? That's your threat?" she said, her words dripping with disdain. "How original, a man using rape to threaten a woman. Surely, you can do better."

Lucian, still inches from her face, didn't speak. He didn't need to. Rage distorted his features and reddened his skin for all to see.

"I'll be waiting," Amanda whispered to him then, trying to sound as confident and as threatening as she could.

Lucian stood tall and looked down on her. His face filled with anger, he spat at her. It landed on her cheek with a wet splat and started to run down the side of her face. She flinched as he did it and wiped it away. The thought of his spit on her face made her stomach tighten with nausea.

He smiled to himself and stepped back. His hands shot up and he clapped them in front of her face. Amanda jumped. He laughed before turning away and walking off.

As she watched him walk away and mount his bike, she forced her breathing to slow.

She stood there and watched them leave, facing their mad-dog stares, unwilling to show any weakness.

Once they were gone, Amanda turned to her bike. Putting her hands on the seat, she bent over and took several deep breaths.

Lucian scared her, there was no point in denying that, but she also felt confident that at least for the moment, he wouldn't try killing her. Something, or someone, seemed to be stopping him.

Liz dropped to the ground and sat there with tears running down her cheeks.

Amanda crouched down next to her.

"You okay?" she asked as she put her arm across Liz's back.

Liz caught her breath and sniffed. "I'm good. Don't worry."

"God love ye, little one," Amanda said and pulled Liz closer.

"Why didn't he kill us? Isn't that what Nomads do?"

"I suppose it is. I don't know why. I've not worked that out yet."

"Well, I'm grateful something's stopping him, that's for sure."

Letting go of Liz, Amanda stood and looked back towards the southern tip of Manhattan Island and the direction they'd come from. She could see the flashing lights of the emergency service vehicles as they arrived at the crashes their chase had caused.

"Yeah," she said, her voice non-committal. She wasn't sure why Lucian seemed to be holding back, but she felt certain about it now. Lucian had his chance—two actually—and he'd walked away. For whatever reason, he wouldn't kill her.

Looking back at Liz, she decided that they needed to leave.

"Come on. We need to get back and tell the others what just happened." Amanda said, helping Liz to her feet.

- Tokyo, Japan.

The shadow moved silently along the corridor. She could see the men up ahead, their guns out and raised to fight off the invisible attacker. She wasn't genuinely invisible, but she knew they wouldn't see her until she wanted them to.

The men, panicked and scared, had even called the authorities. These thugs probably had a few key personnel within the police on their books.

Deciding she'd played with them long enough, she stepped out of the shadows, drawing her katana as she did. It glinted in the meagre light.

The men wasted no time and opened fire on her. She moved the sword like lightning, anticipating the bullets and knocking them out of the air in front of her in a few, smooth movements.

The look of shock on their faces, priceless. She moved and suddenly she stood amongst them, cutting them down with her sword. Bits of them covered the floor all around her as she turned to the older gentleman who had stayed well back.

"W… why are you here?" he asked, his voice quivering as his body shook.

"I'm here to deliver a message," she said.

"M…message? What message?"

She swung her blade, cutting his head clean off. It hit the floor with a dull thud and bounced before coming to a rest on the carpet before the man's body dropped beside it.

"That message." Her earpiece beeped and she tapped it. "This is Black Lotus," she said.

"Mission status?" the familiar voice of her handler asked.

"Mission complete. I'm withdrawing now," she said.

"Report back to base at once. Your father wants to see you."

A New Player

Bronx, New York

Lucian lounged in a reclining chair in a dark, dusty office that perched in the rafters of a warehouse. The room felt dead. Disused for a long time, Lucian used it now to stay hidden but close to the proceedings below. He didn't need to be here for these meetings, but he liked to attend a few of them to keep a close eye on his empire and make sure his employees knew he was around.

Apart from the chair he sat in, everything in the room had a thin covering of dust on it. He'd magically cleaned it before parking himself in it.

He looked down through the dirty glass window that he sat next to. Below him, several men sat in conversation around a table.

He didn't concern himself with the details, though, that wasn't his domain, he left that to others. The important thing was that the client wanted to buy more drugs from him. More cocaine. That was the important thing.

The eyes of a few of the thugs that the buyers had brought with them kept drifting to the workers nearby as they stood at their tables, cutting the drugs, and preparing them for distribution in a variety of strengths. Their hungry glares gave away their own desire for the product.

Amounts and costs were agreed upon, delivery dates set, and the deal was done.

Another successful day for Lucian's business. Lucian's representative, Jalen Toney, shook the hands of the buyers before they were shown to the door with smiles on their faces.

Lucian walked from the office and down the metal stairs to the ground floor.

Jalen walked over to him in that cocky, almost limping manner that many gang members and cool teenagers did these days. Lucian thought it looked ludicrous, but Jalen, despite his occasional personal foible, had always been a capable worker, which Lucian appreciated more than anything else.

The man wore a black suit with a white shirt that he only buttoned up halfway, showing off his toned chest and the large amount of bling around his neck. He wore so much gold that Lucian sometimes wondered how he managed to stand up at all. Maybe the chains were the reason for his lopsided walk.

"They're happy then, mon?" Lucian asked.

"Yeah, they happy. Buying more from us this time than ever before. They doin' well!"

"Great. You did good tonight, mon. How's the latest shipment coming along?" Lucian asked.

"We're on schedule, everything should be ready for the buyers in good time. We'll be left with some spare to shift later, I'm sure of that."

"Excellent."

"Thanks for coming tonight, Lucian. It was unexpected."

"I know, mon. I have other business here tonight."

"Anything I can help with?" Jalen asked.

"Fuck no. Just do your job."

Jalen nodded and stepped back, understanding that he'd been too familiar with his boss.

Lucian didn't care much, but he liked to keep his employees on their toes. Especially the ones who'd attained stature within his empire. They had access to Lucian that others did not, but Lucian didn't want them to think he cared about them. They were all expendable, and there were always more who wanted to take their place and reap the rewards.

Coming here tonight and watching the meeting had been vaguely interesting, but it had not been the main reason for his visit. He had other plans, a meeting of his own to attend shortly. As far as he was aware, this building remained one that Ekua didn't know about, so it made sense to use it.

It also made sense to get here early and see how this branch of his empire had grown.

"As you wish, Baal Lucian," Jalen said, his eyes downcast.

Lucian turned to the four rows of rectangular tables arrayed end to end across the large, open-plan room with workers on either side, cutting the white powder with other white powders, diluting the drug, and increasing the weight of the final product. He didn't care what white powders were used, all he wanted was to keep the profits rolling in and his influence over the city to grow. He left the boring details to his employees.

Satisfied that everything seemed to be going fine, he turned away and marched past the meeting table and into the darkness on the other side of the vast room. Lucian's operation only took up half of this warehouse, but its location, hidden away from casual onlookers, made it a perfect fit for his business. It had been Jalen's choice, and he'd done well.

Despite the darkness, Lucian's Aetheric Sight meant he could easily make out the stairs that sat in the far corner leading up to the upper catwalks in this part of the building.

As he approached the stairs, a side door opened just next to them. Shaun stepped into view just as Lucian had requested.

Shaun waited at the bottom of the stairway, dressed in black from the neck down. Only the pale waxy skin of his deformed head remained on display.

He inclined his head in greeting. Lucian glanced at him, but otherwise made no gesture of acknowledgement. The Vampire fell into step behind Lucian as they climbed the stairs in silence.

A catwalk and another set of stairs later, and they found themselves on the roof.

Most of the other buildings in this area were of a similar size, mainly warehouses and tenement blocks. Nothing really overlooked this building, which was another reason for its choice as a meeting place. In the distance, the lights of Manhattan glowed in the night like a city of the future. Here in the Bronx, the lights were not quite as bright. Neon signs and lit-up billboards dotted the landscape around them, but the warehouse district they were in was very dark with the various business closed for the night.

Lucian's own business being an exception to the rule.

Looking around, Lucian didn't seen anyone else on the roof, meaning, his contact had yet to arrive.

Suspecting that they were being cautious and probably watching him and Shaun right now, Lucian waited and used his Magical sight to try and spot them.

After a few minutes, as Shaun started shifting about in boredom, a sudden dull thud sounded behind him.

Lucian turned. So did Shaun. Several meters away, a figure stood in the shadows. They stepped forward, and her gender became apparent as the light from a nearby sign reflected off the strikingly-designed stealth suit in a way that Lucian appreciated.

This would be Black Lotus. Someone that Lucian had heard of, but had no need for, until now. There was also a nice, juicy side-benefit to having the Lotus come to New York.

Yoh had become something of an obsession for Lucian over the years. He had kept to himself for the most part and didn't do much to disrupt Lucian's plans, but it had become a matter of professional pride that his city not have any Arcadians living in it.

After years of research, he'd finally found out where the Magus had come from, and he also found out about Black Lotus and her hatred for Yoh.

Until now, that had been nothing more than a curiosity. Lucian wanted to kill Yoh himself, not set some assassin on him. But Amanda had changed all that.

The woman walked towards Lucian, a blank slate in his Aetheric Sight. She didn't even show up as alive.

Her boots crunched on the ground as she walked towards Lucian, and stopped a few meters short of him.

Black Lotus stood in her stealth suit, covered from head to toe in pure black, but as they watched, some of the black on the catsuit she wore faded away to white, leaving behind a black and white pattern that looked like stylised Japanese lotus flowers.

The suit even covered her head, only a ponytail of long black hair gave any hint as to her actual appearance.

Strapped to her stealth suit, tactical webbing held pouches and holsters of all kinds, each filled with weapons or other implements of death. Black Lotus was an assassin, an Initiated Riven who worked for a secretive organisation from Japan who took out contract killings that straddled the divide between the mortal world and the Magi world.

Lucian also knew that Black Lotus would not be able to resist the lure of finding Yoh.

"You've found him, Lucian-san," she asked, her voice carrying a strong Japanese accent, even though she spoke excellent English.

"I have. He's here in New York. Shaun can show you where."

She looked over at Shaun, before glancing back at Lucian to offer a brief bow of thanks. "*Hai*," she said, before turning back to Shaun and stepping closer to him.

Shaun stepped forward and offered her a slip of paper.

"Meet me in an hour at this address."

She took it and looked at it before she bowed briefly to Shaun and turned away from the two men. Moments later, she jumped off the roof.

Satisfied, Lucian turned to Shaun and nodded before Porting off the roof and appearing instantaneously in a corridor of The Pit Club, his Magic allowing him to pass through the backdoor built into the club's Aegis.

Lucian started to make his way through the corridors, looking for Raal, Lex, and Aneurin to update them on the latest developments. Instead, he found himself running into Ekua as he rounded the corner and looked into one of the communal rooms.

"Lucian. *Wha gwaan*. I've hardly seen you, mon. Hey, how dem latest Arcadians die?"

Lucian kept his face neutral. He didn't want his thoughts and feelings betraying him. They were coven mates, but their rivalry had been simmering for a long time. Lucian knew that Ekua had progressed in his Magical ability in recent years, to the point where he could potentially best him if he weren't careful. Lucian also knew that Ekua's comment had been designed to bait him. Lucian and his allies had agreed on a story that they had so far failed to find the new Arcadians, in an attempt to stall Ekua for as long as he could.

The moment that Ekua knew the truth though, he would almost certainly go to straight to Nymira, and then Lucian would have some explaining to do. At the very least, he suspected that Ekua would be promoted to Coven leader, and his life would be made much harder, and probably more painful.

And then there was Yasmin, who would likely kill him if Nymira didn't.

"Ekua, mon, these fucks will be crushed. I have my crew on it. They can't hide forever."

"You ain't found dem yet? What da fuck you doin'? If Nymira…"

"She knows." That much wasn't a lie. He had sent word to his master that Arcadians had entered the city and he'd been hunting them down. Better it come from him than Ekua.

"Chill, mon. I know you on it," he said eyeing Lucian carefully.

Lucian left the room, his face a picture of calm, but inside he felt in turmoil. He had to get these Arcadians out of his city soon, without angering Yasmin. They could ruin everything.

He hoped that Black Lotus might be able to kill two birds with one stone. Maybe killing Yoh, who Lucian knew had befriended Amanda, would force them out, or scare them away from New York. Removing that particular thorn in his side would also give him some leeway with Ekua and Nymira again. Letting Lotus do the dirty work also meant that if things got messy, and Amanda was hurt, he wasn't technically disobeying Yasmin's orders. He could blame the assassin.

It was a long shot, and he felt fairly sure that Yasmin would kill him anyway, but what else could he do? He needed Amanda out of New York before his empire came crashing down around him.

He shook his head as he walked away from the encounter with Ekua. The mental gymnastics he had to go through to keep things straight with Ekua and his master, while at the same time dealing with Amanda, took a toll on him.

He headed back towards his quarters and dropped himself into his couch with a grunt born of frustration and exhaustion, silently cursing Yasmin for putting him in this position.

Soon, he thought, soon Black Lotus would confront Yoh, and with a bit of luck, his problems would sort themselves out.

- Online Chat between Chronos and Edge dated April 8th

Chronos: You're close. So close to the truth.

Edge: Excuse me? Who is this?

Chronos: You can call me Chronos. I have read your blog, and the conclusions you have drawn are close. How do you know all this?

Edge: Investigation. I follow the rabbit hole wherever it takes me.

Chronos: Matrix reference.

Edge: Well spotted.

Chronos: You're in the UK, right?

Edge: Correct, how did you know?

Chronos: You're good, but you have a lot to learn.

- Online Chat between Chronos and Edge, dated April 16th

Edge: What's this?

Chronos: An address.

Edge: What's there?

Chronos: If you're careful, your first steps to learning the truth.

Edge: Is it dangerous?

Chronos: Of course. Watch at a safe distance and don't get caught. Got it?

Edge: Got it.

Surveillance

The Bronx, New York

With a whipcrack of air, Lucian disappeared from the rooftop, leaving Shaun standing on the warehouse roof alone.

Shaun frowned and then looked over to where the assassin, Black Lotus had jumped off the roof. Lucian was finally going after Yoh and using an assassin to get the job done, it seemed. Shrugging, Shaun walked to the edge of the rooftop and looked down.

A short way up the road he saw the car that had brought him here tonight. It idled beside the warehouse with Ben still inside. Shaun glanced around briefly to make sure no one happened to be watching, then he stepped off the roof and dropped three stories to the ground, landing easily.

Everything seemed quiet as he walked to the car and climbed into the passenger seat, pulling his hood up to hide his face.

"Back to the stakeout," he said to his assistant, Ben who waited for Shaun to close the door before pulling away.

The roads were quiet, and they made good time driving back to Greenwich Village. For most of the drive they rode in silence, Ben concentrating on driving while Shaun watched the world go by through the tinted windows from the depths of his hoodie. Shaun didn't like being in a car, out in the open, but it was the only way to move quickly around the city while retaining a certain amount of privacy. After all, he couldn't just step onto the next subway train with a face like his.

Eventually, Ben pulled into the back alley of the tenement building they were set up in and came to a stop. Before opening the door Shaun glanced up and down the street. The coast looked clear, so he got out and followed Ben to the service entrance. Ben locked the car and pulled out a set of keys, opening the service door with a squeak of metal on metal and waited for Shaun to step through into the relative warmth of the building. Shaun had been here a few times, but usually left this kind of work to his two apprentices as he preferred to stay underground. But Ben had figured out a way for Shaun to get to the apartment on the fifth floor with almost no chance of him being spotted by using the service elevator, which exited only a few doors down from their stakeout location. The building might as well have been abandoned for all the upkeep that had been done to it. The service areas were nearly always deserted, apart from the occasional bum who broke in to sleep inside. Tonight, the small complex of rooms that made up the service area were empty, so they made their way through without trouble.

The doors to the elevator car stood open, waiting to be used. They stepped inside, and Ben used a key to activate the mechanism that would take them up to the fifth floor. With a *bing* the doors closed and they started to rise.

After a few moments, the elevator stopped, and the doors juddered open most of the way. Beyond, a dank corridor led into the building, lined with apartments on either side. A short way up, through the flickering light, a stairway led to the other floors.

The place looked empty, but they could hear sounds coming from other parts of the building—music, movement, raised voices, the usual sounds of life.

Ben stepped out and looked both ways, before nodding to Shaun. "It's clear, let's go."

Shaun followed Ben out of the elevator car and down the corridor a short distance to the last door before the stairwell. With his key ready, they were inside the apartment before the elevator doors had closed behind them.

The apartment consisted of a combined living room and kitchen, a bathroom, and a bedroom. It smelled like rotten food, dirty socks, and mould and the air felt a little clammy to Shaun, but then, his two apprentices had been living here in relative squalor for the past few days and the whole place was a mess. Food packaging laid about the room, blankets and clothes littered the furniture, but it wasn't unexpected. This would be a temporary living space while they conducted the surveillance that Lucian wanted.

Along the exterior wall directly in front of him, a table had been set up with several flat-screen monitors hooked up to a couple of computer systems. The monitors displayed live feed from the various cameras they'd set up in here and out on the street. DSLR cameras on tripods stood in front of the windows, their telephoto lenses trained on the house they could clearly see a little over a block away. The tenement they were in fronted a street down the road and around a corner from Amanda's house. The other buildings between the tenement and the house were all one or two-story structures. That meant they could look over the top of them to where Amanda's house sat on the other side of the intersection on the far side of their own block. They had a clear view of two sides of the house affording them a view of the front door, and the side door and garage respectively. An alley ran around the back of the house, where another door had three hidden cameras trained on it, recording any movement they picked up.

A couple of other cameras on nearby rooftops made up the rest of the video feeds on the monitors that Vanessa had been watching.

She sat on a chair in front of the table, her legs propped up on the table top, ankles crossed. With a nail file in one hand, she absentmindedly shaved down her fingernails.

As Ben and Shaun entered, she turned to look, and on seeing Shaun, she removed her feet from the table and tried to look a bit more attentive.

Shaun saw it all, but didn't comment, he just stepped forward, looking at the bank of screens.

"Vanessa," he said in greeting. "Anything to report?"

"Just the usual movement. Nothing out of the ordinary," she said handing Shaun a clipboard upon which was a sheet of paper where they recorded who had been seen and when, who they suspected to be inside the house, and who might be elsewhere. They were quite aware that this was all guesswork when any one of the Arcadians could just Port elsewhere from within the house. They had already seen examples of this, like Amanda walking out the front door, only for her to walk out the same door again a short time later, while never having seen her walk back into the brownstone first.

There had been fears that Amanda had discovered she was under surveillance and did these confusing things to throw them off, but after a while, they concluded it was just normal Magus behaviour.

Shaun scanned the paper on the clipboard and felt happy with the evening's work. The only movement had been the three usual residents; Yoh had not been seen today.

Shaun checked his watch. They were back in good time. Black Lotus wasn't due yet, but he needed to inform his apprentices that she would be coming.

Vanessa and Ben had been with him a while now, Ben the longest of the pair, and after getting to know them, he held some genuine affection for them.

Ben had been just a dumb kid who got himself into trouble with his formidable hacking skills. As the modern world had progressed and the digital age dawned, some in the Magi and Scion communities were early adopters of the new technology. They were able to take basic computer systems, and with the aid of their Magical ability, modify them, making them more and more powerful. While many Magi stayed away from this frightening and powerful technology, those who embraced it tended to be those with a younger outlook on life, and it became a way for these Magi to become lords of their own domains.

As they created faster and more powerful machines a small community grew online, hidden within a private encrypted forum they built what they called The Dark Web, or DWeb for short.

Today, the pioneers of this digital Magic were creating lifelike virtual reality worlds that you could plug into with the VR rigs they were developing.

The Dark Web was one of the most secure sites on the internet, but there was no full-proof way to stop breaches in security, and Ben had been one of the hackers who'd made it inside.

Punishment came swiftly for those who broke through DWeb's security, but Shaun thought he saw something he liked in Ben and managed to reach him just before the others did. Shaun had saved him, but he could not protect his family, who were killed without mercy. Ben had been forever grateful to Shaun for saving his life but carried the scars of his family's demise around with him.

Vanessa had been a street kid for a while. She'd run away from home and from her abusive family, and had lived on the streets, getting into drugs and prostitution, before ending up in a bedsit where she saw another resident on a computer system. It turned out there were a few of them and they were part of a community of digital rights activists who used the internet to cheat the system and make a living. They worked with the hacker group, Anonymous, and provided various digital services to those who needed them. They actually earned good money, doing everything from hacking the social media accounts of a cheating partner, to hunting down kidnapped children, or facilitating business deals that would not have been possible otherwise.

Fascinated, Vanessa watched and learned before quickly joining the group and becoming a trusted worker.

Ben happened across her online and the pair struck up a friendship, even though they'd never met. Then one day, Ben got a frantic text. Vanessa's group had landed themselves in trouble and their building had been raided by men with guns. She'd run like others of her group. They'd already been tracked down twice with more of her group being killed. She ended up separated from them and knowing no one else she even vaguely trusted, she contacted Ben.

After speaking with Shaun, Ben agreed to meet her and bring her in. Ben met her for the first time in an out of the way diner and fancied her right away.

Ben warned her that he and his associate would be able to save her, hide her from those who wanted to kill her, but that there would be no going back, this would be a one way trip into the shadows. Desperate, she'd agreed and followed Ben into the tunnels beneath Manhattan and into their hidden sanctuary. There, Ben sat with her and started to tell her some of the truth of the world, about the Scions and the Magi, and with some warning about Shaun's appearance, introduced her to him.

She'd handled it well, and soon settled into life beneath the streets. Shaun's work and contacts kept the three of them living in comfort. Money was never a problem, and they wanted for nothing, really. It wasn't an uptown penthouse with views over Central Park, but when you lived on the fringes of society and, in Shaun's case, looked like Bram Stoker's nightmares, your choices were few.

Shaun walked over to the window and looked out over the buildings towards Amanda's house. Everything looked quiet, so he turned to his two apprentices. He couldn't think of another word that seemed suitable for them, really; they were learning from him, after all.

Scions could pass on their gift to others by pouring their blood into a cut on a human or by allowing them to drink of their blood. Either worked just as well, but the transformation could not be guaranteed. The blood of a Scion, in well over ninety percent of cases, killed the subject. Their blood was toxic, and only a few humans ever survived the process. When it came to passing the gift onto a Magus, the chances of it working were even less, and in either case, there was no way of telling who would survive and who wouldn't. There didn't seem to be a pattern.

Shaun knew this, as did most Scions, so passing his gift on to Ben or Vanessa would be his very last resort.

"Guys, you need to know that we will have a visitor here shortly."

Vanessa raised her eyebrows but said nothing. Ben raised his head in surprise.

"What?" Ben said.

"The meeting with Lucian tonight. Turns out he was introducing me to someone who is interested in finding Yoh. My guess is that she's an assassin, and this won't end well for Yoh."

"Oh, right," said Ben, frowning.

"She?" said Vanessa. "Cool. She must be pretty badass to be able to take on Yoh."

Shaun smiled, which was something that scared most mortals when they saw his mouth full of sharp teeth, not unlike a shark. Vanessa had become used to it, though. "Indeed," he said.

"I thank you for your compliment," said a voice from the other room, its tone creamy with a far eastern accent.

All three of them looked round in time to see a figure step from the bedroom. She wore the same outfit from the rooftop meeting

"Apologies for the interruption, I did not mean to startle you," she said, her movements silent.

"But, how... what...?" Vanessa started.

"Welcome. Thank you for joining us," Shaun interrupted. How she got into the bedroom was of little consequence to Shaun, and it didn't mystify him as much as it did Vanessa. A Magical Artifact could accomplish that with little trouble.

The assassin offered a small bow in response as she stopped in the doorway.

"How may I address you?" Shaun asked. Curious to find out her name or something he could use to find out more about her.

"I am known professionally as Black Lotus. You may address me as such, Shaun-san," she said.

Shaun nodded. "Thank you. Please, if you would come over here."

She stepped forward, her hands clasped behind her back as she walked over to the window.

Shaun gestured outside. "The house on the far side of the junction. A Magus by the name of Amanda-Jane Page lives there with two others, they are friends of Yoh's and he visits most days."

She looked intently at the house before looking at the feeds from the cameras. She pointed to the images coming from the alleyway behind the house. "A rear entrance?" she asked.

"Yes, and Yoh's favorite. He usually Ports into the alley and enters the house from there.

"You don't know where he resides?"

"I'm afraid not. He's a capable Magus and has managed to cover his tracks quite well. This is the only place we know he frequents.

"And the layout of the house?"

"We only know parts of it. Ben, get Black Lotus a copy of the map."

Ben nodded and tapped away on his laptop for a moment until the printer spat out a copy. Ben handed it to the assassin.

She took it from him and looked at it for a few moments, glancing at the house a couple of times before handing it back to him.

"*Arigato*, Ben-san," she said, thanking him in Japanese.

"Err, that's okay," Ben said, unsure how to reply but taking a guess anyway.

"*Domo*, you have been very helpful. I shall await Yoh's arrival in the alleyway."

"Of course," Shaun said.

Black Lotus then walked to the door and left the apartment.

"I thought she might just vanish," said Vanessa.

Shaun smiled but said nothing. Instead, he picked up a laptop and sat in one of the soft chairs as he logged into the Dark Web and navigated to where he needed to be.

He saw his post from a few days ago, asking for anyone to contact him who might be able to help narrow down the timeframe of when Amanda bought the house and hoped that this search would be just as fruitful.

Within a few minutes he'd discovered that Black Lotus worked for an organisation in Japan that did wet work. Their forte seemed to be assassinations, contract killing, body disposal, and other dirty work. As one of their premiere assassins, Black Lotus travelled the globe, taking on contracts of all kinds, killing Riven, Initiated, Scions, and even a few Magi. The general consensus seemed to be that she was probably a Scion and that she used a range of Magical items that her organisation procured for her from the powerful Magi they worked for.

But Shaun couldn't find her real name or her connection to Yoh anywhere. He supposed he might never know, but he already felt better now that he knew a bit more about her. He logged off and closed the laptop.

All they could do was wait.

- Summary of the Laws of Necromancy, by Louisa Hunt.

Within the ranks of the Arcadian Magi, Magic that interferes with the natural order of death, the Soul, and with the Spirits of the dead, is known as Necromancy.

All living creatures have within them an Energy we refer to as the Anima Mundi, and it's this that gives us life.

We know that this energy, upon death, eventually ascends to a higher plane of existence, and the Arcadian Council decrees that interfering with the natural order of this is wrong, dangerous, and can be punishable through expulsion from the Arcadian Ranks (thus becoming a Nomad by default), or death by execution.

Examples of Necromancy include, but are not limited to:

- Bringing someone back from the dead who's Anima Mundi has departed their physical body.

- Forcibly removing an individual's Anima Mundi before the death of their body.

- Replacing an individual's Anima Mundi with that of a Shade (Anima Mundi that had departed a dead body).

- Creating a zombie by forcing a Shade into a dead body.

- Binding one's own Anima Mundi to your Magically animated dead body, thus becoming a Lich.

Vendetta

Greenwich Village, New York

Liz pulled the pint, slowly filling the glass she held while the customer waited for her. She'd been working behind the bar at The Jade Palace for a nearly a week now, making drinks and talking with customers. It had been precisely what she'd needed to do—getting out the house, away from the Magic of her other life, and mixing with ordinary people. Talking with people who had everyday problems and weren't being hunted by psychotic wizards was a welcome release for her.

Even though she worked in the main bar, she almost never saw Yoh or Stella, because they rarely came to the front of the building. It was primarily, a precautionary measure to limit their chances of being spotted, but she supposed it had kept them hidden for this long, so who was she to cast judgement?

As she pulled the pint, she looked down the bar to the young man sitting at the end. He saw her looking and smiled. Liz smiled back.

His name was Jason and he'd been in here every day for the last few and always made it a point to talk to her. She'd seen him before, but when he came in the other day, he'd flirted with her. Touching her hand and looking her in the eyes for a moment longer than he needed to. He was polite and she enjoyed the attention and thought he was handsome and well dressed.

Yesterday, he'd been there at the end of her shift, and afterwards, they went for a drink. She'd been unsure if she should go, or if she needed this kind of attention right now. Liz had thought back to her friends, to Stephen and Ben. Ben had been her first boyfriend. She'd even kissed him before a Nomad had killed him in cold blood.

That had been over a year ago. Maybe she'd never fully get over it. That kind of thing could easily scar you for life. But as they chatted and drank, Liz realised she might actually be enjoying herself. They laughed and talked about all kinds of things. The differences between British and American cultures came up often, frequently ending with them breaking down into giggles.

Towards the end of the night, they even had a dance and indulged in a few gentle kisses.

When she saw him today, there'd been a hint of awkwardness, but it passed quickly and they went back to talking openly again as she served people.

Before long, her shift was done and her manager informed her she could go home whenever she wanted.

After she put her things in her locker in the backroom, she pulled on her coat and stepped back into the bar to find Jason waiting for her.

"I really enjoyed last night. Are you sure we can't go out tonight? I know a great place we can go," he said with a charming smile.

"I know. I did too, but I can't right now. I have some things to do, but maybe tomorrow? I'm off tomorrow, so we could head into town, have a day together? What do you think?"

"Sounds great. I'll call you tomorrow, late morning probably," he replied, opening the door and allowing her to pass through first.

"Great. I'm looking forward to it." She'd sensed the slight disappointment in his voice, so she leaned in and kissed him gently. "I gave you my number, right?"

"You did. See you tomorrow."

They hugged, and she watched as he turned away and walked down the street.

Feeling happy, she turned and walked over to where Amanda sat on her bike waiting for her.

"Well, well, well, found yourself a guy, have ye?" Amanda teased as she handed Liz her helmet.

"His name's Jason, and, I don't know. Maybe. He's nice. I like him," she answered, pulling on her helmet.

"He's a good looking lad, to be sure."

Liz climbed on behind Amanda.

"Yeah, I noticed."

"Bleedin' right, ye did. I saw you kiss him," Amanda said as she checked traffic and pulled out onto the road, doing a U-turn to head back to her house.

Liz didn't answer, she was too busy thinking about how it felt to kiss him. She thought back to the dance last night when the slow music had come on, and she'd put her arms around him.

He'd slid his hands down onto her bum and pulled her closer to him as they moved to the music, enjoying each other's kiss and touch.

After all the bad memories, it felt great to have a happy one. Liz's thoughts drifted, and she thought about the night ahead and her plans.

"Training night tonight?" she asked Amanda.

"That's right. We'll spar in the gym and talk about some Magical theory."

As much as she'd enjoyed last night, and as much as she wanted to spend more time with Jason, she couldn't help but look forward to something a little more routine, something familiar that she could lose herself in.

She looked up at the passing buildings as they sped through the city, enjoying the rush of air and the sense of freedom that the bike gave her and she wondered if this concrete jungle might ever feel like home.

***

"Well done, Padawan. That was great, you're really coming along," Amanda said, trying to catch her breath as she pulled Liz in for a rough hug.

"Thanks." Liz smiled up at her.

Amanda enjoyed seeing Liz looking a happier and more optimistic. After the past year and a half, she deserved a bit of happiness in her life. Something she could smile about. Seeing her step out of The Jade Palace earlier this evening and looking so happy as she'd kissed that boy, had filled Amanda with pride. Liz had come a long way and she'd healed so much. She seemed to be a much tougher person now.

They wiped their faces with their towels and sat on the bench at the side of the gym on the third floor of her house. The entire storey was just one large open space with crash mats on the floor and Japanese décor around the walls. A curious mix of oriental and western themes filled the space. Weapon racks were in one corner, gym equipment in another. The stairs from the floor below and up to the roof were at one end of the room, made from dark varnished wood.

Amanda used this room every day either on her own, teaching Liz, or being taught by Gentle Water. Her sessions learning Magic with her mentor had become less frequent, and they were on more of an even footing than they had been back in those early days in Ireland when everything had been new. Now, Amanda didn't need much tutoring, she knew how to advance her abilities in Magic, knew the ranks she had not achieved, the effects she could not yet do, and she knew how to reach them.

So Amanda and Gentle Water tended to stick to martial arts training. She had become a capable fighter, picking up the art form very quickly. She wasn't that far behind her mentor in ability these days, although he always seemed to have a new trick up his sleeve.

She knew there was a big difference between a sparring session and a real fight, though. Her memories of the train and how Angel had pretty much only used Magic to defeat her, played on her mind when she thought about confronting someone like Lucian. Sometimes, how well you could throw a punch counted for nothing when it came to the Magi.

She'd built her confidence back up since then. Assisting Xain and the boys in their raids had been great for that, and she'd ended up in a few fights on those missions. She always had back up, though, and most of the fights were against Initiated or not very skilled Magi.

Coming face to face with Lucian had been something of a step up from that.

"So, we'd been talking about Time Magic earlier," she said.

"Yeah. It sounds great. So, when I get strong enough, I could go back in time and save my sister?"

"In theory, you can. In practice…"

"No?" Liz asked.

"Almost certainly, no. That would change the timeline and cause a paradox. It's the old, 'if I go back and kill my father before he has me, then I won't be born, but if I'm not born then I can't kill my father,' paradox and so on."

"Aaah, yes, I've heard of that. I think the boys talked about it once."

Amanda knew she was referring to Stephen and Ben when she said 'the boys'. Her way of talking about them without saying their names helped keep the grief at bay.

"Also, there's the small problem of the Weavers."

"The who in the what now?" Liz asked.

"The Weavers. They police the timeline. Little is known about them other than their name and that when Magi get too cocky with Time Magic, they show up and that Magus disappears. It doesn't seem to make any difference how powerful the Magus is. Novice or Arch Magi, everyone's fair game."

"They're not Magi or Scions, then?"

"To be sure, no one knows what they are. You just be sure to use Time Magic sparingly and carefully. Anything to do with going forward or with our current timeline generally seems okay, but going back in time… you do that at your own risk."

"Ah, okay. Well, now that you've scared the bejeezus out of me, I doubt I'll be using that Magic any time soon."

"Speeding up time, slowing it down, pausing it, or looking back or forward through time is all good. I haven't heard of anyone bringing a Weaver down on them by doing any of those things. But yeah, you're not alone in being a little nervous about Time Magic. Gentle Water says most Magi avoid it entirely, just to be safe."

Liz nodded, and they both sat back again, Amanda resting her head on the wall behind her.

"So, how long have you known Jason for, then?" she finally asked.

"Hah. I knew you wanted to ask me about him. I knew this was coming."

Amanda smiled, wondering if this is how a mother felt when her children started dating. "Sorry, I'm just protective of you, I guess. I want to make sure you're okay."

"Yes, Mum!" Liz answered.

"Sorry," Amanda replied with a smile.

"It's okay. I understand. But to answer your question, just a few days. I've seen him in The Palace before, but he only started talking to me a few days ago."

"And he's nice? Do you like him?"

"I do, yes. He's…"

Amanda sensed a flare of Magic—powerful Magic—somewhere close by, with a signature she didn't recognise.

Amanda darted from the bench and ran across the gym. After a few bounding steps, she Ported two floors down into the foyer at the front of the house. She stopped and listened with her enhanced senses.

A noise from the back of the house caught her attention, and then a sudden, loud bang echoed through the house making her blood run cold. If she was right, someone uninvited was inside.

Amanda quickly used her Magic to set her mind to Multitasking. Her secondary mind checked her Aegis and then started pulling in Essentia, preparing for the potential fight ahead.

As she turned and ran down the hallway towards the rear of the house she heard Liz charging down the stairs above her. She used her hands to keep from hitting the walls as she careened around corners at speed. She felt sure the bang had been the back door, slammed open by something. She knew Yoh had been due here any time and he always used the back door. He even had his own key so that they didn't need to keep opening it for him, but Amanda knew Yoh's Magic, and she knew the typical sounds he made as he entered and this sounded nothing like it. Something was wrong. Could it be Lucian again? They'd not seen him since her encounter on the pier. Is that what he'd meant by his little speech? Is this how he'd hurt her?

A couple seconds later, she reached the door to the utility room and burst through it, but stopped short and gasped. Yoh lay on his side, across the threshold of the backdoor, only his upper half having made it inside. A deep crimson stained his grey jacket and seeped onto the floor beneath him.

Then, Yoh moved. A painful grimace on his face as he looked to see who had entered the room. At least he was alive, she thought.

"Don't…" He struggled. "Be careful," he managed before the pain caused him to curl up, gritting his teeth.

Amanda nodded silently, heeding his warning. The attacker was close and might want to finish the job. Amanda's Magical sight took in the room, everything looked as it should. The Aegis around the house that covered the door looked intact with Yoh safely inside it. The room seemed otherwise untouched. She stepped down the two steps and into the room, looking about her carefully. Apart from around Yoh himself, the Essentia here seemed untouched, undisturbed by anything. She looked back at Yoh, her confidence growing.

Something on his chest glowed with a serious amount of Essentia and as she looked, she could see that the flow of magical energy through his body—the flow that kept people alive—had been disrupted. It seemed to move in fits and starts, almost juddering through him rather than flowing cleanly.

With a drumbeat of footsteps, Liz reached the doorway behind Amanda. Amanda held her hand up, one finger extended to get Liz to slow down and take a moment. Liz hesitated for a second before cautiously stepping into the room. She stifled a scream, covering her mouth with her hand when she saw Yoh's crumpled form on the floor.

Yoh moved again, raising his arm and pointing through the door.

"Outside..." he gasped.

Amanda nodded, choosing to stay quiet. Her fists clenched, she edged towards the door but could see little from where she stood so she pulled on the threads of Essentia and worked a little Magic, sending a second set of senses outside. She couldn't see anyone from her vantage point just outside the door, but she needed to be sure.

"One moment," she said Porting outside and appearing in the alley a short distance from the door. She stood at the corner of the house so she could see either way.

They seemed to be clear of anything untoward. She could see Yoh's feet poking out of the door to her right, but nothing else.

She went to move back towards Yoh, only for something to glint in the meagre light to her left, catching her eye. Stepping back, she looked harder and noticed glass on the ground. That was odd.

She moved a couple of steps further along and saw that one of the windows on the rear of the house had been smashed and the window opened.

More disturbingly, with her magical sight, she could see a hole slowly closing in the Aegis surrounding the house. She almost hadn't seen it, the Magic that had created it, and that now faded away before her eyes, had been both powerful and subtle.

Her stomach sank, and a deep-rooted fear took hold in her gut. It felt like her world stopped. She felt frozen in place, unable to act for fear of what might happen. Whoever, or whatever had hurt Yoh, was inside the house.

A scream from the back of the house broke the spell that fear had cast over Amanda, snapping her back to reality. *That sounded like Liz*, she thought, before Porting back into the utility room

The first thing she saw was a figure crouching over Yoh pulling an ornate dagger from his body with a jerk of her arm.

The figure, dressed in an all-black catsuit had a powerful Aegis surrounding her. It suppressed any magical signatures, making it difficult to get a read on her. After seeing her ability to tunnel through the house's Aegis, Amanda had to assume she was a powerful Magi.

On the far side of the room Liz lay crumpled against the wall, alive, but clearly hurt. The attacker looked over at Liz and got up from her position over Yoh, holding out the bloody dagger before her.

"Hey!" Amanda shouted.

The assassin paused and partially turned her head so she could see Amanda and Liz at the same time.

Amanda didn't waste any time, she needed this killer away from Liz before she hurt her, too. With a force of will born from anger and fear, she blasted the assassin with a kinetic blast. She flew sideways across the room, away from Liz. The assassin may have an Aegis, but she could still get knocked off her feet.

The assassin slammed into the wall several feet above the floor and landed with a bone-crunching thump.

She rolled with the fall and barely a second later, was up on her feet and moving to attack Amanda with the dagger in hand. She swung at Amanda and Amanda reacted without thought, using her forearm against her attacker's forearm to fend off the knife, only to be greeted with an electrical shock that made her yelp.

The assassin's attacks rained down without let up or pause. Amanda tried to defend herself, getting electrocuted each time she fended off another blow.

Amanda's second mind went to work and pulled on reality. Working her Magic, she modified the shield she already had in place so it would repel and disperse electrical attacks. A moment later, the shocks were gone, and she redoubled her efforts.

Amanda focused, looking for openings in the assassin's defence. Within moments, she found one and turned the tide of the fight. Amanda went on the offensive, catching the hand with the dagger and twisting it. Grunting, the assassin dropped the dagger to the floor with a metallic clatter.

Claws extended from the assassin's fingers as she came at Amanda again. Each nail was over an inch long and quite deadly-looking as they raked across Amanda's stomach. Using Amanda's natural response to pull away, the assassin twisted out of her hold and pirouetted away, only to turn back to face Amanda with her arm raised. A gun on her wrist fired and something tiny shot past Amanda and then froze in mid-air.

The pellet flared with Essentia, and a second later a powerful gravity well appeared around it, crushing it. The room shook as the Magic grew. Within a few moments, the contents of the entire room would be pulled and crushed into that one invisible point of space.

Amanda's second mind worked frantically to counter the Magic, unravelling it as fast as it grew.

Meanwhile, the assassin pulled the two swords free from where they were secured across her back. Amanda couldn't see the assassin's face under the stealth suit, but she could have sworn that the killer smiled at her.

She ran at Amanda, lashing out with her katanas. Amanda dodged away from the blades. They missed her by inches, but that was enough.

She tumbled and ducked away from the slashes, the women moving in unison, like a carefully choreographed dance routine. The ebb and flow of the fight moved about the room as the pair flipped and spun around each other.

***

With the attacker occupied with Mandy, Liz moved back to Yoh's side and held his hand in hers. His breath came in short, ragged gasps that put her on edge.

She looked up as the assassin drew two curved Japanese swords from her back and attacked Amanda, who was also using her own Magic to counter a growing effect behind her. Small objects, dust and other lightweight items started to levitate and move towards a spot in space where gravity suddenly grew in strength.

Liz knew she could help. Amanda had taught her how to unravel Magic only recently as she progressed from Apprentice to Adept in rank.

She raised her right hand and extended it out towards the gravity well to help focus her will, while concentrating on pulling the Essentia back and away from the effect. The Magic in the gravity well was strong and complex, but between her and Amanda, they began to make progress. The Magic stopped increasing and began to lessen as Liz did her best to remain focused.

A movement to her right caught her eye. Maya entered the room with a look of surprise on her face, which swiftly changed to horror when she saw Yoh on the ground.

Maya ran over to them, her black skirt flaring out behind her before she skidded to a stop and went down on her knees.

"Is he okay? What happened?" she asked.

Liz grunted in her effort to keep fighting the gravity well. "He's… been stabbed. By her," she managed, her tone condemning the assassin.

Maya nodded. "You focus on your magic, I've got Yoh."

Relieved, Liz redoubled her efforts. With a grunt and yell, she helped Amanda rip the last of the Essentia from the gravity well.

The ball of crushed objects dropped to the floor with a thud. Amanda nodded at her in approval, after dodging another of the assassin's attacks. Liz smiled back before turning back to Yoh and Maya.

Maya leaned in and tried to listen to Yoh's breathing. Liz felt helpless. She didn't have the Magical ability to heal people yet. She could only hope Amanda would survive the fight and be able to save him.

Maya moved her head away from Yoh's face.

"God damn it!" she cursed. She turned him easily onto his back so she could check his airway, her Vampire strength making light work of moving him.

"Crap," she whispered. Liz could see why. Blood covered Yoh's face and seeped from his mouth. His airway would be filled with it, too. But it didn't stop Maya, who covered his mouth with hers and breathed into him twice, filling his lungs with air before she used her fingers to find the right place on his chest, put one hand over the other, and started chest compressions.

***

Dodging the swings of the two swords, Amanda felt the gravity well behind her fade to nothing. With Liz's help, they'd killed the effect, and likely saved the house and everyone in it.

Amanda nodded once to Liz as she turned both minds back towards the assassin. Her twin blades had slashed against Amanda's Aegis a few too many times now, leaving it in a weakened state. Cursing, she delivered a kick to the assassin's chest, sending her flying into the far wall. In the seconds of breathing space that gave her, she dumped as much Essentia back into her defences as possible.

The assassin fell, rolled, and in just a couple of seconds, stood before her once more.

Amanda screamed at the figure in black. Using one mind to send a knife of Magical energy into the Aegis that surrounded the assassin, cracking it, she used her other mind to reach out and Port a katana of her own from the weapons rack upstairs into her hand.

The assassin cocked her head to one side as if to say, "Really?" before lunging forward again.

Amanda countered the attack, their swords clashing, the sound of ringing metal echoing through the room. On the offensive now, Amanda's second mind reached out to the washing machine, took hold of it in a telekinetic grasp, and threw it across the room. The assassin didn't see it coming. The heavy metal appliance hit the attacker full force and crushed her against the wall.

The machine dropped to the floor and shifted sideways out of the way before Amanda let it go. The woman collapsed to the floor as well, groaning in pain. Using both of her minds, Amanda ripped the Aegis from her opponent, leaving her defenceless.

The assassin climbed unsteadily to her feet, slower than before, her left arm limp. Now that the assassin's Aegis was gone, Amanda's Aetheric Sight allowed her to see the broken bones in the woman's arm. She also had a few broken ribs and some internal bleeding, but as Amanda watched, she could see them healing. The woman wasn't a Magus, though. She was a Riven, and all her Magic came from enchanted items.

Amanda threw her sword to the ground as the assassin tried to stand. Her Magic ripped the blades from her opponent's hands, followed by her tactical webbing and belt system. Amanda stepped forward and threw a right hook at the assassin that knocked her back against the wall.

Amanda hit her again and she dropped to the floor, unconscious. Blood dripped from Amanda's fist as she stood over her fallen opponent.

"Amanda," said Liz from across the room.

Amanda turned and looked at Liz and Maya. Maya knelt at Yoh's side while Liz sat back on her haunches a foot away, her cheeks glistening in the light from the tears she'd shed.

"He's gone," Liz whispered.

Amanda let out a breath and her shoulders slumped. "Shite," she said under her breath. "I was too late."

"We tried to save him, but she stabbed him so many times. It would have taken Magic to heal him."

Amanda turned to the assassin then.

"Damn it," she shouted, kicking the unconscious woman out of pure frustration.

"Can we bring him back?" Liz asked.

"I don't know. I might be powerful enough, but I'm not sure if Arcadian law would consider it Necromancy or not. I... I don't know."

"Where's Gentle Water? He'd know."

"Paris, I think. I'm not sure. It would probably be too late by the time we got anyone here."

"There is an alternative," said Maya.

Amanda turned to the Scion. She didn't know Maya all that well. They'd spoken a few times and actually got on really well, but the other woman mostly came here with Yoh. They were close and with a pang, Amanda realized that Maya was hurting just as much, if not more, than she herself.

"Go on," Amanda said.

"I'm a Scion, I can turn others into Scions by sharing my blood with them. I know I can bring him back but he'd be a Scion like me."

"You mean, a Vampire?"

Maya nodded.

"I… I don't know," Amanda said, unsure what she should do. Maya's suggestion sounded like a somewhat radical step to take. But then, this was not your average situation.

The idea of bringing people back from the dead played with the natural order of things. The Arcadians called that Necromancy and she knew they took a pretty hard line on that sort of thing. If you were caught dabbling in it, you were branded a Nomad and hunted down. She'd been taught that it was one of the primary reasons that some people defected from the Arcadians to join the Nomads over the centuries.

Becoming a Nomad had lots of other connotations that went along with it, though, so she would not be walking down that path.

Liz stood up and walked over to Amanda. She looked just as conflicted as Amanda felt. It was a pretty heavy choice to lay on their young shoulders. She didn't want Liz to feel responsible for this at seventeen years old. But then, Amanda would only be twenty-one in July this year.

"I'm not sure about this, Amanda," she said. "Can't we get Gentle Water here or a message to him quick enough to find out what we can do?"

"Maybe. I have no idea. He's on a mission for the Legacy and he warned me he'd be out of touch for a few days. Let me try," she said, and concentrated, reaching out through the Link to her mentor. The seconds passed, but there was no answer. She shook her head in defeat.

"Damnit, isn't there anyone else we can ask?"

"It all takes time. We have a minute or two to do this and convincing Arcadians to come to a Nomad city is difficult enough at the best of times," Amanda replied.

"Time is short, Amanda," Maya reminded her.

Amanda tried to organise her thoughts, she needed to make a choice, but her mind was scattered in the face of such a weighty decision.

Technically, she might be powerful enough to bring Yoh back, but she'd never done it before, which meant it might not work or it might take too much time. Time, Yoh didn't have. Then there were the Arcadians and the whole Necromancy thing. She didn't have time to find another Magi who she could ask.

Which left them with Maya. She claimed she could turn him into a Scion. From everything Amanda knew about Scions, she believed this to be true, but she seemed to remember being told it didn't always work. Then again, Yoh was already dead…

Amanda turned to Maya.

"Do it."

"Really?" Liz asked, incredulous.

Wasting no time, Maya went to work, biting her own wrist and dripping her blood into Yoh's wounds and mouth.

"We have no other choice. I'm not going to risk being branded a Nomad for using Necromancy, and we don't have time to hunt for help."

"But he'll be a Scion!"

"He'll be alive, if he survives the transformation."

"What? So this might kill him?"

"He's dead anyway, Liz. We're giving him another chance at life."

They both looked over at Maya, who stopped dripping her blood into Yoh's mouth before pulling away from him. She stood up and stepped back.

"Now, we wait," Maya said.

"How long?" Liz asked.

Yoh's body bucked and jerked suddenly, his movements those of someone in agony.

"Not long," said Maya. "My blood is doing its job."

Amanda watched Yoh, fascinated by the transformation. They could see the Essentia around him doing strange things—moving in odd waves and patterns—as his body reacted.

And then, as suddenly as it had started, it stopped. The Essentia around him calmed and went still, like Yoh's body.

The Magical energy that Amanda could see as a thin golden mist didn't flow through him as it did with a living creature, which meant that Yoh had died. Again.

Amanda felt deflated. His body's movement had brought her false hope it seemed, meaning today would be remembered as the day that Yoh had died.

"It didn't work, did it?" Liz stated.

"I don't think so, Liz. I'm sorry," Amanda said, reaching out and pulling Liz in next to her, hugging her.

Amanda looked at Maya, who continued to watch Yoh, as if she expected him to move. Amanda felt sorry for her. She'd tried to help, but it hadn't worked out.

Yoh sat up, blinking.

Amanda jumped back at the sudden movement.

Yoh groaned and held a hand to his chest. Amanda and Liz ran to his side and eased him up into a sitting position.

"Take it easy."

"Amanda-san, what happened?"

He pulled his hand away from his chest, looking at the thick, wet blood that covered it.

"Where is she?" he asked, scanning the room.

"Over there," Maya said, pointing to where the assassin lay on the floor.

"Ugh, help me up," he said.

Amanda and Liz helped him.

"She's unconscious," Amanda informed him.

Yoh looked at her.

"Did you… do this?" he asked.

"I did."

"*Dozo*," Yoh said, thanking her, "and remind me not to get on your bad side."

Yoh walked a couple of steps and bent down to pick up the dagger on the floor. It was ornately carved, and even drenched in blood, it had a beauty all its own.

"Are you sure you should be walking about?" Amanda asked.

"I'm feeling better already. What did you do to me? Things seem, different."

"You died, Yoh. You were dead by the time I subdued her. We didn't have many options."

Yoh looked Amanda in the eyes, raising his eyebrows slightly.

"What did you do?"

"Maya offered to turn you into a Scion. You were dead anyway, this way you had a chance."

Yoh sighed and looked away.

"Damnit. That explains a lot. I… My Magic seems different. I'm not sure about my connection to it."

"It could still be there, but it will take time to get used to things again," Maya said.

"And it might be gone," Yoh answered.

"Indeed," confirmed Maya.

"That's a sickner," Amanda said in commiseration. "I didn't know what to do. I'm sorry."

Yoh turned back to her.

"Don't worry. You did what you thought was right. At least I'm alive, after a fashion."

He was right, his body remained technically dead. With her Magic, Amanda couldn't detect a heartbeat and the local Essentia didn't flow through him like it would a living being. It also didn't flow through Maya, in much the same way.

"So, I'm a vampire," Yoh said.

"That's right," Maya replied. "I'm sorry, I wasn't sure if it was the right thing to do."

"It's okay. Thank you, Maya. I know that couldn't have been easy."

Maya nodded.

Amanda hadn't considered the connotations that surrounded a change into one of these creatures. Yoh would have a lot to deal with now and had a lot to learn, too. As a vampire, she guessed that meant he would need to drink blood to survive. The thought turned her stomach.

Yoh stepped over to the prone figure of the assassin.

"What are you going to do?" Amanda asked.

"What I should've done a long time ago." His voice remained flat and unemotional as he crouched down over the body, one foot on either side. Placing his hand over the mouth of the woman, he raised the dagger and brought it down hard, plunging the blade into her skull with a cracking sound that made Amanda wince.

The body jerked once before going limp.

"Bleedin' hell!" Amanda gasped, covering her mouth, but unable to look away.

"Oh, God," Liz whimpered and backed away from Yoh. Maya however, remained unfazed by the killing and continued to watch.

He removed the dagger and pulled the hood from the assassin's face before standing up and dropping the blade to the floor.

The assassin looked Japanese, with long black hair tied back in a ponytail and if it weren't for the stab wound at the top of her forehead, she may have been pretty.

As the Magic on her clothing faded, her catsuit changed from pure black, to a black and white design of stylised lotus flowers.

"Who was she? Anyone you know?" Liz asked.

"Yes," Yoh replied. "She was Black Lotus. Her real name was Kimi Takahashi, and she was my sister."

Amanda felt her eyebrows rise. That was not the answer she'd expected. Yoh had just killed his own sister by stabbing her in the head. To be fair, she had killed him first.

"I take it you didn't get along," Amanda said incredulously.

"That would be an understatement. I escaped my family many years ago. They have never forgiven me and have hunted me ever since. You don't leave my father's organisation and live, even if you are family."

"That's fecked up."

"Indeed, it is. But the question remains. How did she find me?"

Amanda's heart sank, as the truth dawned on her.

"Lucian," said Amanda and Yoh in unison, looking at each other.

"Has to be," she said. "He knows where I live, I presume he either knows, or at least suspects you and I have some contact, and although he won't hurt me directly, doesn't mean he won't hurt those I care about."

"Makes sense," Yoh agreed.

"But he didn't do anything to me the other day on the pier," Liz said.

"True. But I was with you, and you came here to New York with me. Maybe you're safe, too."

"I, however, have been a thorn in Lucian's side for a long time," explained Yoh.

"How did he know about her, though?" Amanda asked, pointing at Yoh's sister.

"My father didn't exactly keep it a secret that he wanted me dead. Lucian could have found out about my family's vendetta against me without too much trouble. I doubt he knows I'm related to them, though."

The realisation that Lucian had set this up made Amanda's blood boil. She wasn't surprised. She'd expected something like this to happen at some point. But the reality of it, seeing her friend bleeding and dying before being turned into a Scion, felt much worse than just the threat of it.

Lucian had crossed a line. This time, he'd gone too far.

- Harlem, New York

David pulled his wife closer to him and kissed her. They enjoyed the moment for a few seconds before pulling apart and looking at each other.

"Are you sure he didn't mind?" Susan asked.

"Babe, he must have so many people in his congregation, I doubt Father Noah even notices how often we attend church."

"I just feel bad, like we've taken advantage of him."

"I doubt he feels like that. He probably does christenings for loads of couples who don't really attend church," David answered.

"Yeah, maybe."

"It went well, though, didn't it?"

"It did, thanks for a great day. Hey, I have that lingerie on you like, you wanna get an early night?" she purred.

He pulled her in close, grabbing a butt cheek in each hand, feeling the garter belts beneath the fabric of her dress.

Their baby started to cry upstairs.

"God damn it. He has impeccable timing, I'll give him that. One moment, babe, I'll be right back," he said as he ran upstairs, his mind full of images of what he'd do with his wife. Halfway up the stairs, the crying stopped. David paused, but thought he should pop his head in to check on Oscar anyway. He reached the door, quietly opened it, and looked inside.

Something felt wrong. There was a cold breeze, but he didn't remember leaving the window open. Easing the door wider to let more light in, he looked at the empty cot and then over to the wide-open window. His mouth dropped open in shock as his stomach did a summersault. He felt sick.

"Oscar?" he called, in the desperate hope that their baby who couldn't walk yet might have somehow hidden himself somewhere in the room

"Everything okay, babe?" Susan shouted up the stairs. "This dress won't remove itself."

"Susan, you'd better get up here!"

Hostile Takeover

The Pit Club, Manhattan.

Lucian stalked along the corridor of his coven's Sepulchre where they made their home, hidden deep beneath The Pit Nightclub in Harlem. It had been one day since Black Lotus had started watching Amanda's house in Greenwich Village, a day since she'd left Shaun to supposedly stakeout the house and wait for Yoh. And yet, they'd heard nothing. Shaun's reports had said Yoh visited the house most days. Shouldn't they have heard something from the assassin by now?

This whole thing with Amanda had been dragging on for far too long and was making a mockery of his leadership. How could he be the King of New York if he couldn't keep his kingdom in line?

Ekua had been nipping at his heels the whole time, dogged in his determination to discredit him and his leadership in the eyes of the other coven members. He knew he could count on the support of Raal, Lex, and Aneurin. They knew of his predicament, the threat he'd been under, and the stress it had caused him.

No amount of backstabbing comments could change their minds, or at least he hoped not. So far, they'd been at his side the entire time. They were trusted associates who he could call on whenever he needed them.

Ekua had fostered some support from Joaquin, Lucian's man in Columbia who visited from time to time, and in Bull, but that wasn't difficult. The simple-minded Beast Master followed whoever paid him enough attention. Something Lucian hadn't done over the past few weeks due to recent events.

Ekua also had some support in the ranks of the coven's Initiated, but again, Lucian knew he could swing them back any time he wished.

Still, Ekua could not be underestimated. Lucian had to be on his guard.

Lucian planned to hold another meeting this morning with his close supporters to go over recent events and plan their next move, before dealing with his other business interests.

As he walked up the corridor towards a T-junction, he felt a tingle in his Aetheric senses, a sense of foreboding that warned him something potentially dangerous lay ahead.

Looking up, he saw one of Bull's Scions stalk around the corner. They were huge, wolf-like creatures, their dark, raw-looking skin covered in patches of unkempt black hair. Its yellow eyes were locked on Lucian as it bared its teeth and uttered a low, guttural growl that rumbled along the corridor.

Behind it, Ekua strolled into view, his large frame relaxed and a look of superiority on his scarred face. He wore only a stained white vest top with baggy jeans and trainers, his only visible weapon a keen-looking knife in his fist.

Bull stood in the shadows behind Ekua twisting the blood-stained rubber apron he wore in his large hands.

Lucian stopped walking and waited to see what Ekua might do next, while his Multitasking mind worked overtime to shore up his already robust defences and prepare for the fight he felt must be inevitable.

He noted a second of Bull's wolves closing in behind him, ready to pounce just like the first.

"*Whaa gwaan*, Ekua?" Lucian asked.

"Don't play coy with me, guy," Ekua said, pointing at Lucian. "This has gone on for long enough. Your incompetence has made us look weak, mon. Nymira needs to know what you be doin'."

"You think she don' know 'bout all dis? She knows everyting, mon."

"Bullshit. She don' know shit. I'm here to make you an offer."

"Really?" Lucian asked, incredulously.

"Step down now, name me coven leader, and dis ting will be ended. No more will be said."

"And if I don't?"

"Do I really need to spell it out for you?" Ekua said, indicating the two wolves who had inched closer to Lucian.

"I think if you want leadership of dis coven, you need to come and take it, pussy."

Ekua cocked his head to one side and let out a breath.

Lucian sensed the subtle Essentia pulse that came from Ekua at that moment, a simple discrete message sent to the two Scion wolves on either side of him. A heartbeat later the two attack dogs launched themselves at Lucian—their fanged maws gaping and drool flying as they attacked.

But they never made it. Two huge blocks of concrete, each over a meter cubed, launched themselves from the walls into each of the two wolves, slamming into their sides and crushing them against the opposite walls. Blood exploded from the two creatures, catching everyone in its spray as the two beasts whimpered once, before dropping silent forever.

Lucian wasted no time, part of his mind had reached out to his two most combat-ready allies, Raal and Lex, the moment the wolves had pounced. Sprinting forward, his black cloak and dreadlocks flapping out behind him, he sailed over the concrete block between him and Ekua. Lucian landed deftly before his coven mate just as his two allies Ported into the corridor. Raal stood next to where Lucian landed, while Lex appeared next to Bull and immediately grabbed him, putting him into a painful neck hold to immobilise him.

Before doing anything else, Lucian conjured an Aegis around the entire scene to keep Ekua from escaping. Lucian would finish this today, no matter what.

Magic poured out of Raal, flooding Ekua's Aegis with disruptive energy to try and break it down. Lucian did the same, his Multitasking mind working several effects at once.

Essentia lashed out, striking Ekua's Aegis, pushing it to its breaking point. At the same time, Essentia poured into a dagger that Lucian pulled from his belt. Still another part of his mind flung large chunks of concrete at Ekua that weren't deflected by his Aegis, hitting his body hard and knocking him back, while Lucian advanced.

Ekua did his best. He pulled in Essentia to keep his shield in place, his biggest defence against Lucian's attack and his best chance of staying alive. But it wouldn't be enough. With Raal there, Lucian knew he couldn't resist both of them for long.

Sure enough, seconds later, with a snap of magical energy, Ekua's Aegis fell apart. Lucian moved in quickly, dagger in hand, and punched his coven mate. He struck him several more times, smashing his fist into the other man's face. Ekua defended himself well, getting in a punch and a slash with his own dagger, while he struggled to work his Magic.

Lucian wouldn't let up, though. Every time Ekua tried to work his Magic, Lucian blocked him. He threw two or three of his minds at each effect to dissipate the Essentia quickly, stopping Ekua's Magic before it even started. Lucian's other minds threw rocks and debris along the corridor at Ekua, distracting him and keeping his Multitasking mind as busy as possible.

Lucian kept the pressure on Ekua and a few moments later, Ekua messed up, leaving a gap in his defences. Lucian's kick connected heavily with Ekua's jaw, breaking it with a loud crack, and slamming his head against the wall.

Ekua dropped to the floor, his defences down, as he tried to recover from the brain-rattling kick.

Lucian didn't wait. He reached down, grabbed Ekua by the scruff of the neck, and hauled him up off the ground before slamming him against the wall. Lucian's other hand moved like lightning, the dagger's blade flashing as he brought it across Ekua's stomach.

Blood and ropey intestines spilt from Ekua's gut and splashed to the floor, his insides uncurling into a red puddle at Lucian's feet.

Ekua gurgled as blood rose up into his mouth, but Lucian hadn't finished with him yet.

"Nice try, Ekua. I respect your loyalty to our mentor, and it's for that reason alone I grant you this," Lucian said, holding Ekua up.

In one swift movement, Lucian jammed his dagger up under Ekua's jaw, into his brain, killing him, and granting him a quick death.

After holding him there for a second, Lucian withdrew the blade and dropped the body to the floor. He stood there for a moment, looking down at the bloody mess at his feet. He knew this had been coming. Ekua had always been brash and often did things a little too soon or without enough preparation. He also underestimated the loyalty of the other coven members to Lucian, no doubt thinking that the fight would be one-on-one. But Lucian had been prepared, he'd had Raal and Lex on alert for days now, knowing that he'd need to call them at a moment's notice should Ekua try to kill him.

Even knowing this, knowing that Ekua would try to kill him, he still felt angry. Ekua's death, as inevitable as it had been, felt like a waste to him. Surely, as Nomads, they shouldn't be bickering amongst themselves, but instead, be working together against their mutual enemies. He could have used him in the coming fight with the Arcadians. Ekua had been a skilled and competent Magus, a match or better for the redhead.

His harassment of Amanda and her friends would probably come to a boiling point sooner or later, and when that time came, Lucian would defend himself and if need be, kill her. Yasmin be damned.

But now, Ekua would be no use to anyone, except as food for the remaining three wolves living in the levels below.

Remembering Bull, where he stood with Lex, her left arm around his neck and his right arm held behind his back, he walked over to the pair and watched as Bull struggled against Lex's hold.

"Lucian, I'm sorry. He made me do it. He made me. He hurt me, Lucian. He did terrible things to me, to my babies." Bull looked over at the crushed remains his wolves and sniffed.

"Let him go," he ordered Lex. She released her hold on Bull, who dropped to his knees.

He clasped his hands together and looked up at Lucian through his tears.

"You know I'm loyal to you, Lucian, always. I'm sorry, I had no choice."

Lucian actually kind of felt sorry for this simpleton, who Ekua had no doubt manipulated easily into helping him. The wolves were his life. They called him Beast Master because that's all he did. He looked after these creatures, turned them into the killing machines that Lucian needed them to be.

The death of two of them would be punishment enough; nothing else would even come close to hurting him in the same way. So Lucian crouched down in front of Bull and put one hand on his shoulder. Bull went quiet, probably unsure of what Lucian would do next.

"I know, Bull. You're a loyal and valued member of this coven. We'll clean up this mess for you."

"No!" Bull blurted out.

Lucian raised his eyebrows at the outburst.

"Sorry, but no. I'll do it," Bull pressed on. "They were my babies, let me. Please."

"Of course, Bull, of course," said Lucian. He stood up and looked at Raal and Lex. "A meeting, now, in the main meeting room. Bring Aneurin and Joaquin. I'll bring the others. Go, now."

With that, Lucian walked down the corridor to the stairs and ascended two floors to the topmost private level, just below The Pitt Club. As he did so, his Multitasking mind hunted down Shaun, who he found in his lair with Ben. He reached out and broadcast his voice to the room.

"It's Lucian, drop your Aegis and let me Port you both to the meeting room."

He watched them stop in their tracks, listening to the voice that sounded like an unusually crisp and clear speaker.

Shaun hesitated for a moment but then nodded. "Done," he said.

Lucian Ported them both to the meeting room.

His other minds found his biker gang of Initiated in the garage around the rear of the club. They had no Aegises to worry about, so he Ported them all into the meeting room without warning, just as he stepped into the room. Seconds later, Lex, Raal, Aneurin, and Joaquin all Ported into the room in a succession of whips and cracks of displaced air.

Apart from Raal and Lex, they all looked at Lucian with a mixture of curiosity and horror at his blood-soaked clothes.

"Ekua is dead. He tried to take leadership of dis coven from me, and he paid da price. Anyone else care to join him?" Lucian bellowed, wanting to make it absolutely clear what would happen to those who might try to usurp him.

The room remained silent as Lucian looked over the stoic faces that surrounded him. No one dared move.

"Good," he said, satisfied for the moment even though his blood still ran hot. "Shaun, an update on Black Lotus, please."

Shaun shifted on the spot, clearly uncomfortable.

"Ur, sir, is this the best place…?"

"Now, Shaun!" Lucian demanded, turning away to stalk around the room.

"It's not good news, sir," said Shaun quickly. "She attacked Yoh, and from what we can see, she did manage to kill him, but…"

"But?" Lucian asked, rounding on the Scion. "But what?"

"But, he seems to have been turned into a Scion. We saw a woman who we're unfamiliar with turn him in the doorway at the rear of the house."

Lucian closed his eyes, feeling his anger rise to the surface.

"And Black Lotus?" he asked through gritted teeth.

"She made it into the house, evading Amanda, which is where she killed Yoh before the Scion arrived, but she never came out again."

Lucian let out a long, strained breath as he prepared for the answer to his next question. "Is she dead?"

"That is my assumption."

"Fuck," he hissed. Pulling the gun from his belt he raised it and fired at Ben who stood next to Shaun. He blew a three-inch hole out the back of his head that covered the side of Shaun's face in brains and blood.

Lucian looked at Shaun, whose mouth hung agape as he looked down at Ben's body where it had crumpled to the floor.

For a moment, the room stood silent, the blast from the gun ringing in everyone's ears.

No longer able to contain his rage, Lucian roared and slammed his fists into the top of the oak table, splitting it.

"I want this fucking group of Arcadians out of my city right now!"

"Sir, I might have an idea," said one of the bikers.

Lucian looked up at the young man who'd stepped forward. "What is it, Jason?"

***

Lucian stepped up to the wooden side door of the Church of the Divine Mother, just a block away from The Pit Club. Producing a key from his coat pocket, he unlocked the door and stepped inside, followed closely by Joaquin.

He shut the door behind him and locked it, before navigating through the small rooms and narrow corridors at the back of the church.

"Are you going to let me in on this plan of yours, then, Lucian?" Joaquin asked.

"Of course," Lucian answered. "You're the second part. You and Noah. After Jason does his bit, you're gonna be in charge of logistics, while Noah... Noah will be indulging in his own personal tastes."

"Oh, God," muttered Joaquin, knowing what that meant.

Lucian eventually found his way to a plain wooden door and used another key to let them through, locking it behind them. The room looked like it had once been a storage room, but a huge hole had been carved out of the floor and the back wall that plunged into the ground beneath the church at a steep, but walkable angle.

They paused for a moment, looking down into the dark passageway.

"He's down there?" asked Joaquin.

"That's where he said to come," Lucian answered, referring to his earlier Magical link with Noah, asking to see him.

As they gazed down the tunnel, they could see things, like insects, but much, much bigger skittering over the walls.

"I can't wait," Joaquin said, sarcastically.

Lucian stepped forward, carefully making his way down the roughly carved tunnel into the depths beneath the church. They passed huge deformed cockroaches and other bugs that stayed well out of their way, seemingly sensing they were allowed inside, or maybe they sensed the power of two Magi they didn't want to anger.

Soon enough, Lucian reached level ground and could make out the sounds of someone in pain. It sounded childlike, but the voice was muffled as if gagged.

Continuing on, they passed side-corridors lined with cell doors and heard more moans and pleas for help coming from them. Again, they sounded like children.

Eventually, they passed from the corridor into a room dug into the rock. Parts of it were roughly hewn, others intricately carved with writhing bodies of demons and their victims in the throes of torture and rape.

Tables scattered about the space were filled with books and candles, or were splattered with dry blood and held implements designed to inflict pain.

In the centre of the room, on an altar, a boy no more than six or seven, lay strapped to the stone edifice. He was gagged and covered in cuts, bruises, and bite marks. He weakly fought against his attacker but to no avail. He looked at Lucian and

Joaquin as they entered in the hope of release, his eyes were filled with pain as they pleaded for help.

The man who stood beside the altar had his back to them and was bent low over the boy's legs. Sensing a change in the room, he jerked his head up, tensed for a moment, before relaxing and turning to face Lucian. The man wore a robe that covered his back and upper arms, but fell open down his front, revealing his nakedness beneath.

The man had slicked-back dark hair and hungrily licked his lips. Most of his face and front glistened in fresh blood, smeared by his own hand.

"Lucian, such a pleasure. You caught me in the middle of my breakfast."

"Apologies, Noah, but this is urgent. I have a job for you."

"Business or pleasure?" Noah asked.

"A bit of both. You are to take a trip with Joaquin here. Can you be ready to leave in a few hours?"

"For you, Lucian, anything. May I finish my meal?"

"We'll wait outside," said Lucian, glancing at the Vampire's victim, who looked on in dwindling hope. He looked away and led Joaquin out of the tunnels.

"I don't like working with that paedophile vampire. I find him to be… disagreeable," admitted Joaquin, once he was out of earshot of the Scion.

"Really, mon? And yet your business and his tastes align rather well."

"Maybe," Joaquin admitted. "So, are you going to elaborate on your plan?"

"Once Noah joins us. I can't wait to see the look on Amanda's face when she finds out."

- Near Amarillo, Texas

"Who's that?" asked Reagan from where she sat on Waylon's lap in her short shorts and crop top.

"That," answered Saxon, pointing to the image of the red-haired girl on the screen, "is a Young Magi named Amanda. Y'all may remember, I told you about her when she moved to New York the other week."

"Whaaat?" Reagan exclaimed, but stopped short when Waylon backhanded her arm with a gentle slap.

"Quiet," he said.

Reagan noticed that Forest had been giving her the dead eye from across the room. So she shut her mouth and listened. She knew when she'd stepped out of place.

Forest turned back to Saxon. "And why are we talking about her again?"

"Just got word from Victoria, Amanda," he pointed at the image, "is paying her a visit. You asked to be notified of such an occurrence, so what would you like me to say to Miss Victoria?"

Reagan watched Forest looking around the room at the other members of the coven, the Magi Legion, who were attending this general meeting. This was the final item on the agenda and she was bored. She just wanted to get back to the gun range and show Waylon who was boss.

"Tell Victoria we'll be there—me, you, and Stella."

Reagan breathed a sigh of relief. For a moment there, she thought he'd meant all of them would be going. He could keep stuffy Saxon and Mama Ward, all she wanted was her hunk of a man, Waylon. She turned to him and ran her fingers through his handsome mullet.

"I loves you, babe," he said, his gold teeth glinting as he spoke. He pulled her in and pawed at her breasts with his left hand while kissing her. *"Now, let's get back to that there range. I'm a-gonna whip your cute little behind."*

"You can try, sweet thang, but if I win, we do what I wanna do tonight," she said.

"But if I win..."

"I ain't doin' another threesome, Waylon."

"Rules is rules, though, sweet cheeks. I do for you as you do for me."

Reagan scowled. She didn't know how he'd tricked her into doing it again. He was so smart, that's why she loved him so. For them thar brains.

Bureaucracy

Washington DC, USA.

Amanda appeared in the same Porting room that she'd used when she had arrived here twelve days ago with Liz and Gentle Water. Amanda had called the number she'd been given and requested a visit to the Washington Coven House. She'd been given a five-minute window to Port in, after which, she'd been greeted by Miss Evans again. Nothing had changed in the calm, wood-panelled edifice that stood testament to the might of this Arcadian Magi House. But this time, she didn't feel as impressed. This time, she felt angry that this powerful organisation wasn't doing more to help against the likes of Lucian.

The Arcadians were meant to be at war with the Nomads. They were meant to fight them and drive them back. And yet, here they were, watching from the side-lines and letting Lucian run his little empire however he saw fit, killing any Arcadian who dared step foot in Manhattan with impunity.

Coming to see Victoria and asking for help felt like the obvious first step. Victoria seemed nice, friendly, and sympathetic to what Amanda was trying to do. Amanda hoped she could persuade her to lend a hand somehow.

"It's a pleasure to see you again, Miss Page," Miss Evans said.

Amanda smiled, but it never touched her eyes. She wasn't feeling particularly happy right now.

"And you," Amanda answered.

"I believe Victoria is nearly ready for you," she said leading Amanda down the same corridor as last time.

Amanda looked about her as she walked. The building seemed to be just as busy as last time, looking every part like a government office, with everyone walking around in their pressed suits.

Amanda wore a knee-length black skirt and dark top, black tights, and tall-heeled boots. She wore a light jacket over the top with her scarlet hair tied back in a ponytail. Despite her frustration with this coven, she'd thought it best to at least try to make a good impression.

Reaching Victoria's office, she sat in one of the chairs outside while Miss Evans made herself busy behind her desk. There were no Hollywood stars here this time.

After a few moments, Miss Evans reacted to something on her desk, and she stood up to face Amanda.

"You may go in now, they're ready for you."

Amanda frowned. They? Who were they, she wondered? Standing, she straightened her spine, smoothed her clothes, and tried hard to push any apprehension she felt about walking into the unknown out of her mind.

Miss Evans opened the door, and Amanda walked into Victoria's office to find her suspicions confirmed. Apart from Victoria, there were four other people all sat before the large oak desk in the centre of the room, three of them to her left, and one woman to her right. Victoria stood up from behind her desk as Amanda entered.

"Amanda, please, come in and join us," she said gesturing to the empty chair.

Amanda stepped toward the chair, but the woman to her right who stood apart from the rest smiled and offered Amanda her hand. "I'm Kelly, Victoria's chief secretary," she said. She looked to be in her late twenties with dark hair tied back in a bun and a tailored dress jacket worn over a crisp white shirt and matching grey skirt.

"Pleasure to meet you," Amanda said, taking the proffered hand and giving the woman a tight smile. Taking her seat, she looked over at the other three people she didn't know.

"This is Forest Ward," said Victoria, indicating the stocky man closest to Amanda who wore jeans, a red checkered shirt, a jacket, and a cowboy hat. He had a bushy blond beard and looked at her with steely blue eyes. He nodded once to acknowledge her but didn't offer his hand.

"...Saxon Rey..." Victoria continued, indicating the next man along, who wore a suit and couldn't have looked more different than Forest with his neat hair and perfect teeth. Amanda got the vibe of a slick car salesman from him.

He smiled at her. "A pleasure, ma'am," he said in a thick Texan accent.

"...and Stella Ward." Victoria finished. The woman didn't even look at Amanda, but she guessed from her surname and the ring on her finger that she would likely be Forest's wife. She wore similar jeans and boots with a check shirt and fur-lined jacket.

Victoria sat down behind her desk, and Amanda got the impression that she seemed a little more harassed than the last time she'd been here.

"They represent the Magi Legion Coven," Victoria continued, "and as a part of the American Council, have an interest in what you're doing in New York and why you're here."

"Okay, grand," Amanda answered.

"As I understand it," Victoria continued, "you've had some trouble with Lucian since arriving in New York."

"That's right, he…" Amanda trailed off, the thought of having to explain everything to these people felt like a huge and maybe fruitless task. Now that she sat here, she felt like a whining school girl complaining about someone pushing her in the playground. "Look, it's getting beyond a joke. He nearly killed Yoh yesterday after setting a very skilled assassin on us."

"And you'd like us to do what?" Saxon asked.

"Help, of course!" Amanda said incredulously.

"So, he's not actually killed any of you?" Saxon asked.

"Well, kind of." Amanda didn't know what to say. Having these other Magi here from another coven had completely thrown her off, and after only a few seconds, they were already making light of her situation.

"Kind of?" Is Yoh dead or not?"

Amanda looked over at Saxon and saw all three pairs of eyes on her. Saxon's expression was open and questioning, framed on either side by two very sceptical faces that didn't seem very friendly. "He's a Scion now. It was the only way we could save him."

"Excellent, so he's alive and the attacker is…"

"Dead. She's dead," Amanda answered.

"What's the problem, then?" he asked.

"The problem is that I'm trying to make a life in New York. I'm trying to make a difference, and I need your help. I want to fight back against Lucian, and I can't do that alone."

"And yet you knew you were moving into a very dangerous city with an active Nomad coven who would likely try to kill you. And when he does, you come crying to us for help?"

"I am asking for help, yes."

"Well, I'm sure Victoria will be happy to raise the issue at the AMC meeting next month," said Saxon, referencing the American Magi Council, "but until then, we can't really do much. And I wouldn't hold out much hope, Miss Page. The Legacy is out of its jurisdiction, and as proud Americans, we will deal with Lucian when we feel the time is right. It's a very delicate situation, and if we just ride on in there without planning ahead, things could get out of hand."

Amanda looked back at Victoria, who seemed frustrated by the whole situation but had not yet said anything.

"Victoria?" she asked.

"I'm sorry, Amanda," Victoria answered. "There's little I can do. My hands are tied. We have a system in place and it must be followed."

"This is ridiculous."

"May I ask, Miss Page, has Lucian attempted to kill you yet?" Saxon asked.

"Not as such. He's threatened me a couple of times," she admitted.

"Really?" Saxon said rhetorically.

"Why ain't he killed you yet, darlin'?" Forest asked, leaning in, his thick Texan drawl colouring his words. Amanda leant back a touch, away from the smell of chewing tobacco that accompanied his question.

"I don't... Well, I guess he tried."

"Tried? Look, everyone else who's been to that there city in recent years has been hunted down and killed within days of arriving and yet here you are, alive and well after twelve days. Are you sure he wants you dead?" Forest asked.

"What are you implying?" asked Amanda, her tone guarded, sensing a trap.

"We're not implying anything," said Saxon, breaking in before Forest could say anything else. "We're just trying to find the truth."

"Of course," said Amanda before she turned and addressed Victoria again. "I think we're done here."

"So soon?" Forest asked. "I thought you wanted our help?"

"I do. But you seem scared of one little Nomad," Amanda goaded.

"I ain't scared of no bitch-ass Nomad, little lady. He'll get what's coming to him, you mark my words. Besides, you're the one that came in here whining about him."

"Then help me. Fight with me," she pleaded.

"I'll fight when I'm good and ready. You wanted to live there, so you deal with him."

Amanda stood up, furious at the pig-headedness of this wannabe cowboy, her legs pushing her chair back as she stood.

"I will. And when I've finished with him, New York is mine."

Forest sat back and looked up at Amanda, a smile passing over his face.

"Sure, whatever you say, little lady."

Amanda took a breath and looked over at Victoria. "Good to see you again," she said and turned to the door. As she walked away, Victoria spoke to Kelly, asking her to walk Amanda out.

Kelly caught up with Amanda by the office door and walked through with her. Amanda, frustrated and angry, didn't wait, she just walked away as Kelly shut the door behind her.

"Hold up, Miss Page," Kelly called out.

Amanda stopped and looked back over shoulder at Kelly, waiting for her to catch up.

"Come with me," Kelly said quietly and walked off down the corridor.

Shortly before the Porting room, Kelly opened a door and stepped through. Amanda reached the door and saw another office, slightly smaller than Victoria's, but just as nice.

"Come in," she urged and gestured for Amanda to close the door behind her. "Sorry for that farce in there. Victoria and our coven in general, are always under pressure from the other American covens over one thing or another. The Legion is perhaps the group who opposes us the most and causes the most trouble. They were not happy about you moving to New York and insisted on meeting you the next time you came here. They almost certainly have informants in these offices and they have at least a couple of Initiated openly working here full-time whose job it is to report back. So when you asked to visit, we had to invite them along."

"Who are they, then? Just another coven?"

"Correct. Ourselves and the Magi Legion are the two largest covens in the U.S., and between us, we have the most seats on the American Magi Council."

"And they don't like me very much."

"No. You're a foreigner, and you're intruding on their territory, they're not big fans of that."

"Their territory?"

"Well, by that I mean America, but you get the idea."

"Look, I just want some help to get rid of Lucian. I think it can be done."

"Careful, Amanda. Many have tried. While Lucian may not be the most powerful Magi in the country, his master is another matter entirely."

"Nymira," Amanda said.

"That's the one. The Legion is watching us, and you. They don't want us helping you, and they are fully expecting you to fail and leave, or die any day now. The fact that you have lasted this long has surprised them."

"He won't kill me," Amanda admitted.

"*Won't* kill you?" Kelly asked quizzically.

"He's confronted me twice now, the second time I had no real back up, no protections other than my own Aegis. He could have attacked me easily, but he just had a few harsh words for me."

"That's... unusual." Kelly frowned.

"I know. I'm still trying to work it out. But he has no problem trying to kill my friends in the meantime, which is why this needs to end."

"Of course, and while we can't be seen giving you help directly, we will try to help you in other ways." And with that, she reached under the desk and pulled out a manila envelope and passed it to Amanda. "That's everything we know about Lucian. It's not much. We don't even know where their main base of operations is, but there might be something in there that can help you."

"Thank you," Amanda said, taking the packet from Kelly.

"I hope you're successful. I really do," offered Kelly.

"Thanks. I'll... I'll see what I can do."

***

Ten minutes later, Amanda appeared in her front room with a snap.

She sighed in frustration and rubbed the bridge of her nose to fight back the small headache that was lurking behind her eyes. The guys from the Magi Legion felt like every slimy politician she'd ever seen on TV, and that kind of xenophobia really didn't agree with her.

She dropped the envelope onto the coffee table and slumped onto her sofa, glad to be taking the weight off her feet. She hadn't been sitting down for more than a few seconds before she felt the familiar sensation of a presence wanting to link with her. She recognised the presence right away as Xain and opened the link to him.

~Hi, Xain,~ she sent through the Link.

~Hi, Mandy. We got a voice message on our public phone line for you a short time ago. I've been trying to link with you for the past fifteen minutes, are you alright?~ his voice sounding loud and clear in her head as if he were sitting right next to her.

~I was in a meeting, just got back. What's the message?~

~It's from Alicia, she says she needs your help.~

~Did she say what the problem was?~

~Only that some of her pupils have got themselves into some trouble with Magic and she'd like your help.~

~Okay, Xain, thank you.~

~Pleasure. How's New York?~

~It's great. There are a few problems we're working on, but we'll get there.~

~Let us know if you need a hand. Happy to knock some heads together for you.~

~I'll bear that in mind. Thanks, Xain,~ she answered and cut the link.

She dropped her head back against the sofa and took a breath. Just what she needed right now, something else that demanded her attention.

Alicia had been her friend back when she had been growing up in the orphanage in Donegal in Ireland. Religious, conservative, and basically the teachers' star pupil, she had been everything that Amanda hadn't been, until Alicia decided that she would be Amanda's friend, no matter what. Her influence had calmed Amanda down, and their friendship would always be the one thing that Amanda treasured most from her time in the orphanage.

She'd visited Alicia a little over a year ago, shortly after becoming a Magus, and had given Alicia her contact details at that time and had updated them for the Legacy Mansion in Paris months ago.

She hadn't gotten round to updating them to New York yet, but that would be put right on this visit.

The problem would have to be serious for Alicia to call and ask for Amanda to come to the orphanage, that meant she needed to get to Ireland.

"You okay, Mandy?"

Amanda looked up, snapped out of her thoughts by Liz's voice. Her apprentice stood in the hallway close to the front door. She looked good, wearing a skirt that showed a little more leg than usual.

"I'm fine. Are you going out?"

"I'm meeting Jason. We're going to take in a few sights."

"Happy days. Have fun. I might not be here when you get back, I need to pay a visit to a friend in Ireland."

"Alicia?"

She'd spoken to Liz about Alicia and her past a fair amount over the last year, so she wasn't surprised she remembered who Alicia was.

"Yeah. I shouldn't be too long. Have fun."

"I will. See ya," Liz replied and left through the front door.

Amanda smiled. Liz seemed to be finding her feet here in New York more than ever now. She hoped she had fun. Amanda stood up and looked down at the envelope on the table. She concentrated for a moment and Ported it upstairs into her bedroom for safekeeping.

Now she needed to get to Ireland. She'd done this trip a couple of times now, both to reach Ireland and Paris.

Concentrating for a moment, she Ported from her lounge and appeared on a lush green hilltop overlooking a vast body of water that stretched as far as she could see.

Her ability as a Magi allowed her to Port wherever she could imagine, but her ability level limited her to just shy of a thousand miles, so a trip to Ireland, which in total would be a three thousand mile trip in one jump, had to be done in several hops.

She Ported north into Quebec, on the south coast of Le fleuve Saint-Laurent near to Grand Vallée. Up on the hill, the view took her breath away, and it was always quiet. She only appeared for a few seconds, though, before she Ported north again, appearing on another coastline. This time she was at sea level on a quiet northern beach on Long Tickle Island in Newfoundland.

The temperature had dropped enough that she was feeling the cold. Not that it bothered her, her Magic kept her warm. The view out to sea had a pleasant calming effect on her as the water broke gently onto the beach a short distance ahead. But she couldn't stay, so she concentrated again and Ported another five hundred or more miles northeast and appeared on a rocky, snow-covered mountain top. The wind whipped about her as she looked over the wintery, forbidding landscape of Nunarssit on the south coast of Greenland. Behind her, the North Atlantic Sea that she'd just Ported over, stretched away into the distance, while in front of her, snowy peaks of rock jutted into the sky.

Again, she didn't stay long, just a few seconds to make sure there hadn't been anyone watching before concentrating on her Magic again and Porting once more. She pushed herself towards her upper limit, Porting east nearly as far as she could at her current ability, and appeared on the southern slopes of Snæfellsjökull, Iceland, close to Vatnshellir Cave.

The ground wasn't as rocky as where she had appeared in Greenland, but it felt just as cold. The bleak landscape extended down below her to the sea. There were no trees here, just rocks and tundra, and beyond that, the freezing ocean.

She had come most of the way now, just a couple more jumps and she'd be in Ireland.

Pulling her coat tighter, shivering even though she didn't really feel it, she pulled on the threads of Essentia again and disappeared.

She appeared seven hundred miles south-east of Iceland on a small island south-west of Scarp on the Isle of Harris just off the west coast of northern Scotland.

Although still cold, the air felt noticeably warmer here, and the late afternoon sun felt lovely on her face. The Island uninhabited, as far as she could tell, other than the local wildlife and so was perfect as a Porting location.

This would be her last big jump, so she concentrated on her destination, and with a whip-crack of noise and the fleeting feeling of dislocation and dizziness, she appeared outside her cottage in the Blue Stack Mountains northwest of Donegal.

Everything looked as it should. The small whitewashed cottage had been left untouched for a little while, but Amanda popped back here from time to time either for time alone or just to make sure everything was okay.

It would be just a short hop from here to the orphanage to see her friend.

- Online Chat between Edge & Chronos dated April 19th

Edge: Who are they, the people you sent me to follow?

Chronos: You found them? You stayed out of sight?

Edge: Yes, don't worry, they never knew I was there. But I saw things... I saw them doing things that should not be possible.

Chronos: You've seen it before, though, haven't you?

Edge: What are they? Are there more of them?

Chronos: They call themselves Magi, pronounced Mah-Guy, and yes, there's more of them.

Antarctic Trek

Antarctic

Angel sat in the front passenger seat of the Hagglunds all-terrain vehicle as it made its way over the white-on-white landscape. The vehicle consisted of two cabs on tracks, powered by the engine in the front cab.

It bounced and rattled its way over the snow and ice without much difficulty. Inside the front cab, the cushioned seats made it one of the most comfortable trips she'd ever made.

The heater was turned up on high, and she wore her extreme cold-weather gear that covered her from head to toe, but Angel still felt cold, very cold.

She sat with the driver up front, while Mr Black's other two employees sat behind them. They talked excitedly about their trip and what they would find at the dig site, but Angel had no time for them.

She found their conversation inane and boring, so she kept her distance and had barely said two words to them through the entire trip.

They'd travelled from the Syndicate's island a little over a day ago, hopping from one airport to another, changing planes a couple of times until they reached the final leg of the trip that took them from South America to Antarctica in the Hercules LC130 military cargo plane.

The flying grey beast had two propellers on each wing and skis attached to its wheels. The flight had been one of the worst she'd ever experienced. The plane had little insulation, making it very cold, and there were no luxuries, such as chairs. You were treated no better than cargo and sat wherever you could find a space between the actual cargo in the plane.

Rest had been a pipe dream, something that sounded like a nice idea, until you sat on your bag, freezing cold, the noise deafening even with earplugs in, while you rattled through the sky to your destination.

Hiding within the Syndicate had never been easy. She'd worked hard to conceal her true level of Magical ability, and that meant not keeping herself warm during the trip to the South Pole as that would have been outside the ability level she portrayed.

She wore layer after layer of thermal clothing, but it only accomplished so much in this climate.

Located about a day's ride over the snowfields from the nearest American base in the Antarctic, travelling by land vehicle had always been the best way of ferrying people back and forth. On clear, calm days, they used the helicopter for personal travel, but most of the cargo and equipment arrived to the base on one of the ground transports. Today had not been a clear or calm day. The winds were blowing, which meant they had to travel in the Hagg.

Slowly, the sun had started to set, inching closer to the horizon as the transport approached another ridge of snow, rising up in front of them.

"We're about there, I think. We should be able to see the site at the top of this ridge," the driver said.

This only served to get the other two passengers excited, and made Angel roll her eyes at their constant chatter about how amazing this whole experience had been.

Angel didn't listen, she just peered out the front window as the Hagg made its way over the next rise, eventually cresting the ridge and its nose dipping again, revealing the valley below.

The driver stopped for a moment, letting his passengers enjoy the view.

Below them, the dig site sat at the base of a mountain range, nestled in a valley with steep rises on three sides.

Carved into the back of that valley, and mostly hidden beneath the snow and ice, there looked to be some sort of temple or tomb entrance.

Ornate pillars sat on either side of an arched doorway that rose well over a hundred and fifty feet high which had succumbed to the ice, filling the doorway. The main activity of the dig was happening at the base of the entrance. Tents and sheeting hid the excavation as steam rose from the base of the doorway.

Angel knew from the reports she had read that one of the few Magi that the Syndicate employed had been stationed here on an ongoing basis, with a couple more who visited when they were needed.

She also knew that, although Mr Black employed these supernatural individuals, he didn't really trust them. They were a tool he used to achieve certain ends and were only brought in when mundane methods weren't enough. Still, she could sense the Magic here, powerful Magic that permeated the whole area.

Shifting her vision into the Magical spectrum, the ambient Essentia blossomed into view, giving the vista before her another dimension entirely.

Something powerful rested in the ice. She could see the remains of an Aegis that had been more powerful and subtle than anything she'd ever seen before, left in tatters by the Syndicate's now-departed Magi. The Aegis had effectively hidden this place from detection for millennia while an Illusion had hidden the entrance.

Beyond the shield, Magical signatures could be seen everywhere, as well as the distinctive marks of explosions dotted about the camp.

Traps, thought Angel. Powerful and dangerous Magical traps designed to dissuade people from venturing too close. They weren't hidden, though. These were designed for any mortals who wandered into the area who weren't affected by the Aegis. They were obstacles, nothing more.

She could see tents set up between the traps and safe areas to walk marked out by flags, but the real Magical power came from deep below the surface, beyond the ice door. Something powerful lay deep underground here. She had no idea what it could be, but the taste of that power captured her interest.

The driver shifted the transport back into gear and continued down the slope, eventually coming to a stop next to a number of other parked vehicles.

Angel jumped out and grabbed her bag from the back of the Hagg before walking into the compound alone. She followed the path marked out by flags, through tents and piles of equipment boxes, towards a larger cabin that stood ten feet above the ground on scaffolding. As she walked, she approached a gap in the tents that had been marked off. Flickering lights came from the gap as well as strange noises. She rounded the corner to see a bright glowing point of light flickering and sparking, throwing off arcs of magical energy like miniature lightning bolts and puffs of fire and smoke.

As odd as that might be, it wasn't what troubled her.

As the effect flickered, individual body parts appeared and disappeared, jutting out of the energy. Every few seconds, a man's screaming face would appear, and for that fleeting moment, the sound of his bone-chilling scream could be heard before his head disappeared and the sound stopped just as abruptly as it started.

Angel stood there fascinated by it.

"One of the traps," said a voice to her right. She turned to see a man standing nearby, dressed in extreme cold-weather gear as bulky as her own. "The idiot got too close. One minute, he was standing just a little closer than you are now, the next moment... that," he said, pointing at the screaming apparition in the flickering light.

"And you're leaving him like that?" Angel asked, a little surprised that they wouldn't try to save him. Not that it bothered her, but she always thought the Syndicate's staff were a little more humane than that.

"We have our best Magi working on it. They're a little apprehensive about tampering with it while we conduct the dig. Serves the idiot right, though. It's also an effective deterrent for anyone else thinking of being a wiseass. Anyway, I'm Blake. I was just heading out to meet you. I take it you're Angel?"

Angel recognised his name. Blake Preston had been placed in charge of the dig and would be the person she'd be working with during her stay here. Her job would be to use her Magical perception to help them watch out for any Magical problems that might rear their heads.

Angel took Blake's hand and shook it.

"That's right, a pleasure to meet you."

"Shall we get out of the cold?" he asked.

"Absolutely, lead the way," she answered, eager to get a bit warmer.

She followed Blake through the other tents towards the main complex of prefabricated living spaces. To call these oblong grey blocks with a couple of windows and a door, buildings, would have been a little too generous.

Beyond them, the carved rock face rose above her, ominous and forbidding, hiding its secrets away from prying eyes.

But not for long.

- Online Chat between Edge & Chronos dated April 19th

Edge: Yes, I've seen them before. It's been a while ago, now, maybe twenty years, but yes. I have seen something like this before.

Chronos: Twenty years ago?

Edge: I was travelling the Middle East, and it happened while I visited the Island of Tārūt.

Chronos: Tārūt? You mean, the one that had that earthquake?

Edge: That's the one. I was there when it happened. I was in the middle of the earthquake. I thought she was an angel at the time, but maybe she was just one of these Magi. I've lived in denial for a while over what I saw that day, but recently, I realised I had to know. I couldn't leave it any longer, I needed to know what I saw. Which led to the blog and everything else.

Ritual

Donegal, Ireland.

Appearing on the site of the Saint Mary's Orphanage and Convent School, Amanda passed the orphanage and nunnery and made for the collection of buildings that make up the school.

She'd only had intermittent contact with Alicia since her last visit a year ago, mainly to update Alicia on how she could be reached. She wondered what was so urgent that it had forced Alicia to reach out. Surely it wasn't the same kids Alicia had been concerned about the last time she was here. As she approached the main wooden front door of the school's reception, she wondered if that same woman would be here, and how she'd react to her outfit this time. She'd not been impressed when Amanda had turned up in ripped jeans and a tank top last time. Comparatively speaking, she was dressed rather smartly this time, since she hadn't changed after her visit to DC.

As she approached the building that had been her home for the first sixteen years of her life, all kinds of memories and emotions bubbled up inside her. These buildings had been her entire childhood, and she still had an emotional attachment to them. Back then, they'd felt like a prison, but now that she was free, and she had some perspective on things, her feelings were a little different and certainly more complex.

However, she wasn't sure she would change anything if she could. Her time here had shaped her into the woman she was today.

Walking into the reception area, Amanda was pleased to see that nothing had really changed, and the same woman sat behind the reception desk. Amanda grinned and walked over to her. The secretary looked up and smiled, her reaction to her this time somewhat more welcoming.

"Good morning, miss. How may I help you?"

"I'm here to meet Sister Alicia," answered Amanda.

"Ah, yes, she said you were coming. Amanda, is it? If you'd like to take a seat, I will call her down."

"Of course," Amanda said, and walked to the nearby sofas, where she sat with her legs crossed.

Moments later, the door through to the school opened and Alicia, in full nun's habit, stepped through. Amanda smiled. Alicia had been in training the last time she had visited, but she'd clearly progressed since then. Amanda rose from her chair and walked over to greet her friend.

"Amanda, God bless you, it's such a pleasure to see you again. Thank you for coming," Alicia said.

"Any time, you need only ask."

"Come with me, let's go somewhere we can talk," Alicia suggested, in a slightly quieter tone.

"Of course," Amanda replied, and followed her friend through the door into the school proper. They walked through several corridors and up some steps before Alicia unlocked a door and ushered Amanda inside.

"You have an office?" Amanda asked.

"I've taken on more responsibility within the school, and this happened to be one of the perks."

"Very nice," Amanda said as she admired the room with its wooden bookshelves and desk. Everything felt warm and comfortable. A perfect place to work.

"Thank you. Take a seat," Alicia offered. "Did I interrupt anything?"

"No, no."

"Oh, good. You're just dressed a little more…"

"Ye mean, less like a scruff?" Amanda shrugged. "I scrub up alright when I need to." She smiled as she sat in one of the chairs that faced the desk with Alicia seated on the opposite side. "How can I help you?" Amanda asked.

Alicia took a deep breath, trying to calm herself down almost before she'd even started to speak.

"You remember that group of kids I showed you last time, the ones who were into the occult?"

Amanda remembered and almost immediately relaxed. Alicia had discussed this with Amanda last time, and Amanda hadn't found anything magical at all. Amanda felt sure that Alicia meant well, but in Amanda's view Alicia's personal beliefs were colouring her opinions on this matter.

The four kids were Goth's, nothing more. She also knew from her last visit, that although a couple of them had interest in occult stuff, it had had all looked harmless enough. Even with Magic being real and with some real horrors in the shadows, Amanda wasn't worried about them and had tried to get Alicia not to worry, too.

"I checked last time I came, they're just kids, and they certainly aren't worshipping the devil or anything."

"I know you did, but they seem much more into it now. They're being very secretive, and just looking at their notebooks with all the symbols and runes drawn in them, I'm worried, Amanda. I wanted to ask you because you took me seriously last time. You helped me, and I can talk freely with you. I'm worried the sisterhood might not be so… understanding."

Amanda nodded. Alicia really did look worried, and she didn't want to mock her by dismissing her out of hand. "Okay, sure. I'll have a look. Where are they?" Amanda asked.

"Are you sure? I'd like to help."

"I know you do, but without putting too fine a point on it, I know what I'm looking for, so I do. Plus, this might be a long process of just watching them."

"Alright, sure, but if you need anything…"

"I'll be in touch. So, where are they?"

Alicia checked the time. "They should be in the common room in the sixth form block."

"Okay, grand. Leave it with me. I'll watch them and see what I can find out."

"I can give you access to their rooms again," Alicia said passing over a key ring with four keys on it. "Same rooms as last time."

"I remember," Amanda said.

"You're sure you don't need me?" Alicia asked.

"I'll be less conspicuous alone, trust me," she said.

Moments later, Amanda approached the sixth form block, a small building that contained a common room where the pupils hung out and socialised with their friends between lessons.

The majority of the school sat in relative silence now, lessons had finished about an hour ago, and most of the kids had either left for home or were back in their dorm areas. There were always some after school activities and lessons, though, from what she remembered, and the people in the sixth form often hung out in the common room for a while after the day had ended.

As she approached the building, she let her vision expand, allowing the golden mist of Essentia to swim into view. At first glance, everything here seemed in order, no unusual magical signatures. So, she found a place to stand out of the way, where it was unlikely she'd be disturbed and sent a second set of senses inside the common room. Just as Alicia had predicted, the four kids—although, maybe young adults might be a better term—sat in the corner away from the other pupils.

She remembered their names from last time. Scott sat in a chair, his feet up on a nearby table. Tomo sat on the table next to Scott's feet while Christina perched on the arm of Scott's chair. Next to them, Jake sat backwards on his chair, his feet on either side and his arms across the backrest. They talked easily and quietly, keeping to themselves, discussing TV shows, their fellow students, and other uninteresting things.

As Amanda watched, though, she noticed that the Essentia around Christina had a very slight twist or eddy in it from time to time as she moved. Looking closer, she could see that she must have interacted with something Magical recently, something that had marked her.

Intrigued, Amanda used her Magic and eased into Christina's mind, where she started to gently sift through her memories. She moved slowly and with care, not wanting to cause the girl any discomfort.

It didn't take long until she saw the image of a book in her mind's eye. Looking at a memory like this, Amanda had no idea if the item might be Magical in nature, but she did find a couple of other memories that showed Christina reading from the book and a few strange things happening, such as lights flickering, a pen levitating off the floor, and more.

Magic.

Withdrawing from Christina's mind, Amanda watched as the four of them discussed meeting up tonight to take a look at the book.

Taking a deep breath, she let out a long sigh, feeling a little troubled. Not only had she nearly dismissed Alicia's concerns, she'd also assumed that these kids would not be able to mess with real Magic. She cursed her naïveté and wondered if she'd missed something when she'd last been here. Luckily, it seemed that Alicia was taking things a little more seriously and had done the right thing in bringing it to her attention.

Leaving her second set of senses in the common room, watching and listening to the students, Amanda walked back to Alicia's office.

She greeted Amanda warmly at the door a few moments later.

"So, anything? Anything at all?" Alicia asked.

"They're fine, Alicia. Nothing to worry about," Amanda lied. She had no intention of letting her friend become involved in the machinations of the supernatural world. She would be chewed up and spat out in moments. She wanted to protect her, and the best way to do that was to keep her well away from it all.

Amanda would deal with this and remove the book herself, so that her assertion that they were fine would be true, eventually.

"Are you sure?"

"I am. I searched their rooms, and there really isn't anything to worry about. But, to be really sure, I'm going to follow them about for the rest of the evening."

"It's just, I know what I saw. I know what they wrote in their notebooks."

"Trust me, Alicia, there really is nothing to worry about.

Alicia took a breath, apparently trying to calm herself.

"Okay, Amanda. I… I trust you. I do."

"Good, I'll catch up with you tomorrow. Try to get some rest and stop worrying."

"That's easier said than done," Alicia countered.

Amanda rolled her eyes but smiled. She bid her friend farewell and walked out of the office as Alicia started to clear her things from her desk.

She knew she'd done the right thing. Dealing with the supernatural wasn't exactly the safest way to live your life as a mortal. It wasn't any better for the Magi either, but at least they could defend themselves.

Making her way back to the common room, even with this latest concern, she had to admit it felt good to get out of New York and away from the craziness that had been going on there.

She felt sure she could handle this quickly, before she headed back to the Big Apple. She smiled to herself, realising she felt quite confident looking into this all by herself. She wouldn't be calling for help. She'd be flying solo on this one. The boys, Xain and Orion, would be proud of her.

She still had her second set of senses on the four kids, and it looked like they were still quite comfortable in the common room, so Amanda focused on her view of them and tried to see that strange swirl of energy coming off of Christina again.

The school corridors were empty, and the chances of her running onto anyone were slim, so she focused in on her magical senses and just walked on autopilot through the school, slowly and surely. There wasn't any rush, after all.

A few corridors away from Alicia's office, Amanda rounded a corner and walked straight into someone coming the other way.

They bumped into each other with some force. Amanda stumbled back and grasped the wall as she half fell on her arse. She banished her magical senses to a tiny window in the corner of her vision and looked about.

Paper had spilt everywhere, files were all over the floor, and the man who had been carrying them hopped over them to help her.

"Whoa there, young one, I've got you. Are you ok-so?" the man asked, grasping her arm.

Pulling her up, Amanda regained her balance and looked up at the man who'd helped her.

"Mr Croft?" Amanda said, recognising him.

"Amanda. How lovely to see you again, it's been a while," he said.

"Nearly two years, I think, and you're still here," she said.

"I am, for my sins." He smiled.

"Sorry to bump into you like that."

"Away with the fairies, so ye were," he offered.

"Yeah…" Amanda admitted.

"That's okay. It's awful lovely to see you back here again. Can I help you with anything?"

"No, no, I'm good. I'm helping Alicia with something."

"Is she worrying after her students again?"

"Something like that," Amanda answered.

"I do keep telling her that she needs to back off a bit, let those kids find their own way. They're all perfectly alright."

"I know, I've told her that as well. She does seem to worry, though."

"And she always will," he answered as he crouched down to gather up his things.

Suddenly remembering what she'd done, she immediately crouched down and helped him pick up his stuff, feeling embarrassed once again.

"Here you go," she offered as she handed him the last of the documents that she'd picked up.

"Now, young one. The least you can do is come and have a quick drink with me. I'd love to hear a bit more about your travels. You disappeared so quickly last time you were here."

Amanda looked up at her former teacher and felt taken aback by the offer. Had he just asked her out on a date?

"What? To the pub?" she asked, feeling slightly flustered.

"No, not the pub. Just come to the staff room. Some of your other teachers might be there. I'm sure they'd be interested in catching up."

Amanda relaxed. He hadn't asked her out, he just wanted to catch up. She glanced at the little window in her vision, showing the kids in the common room. Everything seemed okay, and she could excuse herself any time she wanted.

"Oh!" Mr Croft said suddenly. "You thought I'd asked you out on a date."

"Well…" Amanda replied, guiltily.

"I'm flattered, but no." He smiled.

"Sorry," Amanda said, feeling a little stupid. She walked with him the short distance to the staff room, helping him carry his stuff, and followed him inside. With it being the end of the day, only a couple of teachers were in here and she only recognised one of them, but not from her days as a student.

William, the teaching assistant who had greeted her and shown her around the school when she'd arrived on her last visit pottered about at the back of the room. He looked up when they entered, and she noticed his expression go from confusion to recognition over the space of a second.

Amanda placed the files she carried for Mr Croft down where he indicated and stood back.

"Wait there a moment," he said as he stepped up to the nearby cupboards and pulled out a few mugs.

William wandered over, a large smile on his face.

"Hi, err… wait, I know this…" he said, as she looked on. She couldn't help but smile at his attempt to impress her by remembering her name.

"It's Amanda," Mr Croft said, no doubt rolling his eyes while he stood with his back to them, preparing their drinks.

"I knew that," grumbled William. "It's lovely to see you again."

"To be sure, and ye," Amanda obliged. "How's the training going?" she asked. He'd been here on placement, learning the job last time she had visited.

"I passed," he said.

"Will here, is a fully qualified teacher now, Miss Page," Mr Croft said. "It seems that they let any young fool through these days."

"And they don't kick out the old farts, either," Will countered.

Amanda laughed.

"It's great to see you again, Will. Congratulations are in order, I think," she said.

"You're damn right, young one," Mr Croft said as he turned around and offered Will and Amanda each a mug. She could smell the distinct whiff of alcohol quite clearly before she even got hold of it. She took a proper sniff and recoiled from the burning smell that filled her nose.

"Are you trying to get me drunk, sir!" she said in mock horror.

"And if I were?" he asked with a wry smile.

"Tally-ho old chap, I say," Amanda replied, raising her mug before taking a sip of the amber liquid.

The guys smiled and sipped their own whiskeys. Mr Croft clearly enjoying his, while Will struggled to get any of his down.

Amanda enjoyed the taste, even if it did burn her throat a touch.

Mr Croft led them over to the sofas and they all sat down, with Mr Croft ensuring that Will ended up sitting next to her. She found his feeble attempts at matchmaking amusing and went with it.

Will still seemed to like her, and she'd already caught him looking at her a few times. It made her smile and took her mind off things. It felt nice to be appreciated.

Mr Croft started to ask her questions about her travels and she enjoyed telling them about some of the places she'd visited, leaving out all the Magic and monsters she had encountered along the way, while she enjoyed the drink that Mr Croft kept topping up.

Amanda soon found herself deep in conversation with Mr Croft and Will as the whiskey relaxed her. She ended up pressed up next to Will, teasing him with the odd playful touch on the leg or arm. She enjoyed listening to his thoughts as well, such as when he got slightly flustered over her latest tap of his knee. She found it cute and endearing, even if she had no intention of taking it any further.

She enjoyed their company so much, and talking at length about her travels felt so great, that when she suddenly remembered to check on the kids, she realised they were gone from the common room.

Realising her mistake, she quickly made her excuses and left Will and Mr Croft in the staff room, claiming that time had got away from her and she had somewhere to be.

Once outside, she checked to make sure no one would see her, and Ported upstairs, appearing outside Christina's room. She placed her senses inside the room and could quickly see that no one was there. So, she Ported inside the room and took a quick look around. Using her Magic, she looked for items that had a strong emotional investment in them from Christina, which were usually visible by the aura they retained from their owner. After a few moments, she found a necklace that would work perfectly. Its aura glowed strongly, making it a good link for Amanda to use.

Amanda picked it up from her dressing table and held it in her hand, concentrating.

She focused on Christina and used her Magic to reach out to her, to find her, and soon found the direction and distance. Over the next few seconds, she started to get an idea in her mind of where she would be. Concentrating, she placed her senses in that area and quickly scanned around.

The scene that appeared in her mind's eye was a road in Donegal, and her vision was focused on a gap between two buildings on that street. Through the gap, beyond the buildings, Amanda could see several commercial units. They looked somewhat overgrown and disused, which to Amanda's mind made them a perfect place for kids to get up to mischief.

The area seemed clear, so after returning the necklace to the stand, Amanda Ported from the room and appeared in the gap leading to the disused units.

In the twilight, the grounds around the disused buildings took on an ominous and creepy vibe, but Amanda could see better than usual with her enhanced senses. The Essentia through here was clearly disturbed by something. Was it Christina?

She walked along the track of hard-packed earth and stone, but as she moved away from the road, it became steadily more overgrown with weeds, nettles, and thorn bushes. Several paths through the foliage led off to the various buildings, but she could already see that the Essentia around one of them was acting strangely, moving about in ways that only Magic would cause.

She picked her way through the bushes and sent her senses ahead of her, but this time, she used her Multitasking effect to split her mind, allowing her to concentrate on two things at once.

She'd been pushing herself recently to split her mind into three or four pieces, but now wasn't the time to be messing about.

The Magic wouldn't work, though. As she tried to scry into the building, her Magic hit an Aegis of some kind that prevented anyone from looking too close. Frowning, she attempted to Port in closer, but again the aura emanating from the building prevented the Magic from working.

Frustrated, she picked up her pace and jogged up beside the building. She could see a reasonably clear path around either side but had no idea which way to go. Both looked well used, and the local Essentia was so disturbed by whatever was going on inside the building, that the trail that led in here from the road was no more.

Keen to get inside, she picked a direction at random and set off over the grass, mud, and uneven ground.

She turned a corner to see an open doorway and dancing lights spilling out of it. Things were progressing, and she needed to get in there.

She moved as quickly as she could and ducked into the doorway towards the back of the building, which was closest to the road, and found herself, much to her relief, on a solid concrete floor again. Mud did not pair well with stiletto heels.

She couldn't see much from where she stood. Various hulking machines and other disused factory furniture stood in place, and beyond those, the lights that danced towards the middle of the building cast strange shadows over the rear wall.

Despite the deep shadows, she could see quite well with her enhanced vision and moved around the machinery to get a better view of the Magical lights as Essentia surged around the building like a tornado.

As she moved, the scene came into view, and she wished she'd arrived here sooner.

The four students stood at the four corners of a summoning circle, one for each compass direction. Between them, on the floor, a circle had been clearly marked out with runes and candles. Christina held the book in her right hand, reading from its pages while she held her left hand aloft. Of the four, she seemed like the only one of them taking this relatively calmly. Scott, Tomo, and Jake all wore expressions of shock and fear as strange smoke rose from the circle and a flickering, pulsing light hovered in the centre, a good six feet off the ground. As she watched, a dark form materialised within the light and started to grow and take shape.

Amanda had no idea what this thing could be, but it didn't look good.

She'd heard stories of demons and spirits living in the Abyss that could be summoned by Magi or those with the right tools, such as this book.

Amanda stood and stared for a moment, not really sure what she should do. Disrupting the spell would be a good idea usually, but with the spirit here in the middle of the protective circle and being held in place by the Magic that Christina conjured up, disrupting the ritual might actually release the demon into our world, not something Amanda felt keen on doing. So, she watched and waited, hoping for an opportunity to end this craziness.

Christina finished chanting and looked up, apparently surprising herself by what the book had done.

"It worked," she said in a shaky voice.

"Shit yeah, it worked, now what?" Jake said.

"Um…" Christina answered, and opened the book again, flicking through pages as fast as she could.

"Oh, great," Scott muttered to himself, no doubt realising that Christina had no clue what to do next.

"Can you send it back?" Tomo asked.

"I'm looking, I'm looking. Give me a moment."

"You're looking? It's looking… at us!" Tomo yelled, desperation edging into his voice.

And indeed the thing, which didn't look human at all, did seem to be looking around at the four kids. The creature was little more than a black shape with few defining features. The top half kind of looked like a Manta Ray, smooth and sleek, the top of its body bent over like a head. The bottom half of the thing tapered off and split into black tendrils that writhed about like a mass of snakes across the floor. As she and the four kids watched, the thing turned on the spot and regarded each of the participants.

"I don't like this, Chrissy," Scott called out.

"It's in here somewhere, give me a moment, I can send it back," she replied.

"Well, hurry up, I don't want to stay here much longer," Jake pressed her.

"Don't you move! If you move or break the circle then you *will* set it free, that would not be good," she said sternly.

Jake lifted his hands in supplication.

"I ain't going anywhere, yet."

Amanda didn't know a lot about these kinds of rituals. Summoning creatures like this was not something she had ever done. Christina seemed to know what to do, and Amanda had no reason to doubt her, so she fuelled her Aegis and waited, hoping that Christina would pull this together at the last moment.

Amanda saw something move on the other side of the circle, but she found it difficult to make out who or what the new arrival could be through the dancing lights and Magical energy.

She moved sideways, trying to get a better look and saw someone running towards the summoning circle on the far side.

"Shite," Amanda cursed as the figure crossed the edge of the circle and stepped into the same space as the creature.

Amanda's stomach tied itself up in knots as she moved forward to get a better look. The light in the circle danced, and she got her first clear view of the new arrival.

Alicia had stepped into the circle with a cross held out, attempting to banish the spirit by reciting scripture.

"Alicia, no!" shouted Jake, recognising her.

"Feck, no, damn it," Amanda hissed to herself and ran forward. Why was she doing this? A nun reciting bible verses would be about as effective against this Abyssal as a broken umbrella in a typhoon.

Amanda reached the edge of the circle, but as she tried to step into it, she found her passage blocked.

An Aegis surrounded the creature, a powerful one that kept the thing confined and Magi, like Amanda, out. As a Riven mortal, Alicia could cross it without a problem. As she watched, the featureless shadow-creature bent low to give Alicia a good, long look and then grabbed her with one of its powerful tentacles.

"No!" Amanda shouted. The thing turned and regarded Amanda for a moment before looking back at Alicia, who struggled and cried out for help.

"I've found it!" Christina called and gave her friends a wild, mad smile.

"Then use it, get rid of it!" Jake yelled. He sounded desperate.

Christina looked down at the book and started to read. Amanda watched as the shadow's head snapped up to look at Christina. Like Amanda, it must have felt the change in the Magical energy and understood what was happening.

The spirit turned back to Alicia and pounced. The whole eight or nine-foot bulk of black Abyssal spirit shot at Alicia's chest and in a puff of black smoke, passed into her body. She dropped in a heap on the floor, her body shaking as foam burbled from her mouth.

Christina finished her chanting, and the barrier dropped. Amanda ran forward and crouched down next to her friend.

"Ali, Ali? Are you alright? Alicia, talk to me," she pleaded as the four students gathered around them. Alicia shuddered in Amanda's arms. Her eyes rolled back as a black, oily substance flowed over them. Suddenly she went rigid, her eyes snapping back, she looked up at Amanda.

"Help me…" she said, before falling unconscious.

Amanda pulled her close, hugging her friend. "Alicia," she whispered quietly.

"Err, hi, can we help?"

Jake crouched down next to her, concern filling his face as he reached out and touched Amanda's arm.

"Not really, Jake. She needs specialist care now."

Amanda placed Alicia on the ground carefully before looking up at the other students from her crouched position. Jake stayed crouched next to Alicia, Scott stood behind him, looking down at Alicia, also clearly concerned.

Christina stood behind him, her Magic book in hand and a defiant look upon her face, while Tomo stood off to one side, lighting up a cigarette and pacing back and forth, muttering to himself.

"What the hell were you thinking, ye ejit?" Amanda asked Christina as she stood up.

Christina raised her eyebrows at Amanda. "I don't think you're in any position to question me. Did you see what I just did? Imagine what I could do to you."

"Oh, really?" Amanda answered, feeling bemused at this girl's confidence.

"The power I now wield with this book! You're nothing to—'

Amanda raised her hand and the book shot out from under Christina's arm to Amanda's hand where she caught it.

Christina blinked, her mouth agape.

"No. No, please, do continue. You were saying about power?" Amanda asked.

"I, err… that is…"

Amanda took a slow step towards Christina as she struggled to find the words.

"You've played with forces so far beyond your understanding. You have no idea what ye've just done, and now you might have killed someone!" Amanda said as she took a couple more steps towards the girl.

"She looks alive to me," Christina said in defiance.

"*Something* is alive in that body, but it might not be Alicia." Amanda held up the book. "This, stays with me," she said. Tomo stepped up behind her and tried to pull it from her hand.

Amanda twisted. She grabbed his hand and completed her turn in one smooth motion. In less than a second, she'd forced the six-foot tall teenager to the ground, where he landed on his knees. She held his wrist almost effortlessly in her left hand, in an awkward position that made him wince with pain.

"As I was saying, if you try any more funny business, then people will get hurt," Amanda continued. "Now, where did you get this book?" As she spoke, she plunged her Magic into Christina's mind. She didn't need Christina to answer the question. Just by asking, she'd triggered Christina's memories of buying the item.

"You think I'm telling you that?" Christina spat.

~Thank you,~ Amanda answered telepathically to all four teenagers.

"What?" Christina said in shock.

"You already have," Amanda answered aloud. "You bought it at Sligo Nik Naks. Thank you."

Christina's eyes widened and then narrowed as her shock turned to anger.

"Now, are we all good?"

Tomo nodded dumbly, Scott backed off, while Christina practically had steam coming out of her ears. Amanda let

Tomo's wrist go and stepped back to Alicia. Jake still crouched next to her, holding her hand. He looked up at Amanda.

"Will she be okay?"

"I have no idea, but I will do everything in my power to try and ensure it. Ye have my word," she answered quietly. "Now, go back to your dorm rooms and forget this ever happened," she said to the group.

They started to back off and walk away.

She needed to get out of here, and get Alicia to safety, and help. She'd been practising Porting herself and an additional person recently, with mixed but improving results. But she needed to do it for real now. Taking a breath, she concentrated, noting that the Magic that had stopped her Porting earlier had faded to nothing. It had been a product of the Summoning Circle, no doubt.

Looking up, Amanda waited until none of the kids were looking back at her before she pulled on the threads of Essentia. Wrapping them around herself and Alicia, she focused on the bedroom in her cottage. With a quiet whip-crack of energy, they disappeared from the warehouse.

***

They appeared in Amanda's cottage on the north side of the Blue Stack Mountains, Alicia appearing on Amanda's bed.

It had been a bit of a strain to take an additional person, but it had been worth it.

She looked at the unconscious young woman, and then back at the book in her hands. She wasn't sure exactly what had happened with that spirit, but as she looked at Alicia with her Magical vision, she could see something had changed. Alicia's interaction with Essentia seemed different, her aura had shifted, and there appeared to be a deeper, more fundamental shift she couldn't quite place.

She knew very little about spirits or possession, so she would need to find someone who knew more about these things.

"God damn it, Ali, why'd you have to go and do that," Amanda said to the room. She perched on the edge of the bed and looked down at her friend. She could see the Essentia within her, twisting about as if fighting itself. She could see two minds inside of Alicia's body, the thoughts of both erratic, but they seemed to be linked somehow.

This was all new to her, something she had never seen before, so she started to open a link to Gentle Water, hoping he'd be available again, but paused halfway through and looked at Alicia. She wondered about trying to link with Alicia's mind. Would it be possible? Would she be able to help her or would she present a more alluring prize for the demon? She had no way to know, but she knew her Aegis had been brought up to strength for the potential fight in the warehouse, so surely she would be protected.

Throwing caution to the wind, she closed her eyes and reached out with her mind.

Her Magic closed in around Alicia's head and started to press in on the mind she recognised as Alicia's. Slowly, thoughts began to reveal themselves to Amanda, like shouts in the distance that she struggled to make out. They sounded stressed and in pain.

So Amanda sent thoughts of her own into the depths of Alicia's mind, comforting thoughts that she was here for her should she need her.

Darkness swooped in from elsewhere in Alicia's body, the other mind, the mind of the creature, pushing Amanda out and away from her friend.

The creature had power, more than enough to force Amanda's Magic out of the way and defend its prey.

Amanda pulled her Magic back in defeat and finished sending the link request to Gentle Water, she needed him to Port Alicia back to her house in New York in one go rather than hop from country to country.

- Christina's Diary.

What the hell happened today?

I had it. I had it all under control until Sister Alicia poked her nose in.

Now, everything's ruined. Jake won't speak to me. Scott's more distant. Only Tomo seems willing to listen to my side of things. He's pissed too, though. Probably didn't like that redhead humiliating him like that.

But, who was she?

I need to get that book back or find another one like it.

New Information

Greenwich Village, New York

Amanda sat back in the chair. Then after a few moments, sat forward again, her elbows on her knees. She wrung her hands through each other, fiddled with the rings on her fingers, and played with her hair.

"You seem worried," Gentle Water commented.

A half-smile crossed her features, snapping her out of the endless rollercoaster of thoughts that her mind had been strapped to. The recriminations and self-doubt that swam through her head sprang from not being there in time to stop Alicia, or not seeing that her headstrong friend might take it upon herself to try and stop the children in her charge from doing something stupid. Had she been there sooner, maybe she would have seen Alicia. Maybe she could have prevented the kids from starting the ritual in the first place. She'd been distracted by old friends and spent too much time with her teacher drinking and talking. She should have taken Alicia more seriously, followed the kids more diligently, and maybe, just maybe, she wouldn't be sat here next to her friend who had been possessed by who knew what.

Gentle Water sat opposite, obviously concerned about her. Given how much she'd been fidgeting while she sat here in the half-light next to the bed, she couldn't say she blamed him.

Gentle Water had Ported them both directly to New York from Ireland. On first arrival, both Gentle Water and Raven had stood next to the bed, using their Magic to see what they could do. Amanda had watched, following what they were doing closely, learning as she observed.

Between them, they tried to pull the creature out, to separate its spirit from Alicia's Anima.

They tried several times, using different methods, but nothing seemed to work. They didn't want to force it, to rip it from her against her will as that would almost certainly lead to some kind of damage, maybe even death.

As time passed, it became clear that no amount of Magical might would remove the thing and leave Alicia undamaged. The spirit seemed to be just too powerful, too clever, and maybe permanently merged with Alicia now.

After a while, they gave up, and the choice was made to wait for Alicia to wake up.

While Gentle Water stayed with Alicia, Raven had agreed to Port Amanda back to Ireland so she could check out the bookshop where Christina had acquired the book.

It turned out to be little more than a collection of odd bits and bobs from cooking implements to chairs, tables, handmade ornaments, and books.

She'd inspected the books, but there wasn't any residual Magic to be found. Dejected, they'd returned, and Amanda had taken up her perch beside Alicia.

"I'm more than a little worried, I have no idea what that thing is inside her or what it's doing to her."

"We here for you, Amanda, we do anything we can. You know that."

"I know, you've already done so much. I don't tell ye often enough how much I appreciate everything you've done for me," she said.

"Thank you, but, no need thanks. You my apprentice, I always help you."

"How long do you think she will be unconscious?"

"There is no way to know. She fights a battle deep inside her mind. A battle she must fight alone. The outcome will be clear soon enough."

"I just hate this waiting, not knowing what's going on."

"She know you here. Trust in that and in her strength, and she will prevail," he said.

Amanda nodded. Her mentor's wisdom always helped her in times of stress. She didn't know what she would do without him. He'd been there after Georgina's death back in Ireland, and through his gentle guidance, he'd pulled her through the grief of that loss.

He'd been there for her every day since then, as a mentor, a friend, and in some respects, a surrogate father. The nuns in the orphanage had to some extent, played the role of mothers, but she'd never had a true father figure. Not that she felt she had suffered because of it, but it felt good to have someone like

Gentle Water, who she trusted with her life and who she knew would be there for her in the darkest times.

She did wonder who her parents were sometimes, though. Why had they chosen to leave her on the steps of the orphanage? What had been going on in their lives that led them to make that choice? She'd never considered looking for her real parents, not really. Not in any seriousness. It just didn't play on her mind at all. She felt content with the friends she already had.

Alicia remained motionless, looking serene and almost at peace, on the bed before her. Her body standing in contrast to the chaos of her mind. Looking back at Gentle Water, Amanda realised that she'd filled him in on what had happened to her, but hadn't asked about his trip.

"How was your visit to Paris?" she asked.

"Good. Thank you. There is not much to say. It was diplomatic mission for Legacy Coven. All very boring. Where is Liz?"

"I don't know. I've not seen her. She's probably out somewhere," Amanda guessed. "She's being a dirty stop-out."

Gentle Water eyed her for a moment, probably pondering the turn of phrase she had used.

"If you say so," he said finally.

"Urgh," moaned Alicia from the bed.

Amanda jumped up and looked down at her friend. "Alicia, are you alright? Don't move," Amanda said.

"Amanda, where am I?"

"My place, you're safe. Keep still, how do you feel?"

Alicia tried to sit up, but struggled to do much more than lift her head a few inches from the pillow before dropping back down again, breathing heavily from the effort.

"Relax, rest. You're in good hands here," Amanda said softly, taking her friend's hand in hers.

"I'm... tired," Alicia gasped.

"Then rest. There's no need for you to do anything." Amanda said, wishing she could do more. "Do you remember what happened?"

"Not much. Just bright lights and then darkness and a really odd dream."

"Dream?" Amanda asked.

"To be sure, a dream of... smothering. It was dark and I felt like I was fighting something slippery, something..." Alicia shivered suddenly. "I... I can't really remember much else. Just the students... oh, my word, the students! Are they okay?" Alicia asked, suddenly animated and trying to sit up all over again.

Amanda gently pushed her back down.

"They're fine, I made sure of it. They got back to the school safely, there's no need to worry."

Alicia relaxed back onto the bed.

"Thank you, Mandy... thank you..." she said, her voice trailing off as she slipped back into sleep.

Amanda let out a heavy breath and then stood up straight.

"She seemed... okay," Gentle Water said.

"Hmmm," Amanda said, her tone noncommittal. "We'll see."

The doorbell rang.

Amanda looked over at Gentle Water, her eyebrow raised.

"Did Liz forget her key?" Amanda asked walking out the room with Gentle Water not too far behind. Heading downstairs, Amanda walked to the door, looking into the other rooms as she went. From what she could tell, only herself and Gentle Water were in the house. Raven must have gone out.

"It's not like you to forget your key, Liz," Amanda called out as she approached the door. She automatically sent out her senses to check who had rung the bell, a habit she'd made a point of getting into since her encounter with Lucian on this very spot. It came as something of a surprise to see Yasmin standing there, looking straight into the Magical senses Amanda had just placed outside the door.

Amanda froze, stopping mid-walk just a foot from the door. She sent a lightning-quick thought to Gentle Water to warn him. Just a single word. ~Yasmin.~

The message brought Gentle Water to a sudden stop, as well. He looked over at Amanda, a look of surprise and fear on his face.

"Hello, Amanda," Yasmin said, still looking straight into Amanda's second set of senses. "I came here to talk. I have something to tell you. I wish you no harm."

Amanda didn't answer. She just listened to Yasmin's voice, biting her lower lip as she thought.

Yasmin the Dark. One of the most infamous Nomads of all time now stood a few feet from her on her doorstep. Yasmin was wearing a skin-tight black catsuit and had a wet sheen to it that glistened in the city lights. From her shoulders, down her back, and around her legs inky black smoke fell languidly about her, as if moving in slow motion. Her sharp features and well-defined cheekbones stood out proudly, giving her face a cruel countenance, framed by the waves of dark hair that hung about her head like a lion's mane.

Amanda couldn't help but admire her. Yasmin looked stunning. Powerful, dangerous, not to be underestimated, but stunningly attractive all the same. And yet, no one on the street paid her the slightest bit of attention. A Magical effect, no doubt.

"I know you're there, Amanda."

Amanda shifted on the spot, unsure of her next move. Yasmin, by all accounts, had reached the rank of Arch Magus, the highest level that a Magi could become. By that point, one wielded almost godlike powers, so it seemed odd that she would be standing on Amanda's doorstep like this. But only because ringing a doorbell seemed like such an ordinary thing, below the notice of such a powerful being. But here she stood, just a few feet away, on the other side of a door that, compared to the power that Yasmin could bring to bear, might as well have been tissue paper.

"What do you want?" Amanda called through the door, finally. Realising that keeping silent wasn't actually doing them any favours.

"As I said, I have information. Now please, open this door so that I may come in and we can talk. It's only polite."

"What guarantee do I have that you won't…" Amanda mulled over her choice of words for a second. "Break my trust," she said in the end.

"None. But you have two choices. Either open the door and let me pass through this Aegis, or I rip down your Aegis, destroying the weeks-worth of work and walk in anyway, a little more pissed off then I am right now."

Amanda raised her eyebrows at Yasmin's candid answer. She hadn't expected that, but Yasmin made excellent points, and Amanda had no desire to annoy an Arch Magus, or to have to rebuild the house's Aegis.

She reached for the door and opened it, while her mind sent out the signal to the Aegis to let Yasmin through.

Yasmin stood in the doorway, hands behind her back, feet apart in a commanding pose. She looked down at Amanda, then across to Gentle Water and back. She smiled, but the emotion behind it remained inscrutable.

She stepped inside, the smoky cape dissipating to nothing behind her as she walked into the foyer, her heels clicking on the hard tiles as she moved.

"Lovely place you have here, Amanda. You must feel right at home."

"I do," she said curtly, not really wanting to get into a conversation with this infamous Nomad. "You said you had information for me?"

"Not you, too," she sighed, "No one ever wants to indulge in a little pointless conversation, it's always right down to business. Such a shame."

"I... um..."

"Of course, I understand why," she continued conversationally. "My reputation precedes me, and judging from your body language you're no doubt feeling a little threatened by my presence." Yasmin continued to look around the hallway and into the adjoining rooms, talking in an offhanded and light-hearted way. "A perfectly reasonable reaction. You want to get this over with and for me to be on my merry way. Is that right?" Yasmin sounded almost pedantic during her little outburst.

"Well..." Amanda answered, agreeing without actually saying so.

Yasmin stepped up to her, coming in close and invading her personal space, her voice low and measured, threatening almost. "Of course, it is. But I am not here to hurt you. I have no desire to see you come to harm. I'm here to help," she said quietly, her face mere inches from Amanda's.

Amanda looked up and met Yasmin's gaze, having pointedly avoided it so far. "And what exactly are you here to help us with?"

Yasmin smiled, her eyes glittered with mischief in reaction to Amanda's retort. She seemed to be enjoying the verbal sparring.

"There it is," she said in a happier tone. "There *is* a little fire in you. I like it."

Amanda took a step back, putting some space between them and raised her chin a bit. She could feel the intense power and Magical energy that radiated from Yasmin, and yet, she didn't feel like she was in any immediate danger. Her confidence growing, she relaxed a little.

"I'm pleased for you," Amanda said, a little sarcasm creeping into her voice.

Yasmin smiled. "Of course, I'm stalling. Okay, let's get down to business. Lucian has gotten somewhat more ambitious and has kidnapped your apprentice, Elizabeth Fox."

"What!?" Amanda exclaimed, her confidence suddenly smashed to bits with a single sentence. "When, where?"

"The details of her capture are unimportant. Suffice to say, she's no longer in New York."

Amanda turned away and immediately sent out a link to Liz. Her mind reached out and tried to talk with her apprentice, but she found nothing. She couldn't sense her in any way, which most likely meant she would be hidden behind an Aegis somewhere or she was too far away from Amanda's Magic to reach her.

Amanda glanced back at Yasmin, who stood a short distance away, her hands clasped behind her back again, and smiling, clearly enjoying the moment.

Thinking for a second, she reached out and Ported a small but valuable item from Liz's room, into her hand before reaching out once more and trying to sense her location, hoping that an item with a greater attachment to Liz might bolster her Magic.

She was annoyed, but not surprised, to find she still got nothing. As a last-ditch effort, she tried to call Liz's phone. But that failed too. She stabbed the button to end the call and forced herself to take a breath and calm down. Her hand shook with both rage and fear, and she found it difficult to catch her breath as thoughts about what she would do to Lucian raced through her mind. This was it, he'd gone too far now.

She stopped and looked into the middle distance, her mind racing. Then a thought occurred to her.

Amanda turned back to Yasmin.

"You know where she is, don't you?"

"I have a vague idea, but I didn't follow it up. Not for me to do, you know. But I do know someone who does know where she is. Which leads me quite nicely to the next bit of information I have for you. Your house is under surveillance," purred Yasmin with an air of triumph.

"I thought as much, by whom?" Amanda asked, this new bit of information side-tracking her anger over Liz for a moment.

"He's a Scion. His name is Shaun Murray, and he's in…" Yasmin walked over to a nearby window and pointed out of it, "…that apartment, right now. He works for Lucian as an information gatherer and knows intimate details of Lucian's operation. He's also harbouring something of a grudge against Lucian right now. I'm sure he would be more than willing to switch sides."

Amanda looked out at the apartment window, her keen eyesight able to pick out the faint hint of camera lenses in the darkness of the apartment.

She eyed the window a moment longer, gripping the windowsill in anger before turning to look at Yasmin, who had wandered over to the front door.

Moving away from the window, Amanda stepped over to Yasmin, a question suddenly popping into her head that had been troubling her since arriving in New York.

"I have a quick question."

"Oh? Do continue."

"Did you tell Lucian not to attack us?"

Yasmin smiled.

Amanda studied that wickedly seductive smile and knew Yasmin had been behind it. For some reason, she had told Lucian not to kill her, or maybe even not to hurt her.

"May I ask why?" Amanda asked, hoping that the lithe woman in black might give up some small bit of information.

"Be seeing you, Amanda," Yasmin said, and disappeared, Porting from the hallway with a snap.

Amanda stared at the spot Yasmin had been standing, before walking over and closing the door behind their departing guest. She might not have actually given Amanda much information verbally, but it did seem that she had some kind of vested interest in Amanda, a reason to keep her alive. As useful to know as this was, the why of it would have been more interesting. She put that to one side for now, though, she had much more pressing matters. She needed to find Liz, and as her thoughts settled on this issue once more, the anger and frustration also started to return. She turned to Gentle Water.

"Go, I will watch Alicia," he said without her needing to say anything.

"You're sure?"

"I am sure."

"Thank you," she said, before concentrating and placing her senses in the apartment to make sure she wasn't Porting into trouble. A second later, she appeared in the main room of the apartment.

Two people were in the room with her, a woman who sat at the computer desk, her arms crossed on the desktop, and her head resting on those arms. Across the way, a man dressed in all black paced up and down the room. The man's disfigured face marked him as a Scion, as did his magical signature. Amanda could see no heartbeat and his body, although up and moving about, would be considered medically dead.

She'd seen this before in Maya, and also more recently in Yoh, who were both Vampire Scions. She guessed this would be Shaun.

The Vampire stopped pacing almost immediately and looked up at Amanda, caution on his face. She stared at him, not trusting herself to start the conversation lest she start shouting at him.

"Well, I knew we wouldn't remain undetected forever. Welcome, Amanda. I'm Shaun, and this is Vanessa."

Vanessa sat up with a start at Shaun's voice and jumped again when she saw Amanda standing just a few feet from her.

"Holy shit, you're here!" Vanessa exclaimed.

"You know who I am?" Amanda asked. It seemed like Shaun wanted to talk, so she indulged him.

"Hell yeah," Vanessa answered.

"You're Amanda-Jane Page," the Scion said. "You're a Magus from Ireland originally, and you live with Gentle Water and Elizabeth Fox—your mentor and your apprentice, respectively. Yes, we know who you are. We've been watching your house for a couple of weeks now."

"Which means that ye know why I'm here," she said.

"My guess, either to kill us or to ask for our help. I'm hoping for the latter, ideally."

Amanda walked around the room a little bit as she talked, taking in their surroundings. The place looked like a bomb had hit it. There were food wrappers everywhere, crumbs crushed into the carpet, and half-finished drinks dotted about the place. Walking helped her control her anger, gave her something to focus on that wasn't violence.

"You work for Lucian?" Amanda continued.

"I do, as well as others, occasionally."

"And you have intimate knowledge of his operation," she asked, keeping her voice as level as she could.

"That's correct."

"How's that arrangement working out for you?" she asked, stopping in the middle of the room to look at him.

"We are... in a period of review," he said, guardedly.

"Well, I require your services, and would appreciate it if you would work for me," Amanda said through gritted teeth as she forced herself to complete her circuit around the small space.

Shaun looked at Vanessa, who shrugged, and then back at Amanda.

"What do you want to know?"

A smile played over Amanda's mouth. That seemed easier than it had any right to be. What had Lucian done to Shaun that would cause him to turn his back on their partnership so quickly?

"Lucian has kidnapped Liz, and I have been reliably informed that you know where she is," Amanda stated, her anger at Shaun subsiding slightly.

Shaun nodded. "I think I do." He walked over to a nearby computer. A few mouse clicks and keyboard taps later and he pointed to the screen. "She'll be in there."

Amanda stepped closer to the screen and watched as Shaun zoomed in and out of the map, showing a satellite view of a palatial mansion in the heart of Columbia.

"And Lucian, where does he hide?"

"The Pit Club, in Harlem. I can get you in, avoiding his protections," Shaun offered.

"Really? Then I will be back for that later. In the meantime, I think you should pack up," she said, gesturing to the camera gear still trained on her house.

Her anger was no longer focused on Shaun and what he'd done. He seemed reasonable and probably had little choice in the role he had played in recent events. Lucian, however, was a dangerous and unstable man. He had crossed a line by kidnapping Liz, and Amanda was determined to make him pay.

"Gladly." Shaun smiled his toothy grin and handed her a cell phone. "My number is on it. Call me when you need me again." The phone beeped suddenly in her hand. "And that's the address of the mansion in Columbia I've just texted to you."

"Thank you. I'll be in touch," Amanda said, before Porting away a heartbeat later.

- From "A history of the Dark Nomads", by Trevelyan.

The legends of Yasmin seem endless. If you believed them all, you'd think that she alone caused all of the major incidents you have heard of throughout history.

According to some, she is behind the fake moon landings, JFK, and worse. But the fact is that Magi rarely cause these events, they sometimes get caught up in them, but they rarely cause them.

With that said, we do have reliable eyewitness testimony that places Yasmin at a few well known moments in history, such as the Fire of London. Did she cause it? I suppose we'll never truly know, but I'm not surprised to hear of a Nomad taking advantage of an unfortunate situation such as that.

For instance, we do have photographs of Yasmin that place her in the Nazi death camps of World War II, wearing an SS Uniform.

Death on such a grand scale will always attract Nomads like moths to a flame.

One Woman Army

Columbia

Amanda appeared on the street of the affluent gated housing estate on the edge of Medellin, Columbia. The sun had set hours ago, but the air was still warm.

The houses around her were all large, opulent affairs. Here, the wealthy and privileged shut themselves away from the poverty and gang violence in the city streets—violence that some of them probably funded or helped create. She doubted her target was the only criminal figurehead living here, amongst the legitimate business owners and the trust fund crowd. Part of her loved the idea of a one-woman crusade, travelling around the world, righting wrongs, exacting retribution against those who preyed upon the weak. She could be a Magi Superhero.

It would no doubt remain merely a fantasy, though. Operating that openly would, at the very least, be frowned upon by the Magi Council.

For today, though, she had her eyes on only one target. The house on the other side of the road.

The whitewashed home sat in a beautifully landscaped garden, surrounded by cruel-looking black railings over six feet high, topped with keen-looking spikes. She could already see a fresh, but weak Aegis surrounding one wing of the enormous house, leaving the rest of the building unprotected.

Amanda's sharp, Magically-enhanced eyesight cut through the darkness, allowing her to see as clear as day. She could make out several men walking the grounds, mainly close to the house, although there were a few at the gate as well.

Cameras were everywhere. She could see the electricity flowing along the powerlines feeding the electronics that watched the perimeter and the outside of the house. She assumed they probably had motion detectors as well.

She took a breath, psyching herself up for the fight ahead. Coming to New York and facing off against Lucian had tested her confidence, both in herself and her Magic. She'd doubted herself a few times, but things were different now. She couldn't hide away any longer. She had to step up and stand up for what she believed in and help her friends.

Coming here was a rash choice she guessed, but Liz needed her, and whether she felt totally confident in doing this or not, she had to try.

Liz would do the same for her, and time was of the essence.

Using her Multitasking she managed to split her mind into three and began quietly building an Aegis around the whole compound. It wasn't that powerful, but it would stop any Magic entering or leaving the grounds, and she'd know if it was broken by anything. As that grew, she began to work in other elements, cutting off the phone lines and the mobile signal, cutting off the people inside from the outside. Finally, she also added in a one-way sound dampener. She didn't want the fighting that was sure to follow to attract the authorities.

As she walked up the street toward the gate, she put the finishing touches on this shield and brought the strength of the Aegis up to, and then beyond, the power of the Aegis the Nomads had erected.

She could easily make out five men, all of them carrying submachine guns quite openly over their suits. She could see one of the men fiddling with his walky-talky and getting angry with it as she started to cross the street and walk directly towards the main gate.

As she drew nearer, a couple of the men noticed her and alerted the whole crew, a pair of them broke off from the group and approached the gate while the others spread out behind them.

Amanda had no desire to talk to these guys, this was a business trip, and there wouldn't be any small talk.

She called on her Magic and with judicious use of some kinetic energy, the two front gates flew off their hinges as if hit by a speeding truck, directly into the men behind them. The two closest guards hit the ground bloodied and useless, another man took a blow to the face from one of the flying gates and dropped, squeezing off a few rounds from his gun before falling unconscious.

The other two men dodged the gates and wasted no time in opening fire. Their guns had no enchantments on them, though. The shots bounced harmlessly off of Amanda's Aegis with a slight crackle of Magical energy, which Amanda ignored as she broke into a sprint.

She closed in on the closest guard, moving faster than he could follow, and punching him in the gut. The force of it winded him, doubling him over. She kneed him in the face, crushing his nose in an explosion of blood.

The second man adjusted his aim and fired—the shots pinging off Amanda's shield. A few of them struck the guard Amanda had attacked, killing him. She turned her attention to the last guard and leapt at him. She spun and kicked him in the face. His jaw snapped as he fell. Teeth bounced off the concrete as he hit the driveway and stopped moving.

Amanda scanned the grounds. She still wore the same dark outfit of a fitted top and smart skirt that came to just above the knee. The skirt now sported a small rip up one side from her acrobatics. She grabbed each side of the tear and pulled, ripping the skirt all that way up to her hip, giving her full and free movement of her legs.

Walking towards the house, her heeled boots clicked on the driveway and her bright red ponytail flared out behind her as she pulled off her coat and flung it away.

As she advanced, she set one of her minds to breaking the Aegis that covered the east wing of the building. She hammered it with Essentia in one spot, looking to break through.

As she neared the house, a couple more guys ran out of the shadows, not noticing Amanda until they were too close. The nearest guy skidded to a stop, seeing her at the last moment. He tried to bring his gun to bear but never got there.

Amanda moved quickly, disarming the man and breaking a couple of his fingers on his right hand as she took his gun. She threw it away and put his arm into a lock.

She held the man between her and the second guard as he approached. He aimed at her, holding the submachine gun high to sight along the barrel. Amanda moved, jumping and kicking the gun from his hands, and sending it flying into the darkness.

The sudden movement and spinning motion proved too much for the shoulder and elbow joints of the man she held, which broke and dislocated with a couple of sickening pops. The man fell to his knees in agony, holding his arm.

Turning to the second man, who had pulled his pistol, she took hold of his hands and twisted. She forced him to pull the trigger and shoot himself in the leg three times. As he screamed. She ripped the gun from his hands as he fell to his good knee. Flipping the gun, she hit him on the side of the head with it, knocking him out cold before sliding the barrel on the automatic and taking it apart.

Behind her, the man with the ruined arm huffed. She spun on the spot and kicked the side of his head with her black suede boot, moments before he raised his sidearm to shoot her. He fell and went quiet.

She followed the path where the two men had appeared and went up three steps bordered by bushes. She emerged onto a lit marble patio with a front door framed by columns of white stone.

Two men waited on either side of the door. One knelt, the other stood, their high powered MP5s trained on Amanda. They didn't waste any time and opened fire. The Weapons sprayed her with bullets that ricocheted off her shield, leaving her unharmed, but destroying the foliage and plant pots beside her.

Their weapons ran dry with a clicking noise.

"My turn," Amanda said. With a quick tug on Essentia, both men were slammed into the wall behind them and dropped to the porch where they lay inert.

As a general rule, Amanda tried to avoid killing whenever she could. The thought of ending someone's life was not an idea she relished. But when it came to the Nomads, the horrific stuff they did, you were usually saving the lives of others by taking that final action.

Few people really deserved to have their lives ended, but when it came to the Nomads, the Arcadians were the only ones who could do the job. They were the last defence against the rising darkness. Royston and Gentle Water had assured her that the killing of Nomads and their covens, including the Initiated humans who served them, had been officially sanctioned by the Magi Council. Not that this really made things any better, so Amanda always tried to subdue her foes whenever possible, keeping her conscience as clean as she could.

She hoped she could complete this mission with as little killing as she could, but it wouldn't be the first time she'd taken a life during her time as a Magus.

Satisfied that these two were no longer a threat, she made for the entrance and purely for dramatic effect, used her Magic once again to blow the doors off their hinges. They flew inside and clattered into the hallway, breaking a couple of ornate vases as they went.

As she walked into the large vestibule with its pair of curved staircases leading up to the second floor, Amanda immediately felt Magic ahead. Looking up, she noticed two Magi stood at the top of the stairs, one on each flight, both of them carrying enchanted automatic weapons. At that moment, a squad of security guards ran into the room on the ground floor. They raised their guns and opened fire without a word of warning.

Amanda broke left, sprinting, she jumped high and fast. Shifting her personal gravity with a subtle working of Magic, she landed on the wall and set off again. Plaster and stone exploded all around her as she ran towards the Nomad on the left-hand stairwell. The man wore beige trousers, an open black shirt showing off his chest hair and chewed on a cigar as he gritted his teeth and fired his weapon.

"Come to daddy, you bitch. I'm gonna show you how we do things here in Columbia," he raged, but Amanda ignored it.

She leapt from the wall. Bullets, both Magical and not, slammed into her Aegis. Spinning and kicking him across the face, he fell back against the bannister. She lashed out again, kicking the gun from his hands. His Aegis sparked at being hit but held firm.

The gunfire from the guards and Magus faltered as she got in close to the Nomad. She noticed the guards begin to move, attempting to get another angle on her.

Amanda swung for him again, but with a cruel grin on his face, the Nomad blocked it, their Aegises flaring as they fought. She backhanded him with her other fist, wiping the smile from his face and sending the cigar flying from his moustached mouth.

Moving too quick for him, she punched him in his gut, releasing a powerful Essentia strike that pummelled his Aegis. The Magical shield faltered but held, barely. She used the same hand to grab his neck, their Aegises flaring wildly as she then jumped up the stairs to the balcony at the top, carrying him with her.

She landed with her knee on his chest as his Aegis finally disintegrated and his ribs cracked audibly.

A movement to her right caught her attention as the other Nomad approached. She was a swarthy young woman with long dark hair, skin-tight jeans, heels, and an over-bust corset. She reached the top of the stairs and fired, scattering bullets at Amanda.

Amanda flipped from the downed Nomad, somersaulting and cartwheeling around in an arc like an Olympic gymnast, only faster, before boosting from the floor in front of her attacker. Amanda's boot connected with the woman's jaw as she leapt up. Essentia hammered the Nomad's Aegis as the pair flew up over the balcony. Amanda lashed out with her Magic. She hit the falling Nomad with a kinetic blast that slammed her to the floor below and ripped her Aegis apart.

Amanda landed next to her with a final punch that broke several bones in the Nomad's skull.

The small squad of guards had split up ascending both flights of stairs to help their employers. They stopped and looked down at Amanda, many of them looking at her with a mixture of fear and awe.

Some of them opened fire, others backed off.

Standing up, ignoring the gunfire directed at her, she sent out a wave of neuro-disruptive Magic and knocked the Riven guards out cold.

The gunfire stopped, and a silence fell over the house as Amanda caught her breath, the rise and fall of her chest slowing.

Looking down at the broken woman at her feet, she kicked her in anger and frustration. Amanda then brushed off some dust from her skirt and noticed a couple of ladders in her black tights. Deciding there was nothing for it, she sighed and headed deeper into the house, towards the east wing and the Aegis that protected it.

The next couple of rooms were devoid of people but well-appointed with expensive-looking furniture and decorative ornaments. The spoils of war, perhaps?

She emerged into a corridor that led to a large wooden door and the edge of the Aegis she'd been working to break through since she'd arrived. The Aegis looked weak from her constant attacks. Summoning all her strength, Amanda released a final spike of Essentia at the Aegis. The whole thing faltered and then failed, dissipating back into the surrounding ambient Essentia as she approached the door.

Catching her breath, she placed her senses beyond the door, seeing a dusky room with just a couple of tiny windows high up on the walls. The paint was peeling, the few chairs and tables were worn and heavily used, and there were clear signs of a struggle with debris scattered across the floor.

The sole occupant of the room was a young, powerfully-built woman who sat in a large, heavy-duty cage. Her legs were tucked in tight to her body, her head down, and her jaw-length black hair was a greasy mess. She wore rags and her skin showcased multiple bruises.

Amanda frowned, wondering if she was seeing things. This all felt very odd.

Beyond the cage, another door led deeper into the east wing, and with the first Aegis down, she could now see a second Aegis shielding everything beyond it. Amanda sighed. They were playing games with her, and she got the distinct feeling that when she walked through that door she would be walking into a trap.

Using her Magical vision, she looked at the caged woman again and realized she was a Scion. This just got better by the minute.

There was nothing else for it, though. She had to go through the second Aegis to find Liz, so she turned the handle and opened the door, walking into the room beyond.

She paused again and cancelled her second set of senses. A musky, unpleasant smell hung in the air, a mixture of rotting food and wet dog that made Amanda curl up her nose. Looking over at the cage, the young woman had lifted her head and was staring intently her.

Glancing around the silent room, she noted the knives, whips, and other strange implements of torture on a nearby table. Looking at the woman again, Amanda could see the signs of torture in the scarring on her arms and legs.

Amanda walked carefully over to the cage and crouched down next to it.

"Hey, how are ye? I'm Amanda and I'd like to help," she said softly.

The woman just looked at her, her eyes wide with a mix of fear and confusion.

"Okay, so, I'm gonna let you out, you're free to go, so ye are. Do ye understand? I'm setting ye free."

The girl just narrowed her eyes at Amanda. Amanda didn't want to use her Magic on her. As a Scion, the girl would recognise it and might not take kindly to it.

The lock to this cage consisted of three large metal bars that were levered into holes in the door by a simple mechanical control about six feet away from the cage, which itself had a padlock on it. Amanda used her Magic to dissolve the padlock, and then moved the lever to the open position. The bolts withdrew from the door with a loud metallic groan.

Amanda looked over at the girl. She hadn't moved and looked as wary as before.

"You're free now," Amanda said, but the girl remained still.

Amanda walked over to the cage and pulled the latch open. With that, the door inched open by itself and swung wide.

Amanda smiled at the girl and gestured that she could leave.

"There ye go, you're free."

The girl looked around and then back at Amanda.

Over the last couple of years, Amanda had used her Magic to enhance her body, which meant she could move faster and was stronger, with better reactions and abilities than almost any Riven human. But when the girl moved, her speed caught Amanda utterly off guard. She leapt from the cage, slamming into Amanda and knocking her back several feet before landing on top of her. Their Aegises flared as they came into contact, rippling with light and energy.

Amanda caught both of the girl's wrists in her hands and watched as the nails on those hands grew into claws at least an inch long. The girl made a guttural roaring sound at Amanda, her mouth filling with huge dog-like teeth that grew from her existing ones. Spit and drool dribbled from her gaping maw as the girl's body grew in size and hair sprouted all over her skin. Her already muscled arms and torso expanded, as her wrists did the same in Amanda's hands.

"Aaah, shite," Amanda grunted to herself.

Amanda used her Magic as a third hand and used it to push the girl's head back, keeping those wicked-looking teeth from biting her. The Aegises of both women fought against each other, preventing them from truly touching each other for the moment, but Amanda knew if they continued to fight, that might change. Amanda used all her strength to push against the raw power of the girl. She'd maybe doubled in body mass while her nose and mouth distended and became more dog, or wolf-like.

A loud bang sounded to Amanda's left. She turned her head just in time to see three men enter the room. Two of them wore all black special forces style clothing with balaclavas, while the third and last through the door, wore light coloured slacks and a shirt. He had swarthy skin and dark hair, tied back in a ponytail, and Amanda immediately noticed his strong connection to Essentia, meaning she faced another Magus. The men wasted no time, the two guards opened fire on Amanda and the Scion the moment they saw them, peppering them with Essentia-infused bullets.

The girl took a good share of the initial opening salvo, the slugs hitting home and slamming into her body while their Magical energy started to overload her Aegis. The few that hit Amanda bounced off her kinetic shield, but not before damaging her own Aegis as well. The girl immediately leapt off of Amanda and withdrew into a cowering ball on the far side of the room.

"Whoa, feckin' hell!" Amanda exclaimed in shock as she braced herself against the attack, and rolled away from it.

The guards concentrated on Amanda, ignoring the werewolf. They sprayed her with gunfire that hissed and popped off her

Magical shields. The bullets slammed into the concrete walls and kicked up dust all about her.

At the same moment, the Nomad called on his Magic, and a huge kinetic blast slammed Amanda into the floor, winding her as it forced the air from her lungs. The tile beneath her cracked like a spider web from the force. Her Aegis held, though, keeping the worst of the attack from hurting her.

At the same time, he released a powerful blast of Essentia at her, trying to overload her Aegis and open her up to further attack.

Amanda rolled onto her front and picked herself up, moving away from her attackers. Using two of her minds, she pulled Essentia into her Aegis to bolster her protections. She gritted her teeth and lashed out with her Magic, attempting to crush the guns the guards were using. The Nomad must have seen it coming though and used his own Magic to block hers.

Amanda grunted in frustration. Her red hair fell about her face in a hellish mess, her dusty, dirty, and ripped clothes looking little better than rags now.

The Nomad blasted her with a Kinetic Ram. Amanda leaned into it, her feet skidding over the dusty floor as they lost their grip. She dropped and put a hand to the tiles to keep from falling over. But her shield held, flaring with energy briefly as it washed over her with minimal pain.

Amanda jumped forward as the two guards advanced on her.

They dropped their weapons, which swung on their straps to their hips as they moved to defend themselves in hand to hand.

Amanda lashed out at the man on her left. He parried her attacks, his wrist guards releasing small Essentia blasts into Amanda's Aegis as the other guard rushed in.

Amanda held her own against both of these highly trained men, fending them off. Momentarily distracted, she missed the concentrated hammer of Essentia that struck her from the Nomad. Her Aegis held, but only just.

The metal cage Magically flew across the room. It smashed into Amanda and the guards sending her crashing into the furniture behind her. The world tumbled around her, crushing her under the debris of wood and metal, until she came to a stop covered by the remains of the attack. What the bloody hell had just happened?

She lay in darkness, battered and bruised. Her Aegis flickered, failing under the pressure of the chairs and tables she was buried under.

A hundred things seemed to press, crush, or stab into her and her right arm felt decidedly wrong. She dare not move it, fearing that the numbness would fade and be replaced with even more pain.

Magic flared close by. A loud crashing of wood and metal followed as the debris shifted and dim light streamed into her field of view.

The majority of the stuff that had been on top of her was thrown off in one magical feat of strength. Now Amanda could make out the figure of the Nomad standing over her.

"Well now, Amanda, seems like your little crusade didn't quite go according to plan. Shame, I thought you would be more of a challenge than this."

Amanda spat blood from her mouth.

"Funny fecker, aye?" Amanda choked and coughed. Talking hurt, but if she could keep him talking, maybe she could turn this around. "What's your name?"

"Heh. Sure, why not? You can call me Joaquin, and I can tell you something else. I'm gonna enjoy this," he gloated.

Amanda's mind swam with pain. She struggled to bring her thoughts together in a coherent way to make some Magic. She shut her eyes and tried to get a hold of herself before this psycho ended her for good.

"Enjoy it? Enjoy what?" Amanda asked, attempting to keep him occupied.

The killing blow never came, though. Instead, Joaquin disappeared from view as Amanda heard what sounded like a very angry and very large dog growling, snarling, and barking mixed with the sound of several heavy thuds.

"Oh, sounds like ye might be busy," Amanda joked, using the time the werewolf had bought her to concentrate.

As the seconds passed, she pulled her thoughts together, finally getting control of herself. Quickly, she restarted her Multitasking effect, setting one mind to healing her broken body.

Her right arm had been crushed and broken in several places. Cuts and bruises called for her attention too. But with a powerful wash of Essentia through her body, the bruises faded, the cuts closed, and with some stomach-churning sounds, her bones knitted back together and popped back into place.

With a grunt, she pushed herself up and conjured a new Aegis. Opening her eyes and feeling much better, she surveyed the room. A little way off to her left, the body of Joaquin lay upon the floor, his torso ripped open and crushed while a look of wide-eyed surprise sat frozen upon his face.

The thing responsible stood a short distance away, backlit by the light streaming through the high window beyond. Its huge furry bulk brought back images of Horlack and the alleyway. Suddenly, Amanda wasn't a Magus anymore, as the fear and terror of that night flooded back. She saw it attack and kill Stuart and loom over her. She hadn't known of Scions or Magi or Magic back then. She'd just been a girl trying to make her way on the streets of New York.

She shuffled back in fear of the half-human, half-wolf thing that towered over her.

"No, no. Not again. Please…" Amanda stammered.

It shrank then, shifting form and changing back into the dark-haired girl that Amanda had found in the cage. She stepped forward, her face moving into a shaft of light, allowing Amanda to see the smile on her face as she offered Amanda a hand.

The images of Horlack faded, and Amanda remembered where she was.

"Here, let me help you up," the girl said in an American accent.

Amanda hesitated for a moment and then took the girl's hand, allowing her to pull her off the pile of debris and back to her feet. She had a surprising amount of strength.

"I'm Celest," the girl introduced herself.

"Amanda," she replied shaking the hand she already held.

"Sorry for attacking you, I... I had no idea who you were or what you were going to do to me."

"Not a bother. I'm just grateful ye came to my aid when ye did," she said, looking down at the remains of Joaquin. "That could have ended much worse for me."

"What are you doing here?"

"The Nomads who use this place kidnapped my friend," Amanda explained.

"They bring people here all the time. If she's here, she'll be through that door," Celest indicated the open door that Joaquin had burst through moments ago.

"Thank you, Celest, ye've done more than enough for me."

Celest raised her eyebrows. "You think I'm going to run and leave you here?"

"Well..."

"I'm coming with you. These men have held me captive and tortured me for weeks. I want revenge."

Amanda looked at the heavily-muscled girl standing before her. She stood a good half foot taller than Amanda, making her an imposing opponent even before she shifted forms. Amanda could clearly see there was no point in arguing, and frankly, after that last attack, she'd be grateful for the help. Celest's clothing had been reduced to little more than rags, though, and did nothing to cover her up.

"Then, may I suggest..." Amanda said as she walked to a table, hovered her hand over the top of it where a pile of clothes appeared.

Celest walked over and smiled. She looked at Amanda and pulled her in for a powerful hug.

"Thank you," she said as she pulled off the dirty rags and quickly got dressed in the newly-created clothes that fit her perfectly. "You could do with a wardrobe change yourself, though."

Amanda glanced down at the remains of her skirt and top and shrugged. "All in good time."

Moments later, the pair approached the door that led deeper into the east wing. The Aegis remained in effect, but the open door created a way—a portal—through the Aegis.

Beyond, they found a long corridor lined with heavy metal doors on either side, each with a barred window set into it. Amanda looked through the first one, finding a small room with a single bed, a toilet, and a washbasin. They were cells. This one was empty, but Amanda wasted no time walking up the corridor, looking in each one. She only walked three doors up before she found one that was occupied. A young woman in her mid-to-late teens lay on the bed inside. She wore only a dirty vest and underwear, and her left wrist was chained to the wall. She could see marks on her arm where they'd injected her with drugs, the effects of which were etched on her face.

"Jaysus," Amanda gasped. With a swift use of Magical force and enhanced strength, she pulled the door from its frame and stepped into the room, crouching next to the girl. "We have to get her out of here," Amanda said.

She'd never seen anyone treated like this before and it made her sick to her stomach. If this was how Lucian ran his business, it became just one more reason to shut him down. This girl needed their help. She pulled the chain from the wall and went to lift the girl from the bed.

"Amanda."

"Yes?" Amanda answered, looking up.

"We should sweep the rest of the building. Take care of any of Joaquin's men who are left. The prisoners are safe here. We need to finish the job first."

Amanda deflated slightly, took a breath, and nodded.

"You're right, let's finish this." Amanda looked back at the girl on the bed and took her hand in her own. "We'll be back, I promise." Amanda stood up, and concentrating, she sent out her senses and counted maybe half a dozen more girls along this corridor. Stairs halfway along led upstairs. The room they led to sat empty, with only a few bits of furniture scattered about the bare floorboards.

Another door up there stood closed, with another Aegis surrounding the room it led to, blocking her magical sight.

"Upstairs, there's another room that's shielded from me," Amanda said as she walked from the cell and along the corridor.

She climbed the stairs and soon caught up with her senses, which she cancelled as she reached the closed door.

Wasting no time, Amanda used her Magic to blast the weak and hastily erected Aegis with Essentia. It fell in a matter of seconds.

Amanda stepped forward and kicked the door. The lock broke as the door swung open and slammed into the wall revealing the room beyond. Beds lined each side of the long room, covered in unwashed sheets. On each bed there were anywhere from one to four children chained to the metal frames, their eyes wide with fear.

The feeling of horror and sickness that washed over her nearly dropped her to her knees.

Young women were one thing, but kids? Amanda could barely process what she was seeing. Some of the children looked as young as three or four years old.

"Amanda," yelped a voice from the back of the room.

Amanda looked up and saw Liz. She sat on a chair, her hands tied behind her back, and her face awash with relief.

Amanda's eyes flicked to a man standing beside Liz just as he lashed out and punched Liz hard across the face. Amanda took a step forward as anger flooded her body.

But Liz, her head bowed to her side from the hit, spat blood on the floor and looked back up, defiant and strong. Amanda felt proud of her apprentice's grit and determination. She might be a captive, but she clearly wasn't going to be a victim.

The man stared at Amanda, his stance ready for her to make the first move. He had black, slicked-back hair, pale skin, and dark eyes. He wore all-black, apart from the priestly white dog collar he wore around his neck. He held a young boy of maybe five or six years old in front of him by the neck.

Amanda could see from the Essentia he had stored within his lifeless body that he was a Vampire.

"Amanda, I presume?" he asked. "It's a pleasure to meet you, your apprentice has told me so much about you, not least of which that you were coming to save her and kill me," he said with a smirk.

Amanda smiled and worked a bit of Magic, creating and then strengthening an Aegis around the room. This Scion would not be leaving here. Not today.

"Maybe," Amanda answered.

"I take it from the presence of Celest, that you have dealt with Joaquin? Shame, I did so enjoy my little visits here." He crouched down next to the boy, placed his right hand on Liz's leg and caressed her inner thigh while pulling the boy's face close to his and licking it.

Amanda moved a step closer, adrenalin pumping hard through her body. She wanted nothing more than to pummel this pervert into a bloody mess. The moment she moved though, the man gripped the boy's neck tighter as claws extended from his fingers, biting into the boy's neck and Liz's flesh where he held her bare leg.

"Ah-ah-ah. Careful ladies, you wouldn't want me to break these precious things, would you?"

Amanda stepped back and took a breath.

"You're right," Amanda answered, "I wouldn't."

Amanda worked her Magic, making use of the Multitasking effect to Port Liz and the boy across the room. They appeared to Amanda's right with a snap. Simultaneously, she Ported herself directly in front of the vampire and smashed her fist into his face. Essentia flared, and the Vampire hit the floor, his face a bloody mess.

"Hi there," Amanda said brightly as she stepped forward, relishing this moment of revenge. "Ye were saying?"

The man moved quickly, springing to his feet. His body started to shift, growing and bulking out very quickly. Not wanting to fight fairly, Amanda called on her Magic and threw him up against the far wall. His Aegis sparked as he smashed into the plaster.

Amanda focused, holding him against the wall, while her Magic tore at his Aegis.

The kids on the beds were screaming and pulling on their restraints. Amanda could hear Liz and Celest trying to calm them down and break the chains that held them in place.

The man had shifted into a half-man half-wolf form, similar to Celest, only smaller. Amanda had heard the legends of Vampires able to shift into Wolves and such—she'd seen the films of it, too—but seeing it in real life turned out to be a great deal more unsettling, even with the knowledge of Magic.

As the man struggled in vain against her Magical grip, his Aegis finally gave way, popping like a bubble.

Amanda pulled on the Essentia inside him, ripping it out from him. A few seconds later, as the energy that fuelled his shift seeped away, his body shifted back to human.

Amanda moved closer, lowering him to the floor.

"Go on, do it. I don't care. Kill me, torture me, I want you to," he hissed.

She didn't speak to him, she couldn't. She couldn't listen to him, either. She blocked it out. That would humanise him, and she didn't want to have any sympathy for this thing. Scion or not, anyone that did this to kids gave up their right to life.

Instead, she hit him as hard as she could. Then she hit him again, and again, taking out her anger and frustration and horror at the things these people did. She didn't count how many times she punched him, but he wasn't making coherent sentences anymore, and his face had been reduced to a bloody pulp.

Amanda let his limp, but still living body drop to the floor and she stepped back. Her fist was grazed and covered in his blood. It hurt too.

"Hey," said Celest, who had somehow managed to walk right up to her without Amanda noticing. "Liz could do with your help. There's a lot of children here."

Amanda looked up. She'd heard what Celest had said, but for a moment it didn't register. Now, with her reverie broken, she looked back at Liz and the kids. Most of them stared at her, their eyes wide, their mouths agape at the violence she'd displayed.

Even though she couldn't think of anyone more deserving than this paedophile, and despite the horrors that these children had faced, seeing them looking at her like that made her feel ashamed.

By beating this man half to death, had she lowered herself to the Nomad's standards? She wanted to save these kids, she needed them to trust her and feel safe while she got them to safety. Being covered in blood would not help that.

She'd done enough. She'd spent her anger. She'd found the payback she'd wanted. Now, she needed to do some good.

Amanda looked back to Celest.

"Sure, I can help. Will you... take out the trash?" She gestured at the bloodied Scion.

"Oh, don't worry, I'll take care of him," Celest said. "You just worry about the kids and the girls downstairs. Get them out of here."

Amanda nodded. "Will I see ye again sometime?"

"Maybe," answered Celest.

"Well, if you're ever in the New York area, stop by," Amanda said, offering her hand.

Celest shook it. "I will."

Amanda and Liz made short work of freeing the children and quickly took them out of the room before Celest shifted form to take her own revenge.

- Columbian News Report.

It seems that a rival gang raided a house on the outskirts of Medellin last night, killing one of the cartel bosses and freeing more than twenty children and teenagers, effectively ending one of the most shocking cases of human trafficking law enforcement has ever seen.

Some local Good Samaritans found the children out on the streets and dropped them off at the local police station.

Pit Fight

New York

Amanda stood in her living room in front of the fireplace, facing her friends. She'd gathered them together this morning after her busy night in Columbia and a few hours' sleep upon her return. Getting a shower after the events in Columbia had been bliss, and she felt much more at home now that she was clean and in comfortable clothing.

"…and that brings us to this morning," Amanda finished bringing them up-to-speed. "As you can see, we've had a fairly eventful few weeks with Lucian and his coven."

"Are you crazy? You could have gotten yourself killed going down there alone," Yoh admonished her.

Amanda acknowledged the comment, giving him a nod and pursing her lips for a moment. Yoh spoke the truth, but the mission had been a success.

"That's great, Mandy, that's a job well done," said Xain from where he sat next to Orion.

"Thank you. I did what needed doing. Not least of which because I needed to bring Liz back, but also because I now understand the depths of depravity that Lucian has sunk to. I always knew the Nomads were bad news, but these ones, they need to be stopped. It has gone on long enough and if we don't take a stand now, who knows how many more lives they'll ruin."

"That's all fine, Amanda, and I agree with you that he needs to be stopped, but the American Arcadians have tried time and again to do just that, and every time they've tried, they've failed," Yoh challenged her.

"And *why* have they failed?" Amanda asked.

Yoh twisted to speak more to the group than to just Amanda, apparently taking it as an opportunity to get everyone up to speed. He probably hoped to get them on his side too.

"Lucian is part of a larger network of Nomads. His ultimate master is Nymira, also known as the Voodoo Queen. She controls much of Central America and the Islands there. Haiti and Jamaica, etc. Nymira has her own coven and she directly sponsors several more. Beyond those, numerous Nomad covens reside in the area and swear loyalty to her. Lucian's coven is one of the sponsored ones and is probably the most remote one that Nymira has her claws into. Whenever we've tried to take out Lucian, he simply calls in Nymira and the other covens who come to their aid. Within moments of us attacking, we're swarmed with Nomads who don't care about innocent lives."

"I agree, we cannot fight the full might of Nymira's army," Amanda said. "But we won't."

"And what makes you think that?" Yoh asked.

"Look. Everything you've told me since arriving about how he deals with Arcadians has suggested that he's always been ruthless. He kills them quickly the first chance he gets, right?"

"That's right," Yoh answered.

"So, why not me? He's had plenty of chances. I've even tried to provoke him…"

"Heh, Badass Red," Xain commented.

"…but he won't do it, he won't hurt me. Why?" Amanda finished, ignoring Xain's comment.

"Yasmin," said Gentle Water calmly.

"What?" Liz asked.

"Yasmin?" asked Yoh.

"That's right, and yes, I do mean *that* Yasmin. She visited here yesterday; she told us where to find you," Amanda said, looking at Liz. "She as good as validated my suspicions that she was stopping Lucian from hurting me. Gentle Water will confirm it, he was here with me."

Gentle Water nodded.

"But, why would she do that?" Yoh asked.

"That's a good question, and I honestly don't know. But I think it gives us an unprecedented opportunity, so it does," Amanda said.

"Because he won't call for back up," Xain extrapolated.

"Why wouldn't he?" Yoh asked.

"Because he's beholden to Yasmin and he can't tell Nymira that, or she'd kill him."

"So, he doesn't have backup?" Yoh said, the idea taking root it seemed.

"That's right. He'll be forced to deal with us on his own, for the first time ever as coven master here in New York. Which means he's vulnerable."

"Are you sure?" Yoh said.

"I'm as sure as I can be, but ultimately, there's only one way to *really* be sure."

"We're in," said Xain, jumping in. Orion nodded next to him.

Amanda smiled. She liked their enthusiasm.

"Thank you," she said. "Our target is The Pit Club, his base of operations, and using a contact I have I can get us into the club by a back door. We'll be able to bypass his Aegis and take him by surprise."

"Unless it's a trap," Yoh suggested.

"Unless it's a trap," Amanda conceded. "Yasmin is a Nomad, after all, and we all know how much they lie. But I'm going. After seeing what was happening in Columbia, seeing all of those innocent lives being ruined by their depravity, to me, the risk is worth it. I can't guarantee your safety, but I am asking for your help. You don't have to come. I know the risks involved, this will be a dangerous mission, so please, think carefully about your answer. Who's with me?"

Orion and Xain raised their hands, to which Amanda nodded, acknowledging them. Yoh sat back and looked at everyone else.

"I will do it," said Gentle Water.

"Thank you."

"Me, too," agreed Raven.

"Count me in," said Liz.

"Are you sure, Liz?" Amanda asked. "With what ye've been through you might want to…"

"No! I'm going. I need to do this," she answered defiantly.

Amanda looked at her for a moment. She seemed unscathed by her kidnapping, in fact, she seemed stronger and more determined than ever before to forge ahead. Amanda felt proud of her. She'd come a long way this past year and a half, and the fact that she wanted to head right back into the lion's den after her kidnapping, spoke volumes.

Amanda smiled at her apprentice.

"Then you're in," she said to Liz.

Maya raised her hand and nodded, to which Amanda smiled before her gaze came to a rest on Yoh. He looked at Amanda, and then around the room at the others. Most of them looked back at him, waiting for his answer.

He sighed and sat forward.

"Okay, I'm in. Let's do this," Yoh said finally.

***

Amanda walked ahead as they passed in single file through one of the city's sanitation systems.

Beneath New York lay a maze of tunnels, sewers, subway lines, and service passageways. People lived down here. A whole community of the forgotten had found a life and even friends in the darkness, which hadn't existed for them above ground. Over the decades, these forgotten people had made their own changes and modifications, adding connecting tunnels, walkways, and more.

In a world where the supernatural existed, this subterranean environment became a natural home. Shaun, as disfigured as he was, probably found a better life down here, away from the revealing light of the sun.

Shaun had given Amanda directions, and they walked along a connecting stretch of the sewer with a makeshift walkway that kept them out of the raw sewage that bobbed along beneath them.

"Had I known we'd be walking through shit, Amanda, I might have had second thoughts about this," Liz said.

"Well, fair play to ye. But I had no idea that the directions would lead through here, either."

The tunnel stank, nearly making Amanda retch. She'd already heard a couple of the others almost bringing up their breakfast.

Moments later, they stepped through a hole in a brick wall and dropped down into a pipe that looked like a sunken service tunnel. Amanda walked along it with everyone following behind her until they came to an iron door. She examined at it for a moment, and eventually found the small distinguishing mark that Shaun had told her about.

"This is it," she called out. She knocked a few times and waited. Nearly a minute later, the sound of heavy metal bolts sliding from their locks could be heard as someone on the other side unlocked the door. It swung wide, and from the shadows, Shaun's face appeared.

"Top of the mornin' to ye, what's the craic?" Amanda said, emphasising her Irish accent.

"You brought your mates, I see," Shaun commented.

"Of course, it wouldn't be a party without them," Amanda joked.

"I suppose not. You'd better come in."

Shaun led them through another dark passageway, filled with junk piled up on both sides, before they stepped through another doorway into Shaun's disused-subway platform home. Although dirty and dark, they did seem to keep the place as clean as realistically possible. There were still a few piles of junk here and there, but it certainly seemed liveable. The lack of fresh air and sunlight didn't agree with Amanda, though. She felt she would probably go a bit stir-crazy living somewhere without windows, but Shaun and his assistant were apparently happy here. Looking around the room, Amanda noted that there were three beds, not two. Amanda could easily pick out the one that Shaun slept on, and she felt sure she knew which was Vanessa's. But the other one, if she had to guess, looked like a young man's bed, judging by the posters and other items on and around it.

Amanda looked back at Shaun, who had been watching her as she scanned the space.

"There used to be three of us," Shaun said, preempting her question.

Amanda glanced at the vacant bed and then back to Shaun.

"Lucian?" she asked.

Shaun nodded. "He shot him, for no other reason than just being angry at… well, angry at you."

"Me?"

"Your arrival here and Yasmin's ban on him killing you. You've pissed him off," he said.

"Bleedin' hell. I'm sorry for ye loss."

"You want to get into The Pit, then?" Shaun asked ignoring her condolences.

"That would be grand," Amanda said.

"This way, then." Shaun led the way towards another doorway. Vanessa watched them go, eyeing Amanda as she passed.

During the previous forty-five minute walk through the tunnels to reach Shaun's hideout, Amanda and the others had taken the time to fuel their Magical shields and get themselves ready for the fight ahead.

With Shaun taking them through the last stretch of tunnel towards The Pit Club and its underground complex of rooms, Amanda started to feel a bit nervous. Lucian and his coven were going to be the most dangerous group of Magi she'd ever faced. She'd been careless and a little rash during her siege of the mansion in Columbia, and she had nearly paid the price for that when Joaquin surprised her. Luckily, Celest had been there for her when she'd needed it.

Taking her friends with her on this mission had been the obvious choice. Storming in there alone after the events in Columbia would have been foolish, to say the least.

As they turned another corner, passing through another dark corridor, Amanda could now feel the vast and powerful Aegis that surrounded The Pit Club. The huge Magical barrier extended underground, all the way around the subbasement that they were now approaching, and as they traversed this last stretch of tunnel, Amanda could make out a doorway ahead.

Moments later, Shaun stopped in front of it and waited for the group to catch up and pull in close.

"This is it. This is where I leave you," Shaun said. "Beyond this door is The Pit Club. You're on sub-level three of five that serve as the coven's Sepulchre. You'll have to find your own way from here on in. I wish you the best of luck."

"Thank you. You're one in a million. I won't forget this," Amanda said as he unlocked the deadbolts in the door.

"I'll be locking this door. I recommend that you leave through the club above when you're finished." Shaun swung the door open wide. Amanda stood to one side as her friends filed inside. After the last one had passed, Amanda put her hand on his arm.

"Thank you, I mean it," she said.

"I know," he answered returning the smile, before closing the door behind her.

Amanda smiled. He sounded like Han Solo.

She turned to her friends, who waited in the short stretch of corridor. Amanda looked at the closed door behind them and felt that strange feeling of rightness. She knew this was what she had to do.

That didn't stop the nerves, though. She checked her Aegis and her stored Essentia, taking a breath as she did so. She called on her Magic and wove it about her, casting the Multitasking effect on herself, concentrating hard she put as much power into it as she could in order to split her mind into as many parts as she could. She noticed most of the others casting their own Magical effects.

"Let's do this," she said and walked to the front of the group

The door opened easily, and they walked into a dimly lit corridor. Up ahead, they could see doorways and openings branching off into the rest of the club. Coming to a stairwell, they stopped next to it as Amanda looked from the corridor to the stairs and then at her friends.

"Okay, as discussed, we split up into groups. We'll cover more ground that way while still staying relatively safe. Yoh, Maya, you're with me. Gentle Water, Raven, and Liz take the floor below; Orion, Xain, take the floor above. Any questions?" Amanda asked in a hushed tone.

They all shook their heads.

"Then, let's get it done," she said and watched as they broke into their assigned groups.

"Okay, come on," she said to Maya and Yoh, leading them down the corridor.

***

Exiting the stairwell, Liz walked cautiously along the corridor behind Gentle Water and Raven, moving gingerly and trying to stay as quiet as possible. Looking at Raven in his combat trousers and vest, and Gentle Water in his jeans and shirt, she started to regret the baggy jumper she'd chosen to wear this morning. But there wasn't any time for that kind of thinking now as they were inside a Nomad coven house, or what was it Amanda called it? A Sepulchre? Whatever, they were in very hostile territory.

They rounded another corner and snuck along another empty stretch of corridor. So far, they'd found nothing. Which, suited Liz just fine. She felt utterly terrified. Her heart beat like a hammer in her chest as she followed her teammates.

Around another corner, they stopped and listened. There were people up ahead, their voices echoing faintly in the tunnel-like corridor. Liz nervously clenched and unclenched her fists as she followed Gentle Water and Raven, being even more careful than before as they slowly approached a recessed doorway on their left.

Gentle Water stood next to the doorframe, with Raven and Liz close behind. Liz felt the familiar signature of Gentle Water's Magic passing a message to her mind, which she accepted. A moment later, he peeked around the corner and she found she could see what he saw.

It only lasted a second—in that space between two breaths—before he pulled back. In the room beyond the doorway, they'd seen four people sitting on benches around a table.

~They Initiated humans. Their weapons enhanced by Magic,~ Gentle Water told them over the link.

Beyond the youths, there had been another room, and although they couldn't make out what it might be, there had been movement.

~I take these four, you two go to next room. Okay?~ Gentle Water asked in their heads.

They both nodded in agreement. Gentle Water held up three fingers and proceeded to drop one at a time about a second apart. After the last one dropped, he ran into the room. Raven followed, and Liz stuck close to him as he ran in.

She watched Gentle Water sprint ahead and quickly take out the closest of the four men, knocking him out cold with a pedestrian kick to the head.

One down, the rest to go.

Raven drew up short partway through the room and paused as he looked forward, causing Liz to bump into the back of him while her attention remained on Gentle Water.

The collision got her attention, though. She apologised and stepped out from behind Raven, looking through to a much larger room beyond this one.

It was circular from the looks of it, there were cages around the edge of the room, all of them open from what she could see. The central area had a thin covering of straw, mud, and other detritus. In the middle of the room stood a short fat man with a bald head, wearing a rubber apron petting and talking to three huge beasts.

Liz couldn't think of a better term for them than that. They weren't dogs. At least, not any breed she'd ever heard of. These things were huge, nearly as tall as the bald man, their raw exposed skin sprouting patches of fur here and there.

As Gentle Water fought, the noise attracted the man's attention, and he looked up from the beasts and straight at Raven and Liz. His three huge wolf-things did the same and began growling, a low guttural noise that made Liz feel a little weak in the knees.

The man approached them, his three creatures following him as he pulled a large meat cleaver from his belt. Liz used her magical senses and discovered that the creatures were actually Scions. Could you change dogs into Scions? Or were these once humans, maybe? Liz had no idea, but they made her blood run cold, whatever they once were.

Raven strode straight toward the man, both men gathering Essentia and working their Magic as they went. As they neared each other, the man gestured with his hands, and all three Scion dogs took off towards them. One made for Raven, one headed for Gentle Water, and one barrelled ahead, heading straight for Liz.

She backed up a few steps as the slavering, vicious-looking thing bounded at her. For a moment, she considered running. Fighting a human, and fighting a dog-beast with claws and fangs, were two very different things in her mind. But after that brief moment of fear, she noticed how Raven readied himself for the

Scion who approached him. He wasn't running, he was confident.

Liz stopped backing away and dropped into a fighting stance, bending her knees and balling her fists, hoping she wouldn't forget what Amanda had taught her. She watched the thing carefully, looking for clues as to its choice of attack. As it closed the gap, it suddenly leapt through the air, its mouth wide in a roar, its claws splayed and ready for the attack.

Liz dropped and rolled under the creature. It landed beyond where she'd been standing moments before and skidded as it tried to reorient itself to its prey.

Liz crouched with one hand and one knee on the floor. She watched it look round in bewilderment, having lost her for a moment. She could see Gentle Water across the room. His fight looked more like a dance as he subdued his opponents calmly and, from Liz's perspective, easily.

On finding her, the creature stalked Liz, padding forward, its claws clicking on the stone floor as it growled through gritted teeth. Liz moved, rising from her crouch and readying herself for the coming attack. The thing charged at her. This time it stayed close to the floor and slashed with its front paws. Liz dodged the attack, spinning away. But she hadn't been quite quick enough and on its third slash, the creature's claws caught on her jumper and ripped it open. Liz tried to back away, but the woollen fabric stretched from her body to the nearest front paw of the creature as it landed back on all fours. The downward pull as it landed yanked Liz off her feet. She landed hard on her bum and yelped.

The creature turned and looked at her, then noticed the fabric caught on its claw before returning its even hungrier gaze back to Liz.

Panic rose within Liz's chest as she tried to pull the jumper from her body and release herself. Sitting just a couple of meters away, effectively tied to the thing, it suddenly looked much bigger.

She got an arm out, but she couldn't get the damn top over her head. The creature eyed the threads that were caught on its claws and pulled its paw with the wool attached, back as hard as it could. It yanked at her waist, tipping Liz onto her back as she skidded towards the open maw of the thing.

Reacting rather than thinking, she kicked out, her booted foot connecting powerfully with the creature's jaw, which shut hard on its tongue, the end of which dropped off in a spurt of blood.

The creature backed away, whining as it reeled from the kick, its paws scrambling to keep it from falling over.

Liz jumped to her feet and took hold of the stretched length of fabric in both hands, and with a swift pull, she ripped it from the creature's claw.

A second later, the thing regained its balance and turned to Liz, blood pouring from its open mouth.

Liz gulped and backed away. She looked over at Raven, and then Gentle Water, both of them preoccupied with their own fights and in no position to help her.

Taking a breath, she looked back at the thing and made up her mind.

She turned and ran.

Shooting around the doorway, she sprinted back down the corridor the way they'd come, heading towards the stairwell. She glanced back once to see if it was following her. Not that she needed to, the sounds it made were not subtle.

Reaching the stairs, she charged up them. She took several steps at once, concentrating hard on where her feet landed, so she didn't fall and lose her lead.

Halfway up the third flight of stairs, she realised she'd passed the level that Amanda, Maya, and Yoh were on, she slowed for half a second, debating whether to drop back down and find Amanda, but the sound of the creature bounding up the stairs behind her changed her mind. She continued on up to the next floor, where she exited into the corridor and sprinted along it, watching for clues that might lead her to Orion and Xain.

***

Amanda crept along the corridor concentrating on the ebb and flow of Essentia around her, looking for any clue as to Lucian's whereabouts.

They passed through a few passageways, all of them mostly bare and with little character to them. The rooms they saw were all empty and varied in décor and usage, but were not really useful to them.

In the stillness, Amanda started to make out voices, and as she concentrated, she could feel Magical energy ahead.

Stopping, she listened hard. She couldn't make out too much, but it sounded like a group of people. As she listened, she realised she recognised one of them.

"He's here," she said.

"Lucian?" Yoh whispered.

"I believe he's just up ahead. Are you ready?"

Maya nodded.

"Of course," Yoh answered. She noticed he took a breath his body didn't need. Old habits die hard, she supposed.

Amanda turned back to face the direction of the voices.

"You're planning on killing him, right?" Yoh asked.

Amanda sighed. She hadn't thought about it too much, but she knew it might be her only option. She figured she'd cross that bridge when she came to it. Thinking ahead of time that she would kill him sounded too much like the thoughts of a psycho. Premeditated murder wasn't something she'd ever planned on, but she had also seen just what Lucian and his coven were capable of. Letting him live to continue his depravity just didn't sit well with her. She knew she'd be condemning more people, including kids, to death and worse if she did nothing.

She also knew that Yasmin changed things, but only for a limited time. Lucian was vulnerable, now. But who knew how long that would last.

"It's the only way I can see of stopping this," Amanda conceded.

"You have no argument with me there," Yoh agreed. "I just wanted it to be clear."

"So, are we?"

"Crystal," Yoh answered.

Amanda nodded and walked on. Turning another corner she discovered an open set of double doors where the voices were much louder.

Amanda paused for only a second to gather her courage before she walked purposefully towards a fight she didn't know if she would walk away from. The previous meetings with Lucian, and the battle in Columbia last night made Amanda rethink her fear of facing a Nomad like Lucian. The legends that she'd heard before moving to New York and her previous experience with Angel on the train had dinted her confidence. She'd doubted her ability to fight and stand up to the Nomads. She'd built Lucian up in her mind into something not only horrific but also unbeatable, someone who could kill her so easily that she should avoid him as much as possible. But her meeting with Yasmin and her rash actions yesterday at the Mansion had changed her perspective. Now, she felt much more confident in herself and her abilities.

Besides, there wasn't any going back now.

She rounded the corner, walked through the double doors and took in the room.

Huge and well-appointed with sofas and rugs, they'd apparently found the coven's communal area.

Flanked by Yoh and Maya, Amanda quickly picked out Lucian from the ten people who were relaxing on various sofas which edged the room.

Lucian looked up and cocked his head to one side, causing his dreadlocks to shift and a couple of them to fall across his face.

On either side of him sat the tattooed man and the voodoo woman with the strange runic script tattooed onto her face—they were same Magi who had appeared on her doorstep not all that long ago.

The rest were Initiated humans. Two sat near the female Magus, while the rest sat grouped together.

They all stared at Amanda in stunned silence.

"I knew you'd come, mon, sooner or later," Lucian said, breaking the spell. "How's Liz?"

"You're a depraved son of a bitch, so ye are. A poxy little gobshite that has had his way for far too long," she answered.

"I'll take that as 'she doing fine' then, shall I?"

"Take it however ye like," she answered.

"So, you're what? Here to kill me?"

"If that's what it takes," she said.

She noted that a few of the Initiated had stood up and were just waiting for Lucian's order.

She walked down the steps into the sunken room, watching the people before her. At that moment, feint gunfire echoed through the complex. Just a couple of bursts that made everyone pause and listen.

"Friends of yours?" Lucian asked.

"This ends today, Lucian. I've seen what you do, what your organisation does to young girls and children. It has to stop."

"Stop? Ha! It'll never stop, mon. You take me out, another *Qwenga* will take my place."

"Not in New York."

"You think you can take New York from us? Nymira will hunt you down."

"Maybe. But we both know that Yasmin will have her say, don't we?"

Lucian's face darkened at the mention of Yasmin's name.

"Kill them," he said to his men.

She knew she'd pissed him off, but that's exactly what she'd wanted.

The group of five Initiated humans raised their guns and opened fire. The entranceway where Amanda and her friends stood exploded in debris and dust as the bullets ripped the walls apart. They ricocheted off of their force shields, leaving them unharmed. Emptying their clips, the gang dropped their weapons and charged, stepping on and jumping over the furniture, pulling knives and more guns as they came.

With a mental link already open to Yoh and Maya, Amanda sent them a quick thought.

~Deal with them, Lucian's mine.~

~Have at him,~ Yoh replied.

~He's all yours,~ Maya agreed.

"Hey bitch, we gon fuck you up now," one of the gang members shouted at her, a wicked smile on his face. She felt sorry for him, he had no idea what he was getting into.

Waiting a second or two more, until the Initiated were just where she wanted them, Amanda ran forward and jumped. Taking advantage of the high ceiling, she boosted over the top of the approaching group, landing behind them on top of a table a few meters away from Lucian.

Behind her, Yoh and Maya immediately attacked the gang. They moved like lightning, cutting them down with little difficulty. In the distance, gunshots echoed through the complex. Amanda guessed that Orion and Xain were having fun.

Focusing on the small group in front of her, Amanda stood tall. "You and me, Lucian, let's go," Amanda said from her vantage point.

Lucian cocked his head to one side and raised his eyebrows. "Really? You expect a fair fight from me?"

Something about his comment and a facial tick made Amanda glance behind her. One of the two Initiated who'd been with the voodoo woman was sneaking up behind her, knife in hand. Amanda spun and kicked out, landing a solid blow to the side of the woman's face. The blow slammed her head onto a tabletop before she collapsed to the floor. Amanda turned and looked at Lucian with his two Magi allies, and the one remaining Initiated.

The tattooed Magus beside Lucian pulled out two daggers from the back of his belt and took a step towards Amanda.

"And what do I call you?" Amanda asked.

"The name is Raal and I've been looking forward to this."

"I bet ye have, pretty boy," she replied as she raised her hand. With a swift working of Magic, she blasted Raal with a massive lightning bolt.

The blast hit Raal's chest, knocking him off his feet and causing him to drop his daggers as he landed. Electrical energy played over his body as his Aegis did its best to protect him.

The burn on his chest still smoking, Raal rolled with the fall and then leapt back to his feet. Her focus on Raal, Amanda hopped down off the table. She set one of her minds to sending constant Essentia strikes at him to take down his Aegis.

At the same time, she pulled down another blast of electricity from the nearest light fixture and sent that at him, causing him to stumble. She stepped in and threw a punch as he recoiled from the electrical blast. He caught her fist, blocking the attack and spun away. He got in a quick Essentia strike as he moved, punching her in the gut, making her Aegis flicker as it deflected it.

She didn't need this fight. Raal no doubt wanted to prove something to Lucian, but to Amanda, he was little more than a hurdle or cross. The real opponent stood a few meters away, watching. She didn't like being distracted like this. He was playing with her, wearing her down before he stepped in. She held no illusions that Lucian would let this fight play out fairly. She expected him to attack at any moment.

Amanda spun and elbowed Raal in the face. She followed it up with a punch and more attacks against his Aegis while bolstering her own defences as much as she could.

Raal blocked her next strike and delivered his own that hit home, hard.

She sensed the flare of Magical energy from Lucian, and in the next moment, the familiar feel of a Magical attack against her Aegis. She went with the momentum from Raal's punch and gained some distance from him. Standing a couple of meters away from Raal, she refocused all her Magical might to defending against Raal and Lucian's attacks against her Aegis. She flooded her shields with power to keep them from collapsing and leaving her defenceless.

Blood trickled down from her nose and into her mouth. Raal's punch had hit home all right.

"By the end of this, I'll be prettier than you, I think," Raal taunted.

Amanda looked up from under her eyebrows and spat the blood out of her mouth. It hit the floor at her feet as she stood tall.

Amanda didn't answer. She let her body language do the talking as she moved back towards Raal and attacked. He blocked her again and hit a quick one-two into her gut. Her Aegis flared as it strained to resist the attacks. He followed with an uppercut that struck her jaw like a freight train and knocked her to the ground as Lucian blasted her with magical energy. Landing on her side she quickly rolled away. She got her feet beneath her and rose into a crouch, looking up at Raal once more.

She wiped her mouth with her back of her hand and saw the blood smeared along her forearm. That didn't exactly go according to plan, she thought as Raal let out a gloating laugh.

"You're no match for us," Lucian mocked her. "You're going to die here tonight. You know that, right?"

Amanda pressed her lips together in consternation. Was he right? Had she taken on too much this time?

***

Liz sprinted through the corridors, making quick turns this way and that, doing everything she could think of to try and lose the nightmare creature behind her.

She ran past the rooms on either side too fast for her to see inside. She hoped she'd find Xain and Orion, but so far, no such luck. She could hear gunfire, but it bounced around the corridors, making it impossible to tell where it came from.

Instead, she just ran.

A few more turns and she started to think she might have lost the wolf-creature. She slowed and came to a stop at a crossroads, leaning against the wall with her hand, fighting to get her breath.

She listened as best she could, but failed to hear any kind of noise that sounded like that thing. Instead, she could hear talking in a nearby room. It came from an open doorway just a short distance away, and she felt sure she recognised the voice.

Pulling off the remains of her jumper, leaving her in just a vest and leggings, she walked towards the sound and listened some more.

"We need to head downstairs. We need to join the fight," said the voice she thought she knew. Her heart plummeted into the pit of her stomach. It sounded like Jason. The guy she'd met at The Jade Palace and gone on a date with.

Other voices answered him, some in support, some not, but she didn't take much notice of what they were saying, as she walked up to the doorway and looked inside. Jason and four or five others were leaving through another door on the far side of the room, talking as they went. Jason was last, and just before he walked through the doorway, he glanced back.

He paused, staring at her, an expression of surprise, and something else on his face. Guilt, maybe? She couldn't be sure.

He put his head out the doorway and called to his mates. "I'll be along shortly, got something to take care of," he said before turning back to the room.

"Liz…"

"What the hell Jason? You're with Lucian?"

He shrugged. "Well, obviously."

Liz's mind raced as she thought back. She'd gone to meet him, to go on a date, but before she'd even gotten there she'd been jumped on the street and kidnapped. She'd been played. It wasn't just chance that Lucian's people had found her. Jason had lured her out.

"You... You bastard. You did all of this on purpose, didn't you? Where do you get off doing that to me?" she yelled.

"I'll do what I damn well like to you, and you'll fuckin' like it, bitch."

Liz raised her eyebrows in response, not quite expecting that kind of language from him. "Is that right?" she asked.

He sauntered across the room towards her, slowly, without any urgency to his movements. "Babe, you think you're the first dumb blonde I've seduced for the Harbingers? Lucian's contacts need idiots like you for their business. Sure, it was a little different with you being a Magi and all, but you fell for it, just like all the other dumb fucks. You're all the same." He sneered.

Liz backed out into the corridor and Jason followed, a cruel smile twisting his lips. He leant against the doorjamb and crossed his arms, looking all too pleased with himself. She noticed a gun in his hand, and the way his thumb played with the hammer. He probably felt powerful, like he was in control. Liz took a deep breath and pushed her fear away. She needed to take control of the situation, and show him she would not be intimidated.

"I don't think you'll be tricking any other girls with your lies after today, *babe*," she said, mocking his use of the word.

"Is that right?" he replied, mocking her back as he raised his gun.

He moved fast, but Liz reacted quicker kicking the gun from his hand before he could pull the trigger. It fell to the floor and skidded a short distance away. While he stood there bewildered at losing his gun, Liz kicked again and connected with his face this time. He fell back against the doorframe with a grunt, holding his mouth as blood poured from his nose.

Liz stood tall and took a step towards him.

"*Damn* right! I can take you down," she said.

She went in for another punch, but he blocked her with his forearm. He grabbed her hand and twisted, forcing her into a crouch.

"You broke my damn nose," Jason spat. He kicked her in the stomach and let her fall to the floor, releasing her hand. She looked up as she gasped for breath and saw him gingerly touch his nose. He winced and then turned his angry gaze back to her. "Come here," he said, fury making his voice shaky. Grabbing her arm, he hauled her to her feet. Liz gritted her teeth against the pain in her stomach and now her arm.

"I'm going to have some fun with you," he hissed. Liz looked at him through tear-filled eyes and saw something move behind him. The Scion wolf stalked into the corridor and eyed them hungrily. It paused for a moment, its saliva hanging in long, gooey strands to the floor, before it charged at them and leapt.

Liz pulled back, trying to get away, keeping Jason between her and the beast.

The wolf landed on Jason's back and threw him forward with a roar. Liz fell too, pushed to the floor by Jason's grip. She rolled with the momentum and stopped a couple of meters in front of him. Jason was on his stomach, the beast on his back. It sank its enormous teeth into his shoulder while raking his back with its claws.

Jason screamed in agony as he thrashed about in panic, trying in vain to dislodge the wolf.

Shuffling backwards on her bum, Liz's hand knocked against something. She looked down and saw Jason's gun. Picking it up she pointed it at the beast and wondered where to shoot it.

She called on her Magical sight in order to determine where the best place to shoot the thing might be. A few options presented themselves, but the one place that seemed to call to her the most wasn't actually on the creature at all. In the wall, an electrical cable sat very close to a water main. She opened fire. After the third bullet, water started to spray from the pipe. After the fourth it burst, drenching Jason and the wolf.

The Scion flinched away from the water in surprise, nearly releasing Jason, who tried to pull himself free.

But Liz kept firing, altering her aim slightly to hit the electrical cable above it. A few rapid-fire shots later and the broken cable swung free and contacted the water. Thousands of volts shot through the water, shocking Jason and the creature.

Both of them spasmed on the floor and then went still.

Breathing hard, she stared at the pair. She couldn't quite believe what she'd done. She'd beaten them, and she'd survived. She couldn't wait to tell Amanda.

Liz decided it might be best if she kept the gun with her. She really didn't like firearms much, but she could see the appeal for a dangerous mission like this. Even with Magical abilities, sometimes you just needed to blow them away.

Straightening up, she listened for the staccato gunfire and headed toward it.

***

Amanda threw a couple of punches at Raal. She followed this with a swift kick to his ribs, which knocked him sideways. Her Essentia hits flared and sparked in her Aetheric Sight as she fought.

Raal staggered to the side but stayed upright. Brandishing his knife, he attempted to get in quick as Amanda brought her leg back down from the kick.

Amanda saw it coming and caught the attack without too much difficulty.

All the while, her other minds did their best to shore up her Aegis. Lucian and Raal threw more and more Essentia at her. They hammered a spike of Magical energy into her defences in an attempt to break them down. She held them off, much to their apparent frustration.

Feeling comfortable that her Aegis would hold for the time being, she concentrated on the fight. She caught Raal's fist. Using his own strength against him, she twisted him around into a hold with one hand pinned, the other holding his knife to his throat. She forced it closer, making its stored Essentia fizz and pop against Raal's Aegis.

With Raal pinned, she looked up at Lucian. She watched him send the other Magus off to fight Yoh and Maya as he backed off even further.

"I told you, this ends tonight, Lucian," she threatened him.

"Actually, no, it doesn't," Lucian replied as Essentia flared around him. He was Porting away. Energy surged from an unknown source. It washed over Lucian's casting and caused the effect to fizzle and die.

Amanda looked around. Lucian did the same, a look of confusion on his face. Amanda suddenly realised who it might be.

"Seems like someone doesn't want you to leave, Lucian," she said, unable to hold back the grin that spread across her face.

Lucian scowled at Amanda. He backed off a few steps, then turned and ran. He burst through the far doors and disappeared from sight.

"Feck," Amanda cursed to herself. She couldn't lose Lucian now, not after coming this far. With Lucian gone and his attacks on her Aegis no longer worrying her, she quickly refocused. She redirected her Magic and dedicated her three minds to ripping Raal's Aegis apart.

"Give it up, Raal, you're done," she warned him.

"No, you can't…" he grunted.

The extra power she brought to bear overwhelmed Raal's defensive shields in a matter of seconds, and they quickly faded to nothing.

Wasting no time at all, Amanda reached inside his head with her Magic. With a quick working, she knocked Raal unconscious and let his limp body drop to the floor.

"Finally," she gasped as she bolted across the room. She sprinted straight for the same door Lucian went through just seconds before. Crossing the room, she vaulted over a few sofas and managed to glance back at the fight in the doorway. Liz, Xain, and Orion had just arrived to help Yoh and Maya. They could handle the remaining Harbingers between them

Lucian had probably seen Liz and the boys arrive a few seconds ago, which had led to his swift exit.

Using her Aetheric Sight, she followed the trail of disturbed Essentia through the corridors beyond the room. He only had a few second's head start, and this Magic had left a wake of churning Essentia behind him. She passed a larger knot of disturbed energy, noticing the Flux Magic signature it gave off. He'd tried to Port again, but the trail continued on, telling her he'd failed.

Amanda felt sure that was Yasmin's doing.

Pushing on, Amanda ran faster than any athlete could manage, taking corners at speed. She shifted gravity as she needed it and ran along the walls to get around some of the turns.

Ahead, an old metal door stood ajar, and the trail of disturbed Essentia faded from view. Skidding to a stop just before the door, Amanda frowned. Had he gone through the door? She concentrated and worked some Temporal Magic.

Essentia surged as she looked back in time to when Lucian passed through this way. She saw him charge into the corridor, clearly frustrated as he reached the door. He took a breath and worked some kind of Magic. A second later, he faded from view. Then the door opened all by itself.

He was invisible.

Amanda cancelled the Time Magic effect. If he couldn't run or Port away, he was going to hide, it seemed. He'd only come through here maybe ten or twenty seconds ago at most. He didn't have much of a lead, and he now needed to be much more careful and quiet if he wanted to get away from her.

Amanda stepped slowly through the doorway, her Aegis back to full strength. On the other side of the door, Amanda found herself back in the sewers and subterranean passages beneath New York.

A metal staircase descended from the steel mesh platform she stood on. She was inside some kind of wide, brick-lined shaft with rusty pipes snaking down the walls. Her Aetheric Sight penetrated the darkness, revealing everything, but not Lucian. Where was he?

Amanda approached the top of the steep stairs and looked down. Rather than trusting the rusty structure, she vaulted the railing and fell lightly to the floor below, her Magic making her landing gentle and silent.

Passageways led off into the darkness in several directions. Pipes lined the walls with the occasional pump or some other bit of mechanical engineering jutting out into the walkways. Puddles covered the floor as mist and steam hung in the still air.

Amanda noticed eddies in the steam down one passage. She smiled to herself. He was being careful, but not careful enough.

Walking into the tunnel, she rounded a corner and spotted Lucian up ahead. No longer invisible, he was little more than a dark shape in the shadows.

"I should have you arrested for stalking me!" he rumbled to her as Magic flared out of him and slammed into her Aegis.

He wasn't holding anything back. His Magic hit Amanda hard, flaring brightly in her Aetheric Sight as it raked across her Aegis. The attack faded suddenly. She looked up, but Lucian had disappeared again.

She spun around, hunting for him, but couldn't see him. It was a game of cat and mouse, apparently.

Stalking forward, she entered a wider section of tunnel with passages and tunnels leading off from it. She dropped down onto the damp concrete, splashing in a puddle as she landed.

Moments later, she had a strong feeling that someone was near. Magic blasted her Aegis. Amanda yelped.

As if out of thin air, Lucian appeared right beside her and hit her in the kidneys.

She staggered and backed off as she struggled to stay on her feet. Looking up, Lucian was gone again. She cursed. She needed to focus and not get too flustered. Taking a breath, she gathered her thoughts and tried to sense where he might be.

He appeared right beside her.

Lucian's Magic flared, and a kinetic blast slammed into Amanda. She was sent flying and landed awkwardly.

Gunfire rang out in the darkness.

Ignoring the pain, Amanda scrambled to her feet. Looking up to see who'd fired, she spotted Shaun in a side tunnel holding a smoking gun.

"Shaun?"

"In the flesh," he answered.

Just a few feet away, Lucian dropped to one knee, his Aegis fizzling from the Essentia rounds Shaun had used.

"Thanks," she said, looking back at Shaun. Behind him, a bloodied Raal stumbled into view.

"Shaun, move!" Amanda yelled.

Raal grabbed Shaun's wrist, disarmed him, and threw him out of the tunnel like a rag doll. He landed on the damp stone floor not too far from Amanda with a grunt.

"God damn it," Amanda hissed.

Raal stepped towards Amanda and raised Shaun's gun. Amanda rushed Raal. She caught his gun hand in hers and raised it. Twisting around him, she got him into another hold, his gun pointing up beneath his jaw.

"For what you and your coven did, you deserve much worse than this," she hissed and pulled the trigger.

Blood splattered onto her face as the ear-shattering noise of the gun made her flinch.

She released him from her grip and let Raal fall face down into the sewage and muck at the feet.

Amanda starred at Raal for a moment, waiting for something inside her to change. She waited for the guilt or horror of her actions to surface. Instead, she felt a sense of relief. She'd killed a Nomad, and the world was better off without him.

Beyond Raal's corpse, the scowl on Lucian's face darkened, and she could see his fists balled in rage. He still wore his shades, but she didn't need to see his eyes to recognise the fury inside him. Amanda slowly rose from the slight crouch she'd been in, watching for Lucian's next move.

Magic flared. Invisible energy slammed into her. It launched her violently through the air as if a car had hit her at eighty miles an hour. She flew across the room and hit a makeshift wooden partition, smashing straight through it in a shower of splinters and pain. Her Aegis cushioned the blows. She landed halfway through the next room, tumbling and rolling through dirt and puddles. She came to a stop in a crouch, gasping for breath.

Looking up, the rest of the wooden partition exploded out into the room as Lucian leapt through the flying debris, landing a few meters away.

"It's all been fun and games so far, bitch, but you goin' down now. Let me show you what we do to Arcadian scum like you," he scowled.

Amanda pulled herself up to her feet, a hundred cuts and bruises calling for her attention, but she ignored them. This wasn't over yet.

"Bring it!" Amanda challenged him.

She lowered herself into a ready stance, as she watched Lucian draw a knife from his belt as he walked.

A few feet from her, he went in for the first stab. She closed the gap. Getting in close to him, she used her forearms to block his swings. She knocked his attacks away and countered with strikes of her own. Amanda's Aegis flared with energy as Lucian's Multitasking mind sent attack after Magical attack at her, wearing down her Mystical defences.

Amanda's extra minds worked double-time to bolster her shield and keep Lucian's Magical attacks at bay. He was a skilled Magus, clearly a higher rank than she was, but she was resisting him. She knew her connection to Essentia was a strong one—stronger than most, or so Gentle Water had said.

As she fended off another attack, she wished he'd make a mistake. Something she could take advantage of, giving her the upper hand.

His Essentia strikes faded, and he hit her with another Kinetic Ram. She stumbled back, off-balance for a moment.

She wondered where her friends were. Were they close? Would they find her? She called out through her Mental Link.

~Yoh? Maya? Liz? Anyone? Are you coming?~

There was no answer. She frowned. She hoped that meant they were still inside The Pit Club and its Aegis, and not something worse.

"You're good at this, Amanda, a regular Bruce Lee," Lucian complimented her as he approached, tossing his knife and catching it. "You should consider joining us. We could use you, girl."

"Thanks for the offer, but I'm afraid I have issues with torturing children, so…" she said in disgust.

Lucian punched and slashed at her. In his overconfidence, he let his arm hesitate a moment too long. Amanda saw it. She grabbed it, planted her feet, and twisted it into a lock. Both of their Aegises flared with a rainbow of light in her Aetheric Sight as they came into contact.

Lucian roared in frustration as she twisted some more. Lucian's Essentia surged, and a Kinetic Ram slammed into her chest, sending her flying.

She hit the floor on her back and skidded over the cracked concrete. She could feel several cuts through the shredded back of her top.

For crucial seconds, she laid there winded, fighting for air, until she finally caught her breath and sucked in a lung full.

Lucian turned, his face filled with fury as he healed his arm.

"I have you now," he said. Reaching up he grasped at nothing and then swung his fist down. His Magic surged once more, as another force blast slammed down upon her.

Amanda raised her arm to protect herself. She flooded her shield with energy as the attack stuck home, hitting her and the ground around her.

The old, weak floor couldn't take the punishment though, and gave way in a violent disintegration, taking Amanda and Lucian with it.

There was a sudden feeling of weightlessness until gravity took hold of her and pulled Amanda down. Stone broke apart all around her, pelting her with bits of concrete while dry, bitter particles filled her nose and mouth.

She landed on the pile of rubble that had fallen away beneath her. Jagged edges stabbed into her back, making her wince in pain. She rolled and got to her feet, skidded down the pile of rubble, dodging the occasional falling rock. Reaching the floor, she peered through the dust cloud, wondering where Lucian might be. She didn't want to get caught off guard as she crept through the haze.

She picked her way over the rocks, using her hands for balance, staying as quiet as possible.

She made out movement through the haze ahead and moved towards it. It was Lucian, reaching the floor after climbing down the rubble.

Reaching a more even surface she walked with purpose towards the Nomad, refilling her Aegis as she went.

The dust cloud thinned and Amanda slowed as Lucian watched her approach. Her breath caught in her throat as she saw his face. She'd met Lucian several times now, and every time she'd seen him, he'd been wearing his shades. They were deep black wrap around ones, and she'd taken them for granted, assuming they were just a fashion statement.

But the fall had knocked them off. Seeing his face without them might have been interesting enough on its own, but seeing what they had been hiding changed everything.

Lucian didn't have any eyes.

His sunken eyelids were sewn shut and surrounded by scars. She'd noticed the hint of scarring on his skin around his shades before, but again, hadn't thought much of about it.

This revelation stopped Amanda in her tracks. She stared at him for a moment, re-evaluating everything she thought she knew about him.

So, if he had no eyes, how did he see?

She took a quick step back as Lucian took a step toward her.

"Getting scared, are we?" he taunted, but Amanda didn't listen.

Quickly, she focused on the Essentia around him, and easily found the Magical set of senses that hovered just in front of his face, and crucially, outside his Aegis.

Of course, she thought, he used Magic to see. He didn't need eyes. And now that she thought about it, she'd seen this casting on him each time she'd met him, but had thought nothing of it.

Magi often used additional sets of senses to get a second view on things, look round corners, and more. This ridiculously common effect nearly always went unnoticed it was so commonplace. Seeing things from an alternate viewpoint could be useful, but Amanda had never thought of countering such an effect as it had always seemed inconsequential.

Lucian, however, needed those senses to see. Without them, he would be blind. But he had no need to worry because the commonality of the effect pretty much guaranteed that they were discounted.

Amanda smiled. She could counter the Magic and blind Lucian in less than a second, but she waited. She wanted to do it just as she attacked him, causing the most confusion that she could.

Roaring, she ran straight at him, catching him off guard and landing a punch right on his jaw. As she attacked, she put as much Magical power into disintegrating his Magical senses as she could.

The effect dissolved into nothing instantly.

Amanda saw Lucian's reaction right away. He stiffened in shock and took a few staggering paces back. She had no time to waste. She gave him no quarter and threw everything at him. Essentia strikes, punches, kicks, she even shouted at him, yelling incoherently. Anything to keep him off balance and make the most of his confusion because she felt sure it wouldn't last long.

Lucian's defences were strong. They held up against her attacks as he tried to create his Magical senses again. Amanda saw it form and countered it easily, unravelling his Magic before it went anywhere.

"Aaaagh, fuck off!" he shouted, his Essentia flaring again. A wave of force energy shot out in all directions. The kinetic shockwave hit Amanda and knocked her back, skidding and stumbling away as she went.

Lucian stood tall during the brief lull in her attacks. He pulled Essentia back into him and worked his Magic.

"Clever girl, no one's figured out that I'm blind before today. I respect that. But you should know, I can't let you leave here now."

"No!" Amanda yelled, seeing her chance to beat him slipping through her fingers. His Magic worked again and his senses started to reform, this time, inside his Aegis.

Gunfire rang out. Lucian's Aegis lit up as bullets ripped into it, peppering his Shield with tiny destructive rounds of Essentia.

Amanda looked up and saw Liz holding a gun in both hands as she fired her clip until it clicked empty. Lucian dropped to his knees with a roar, his Aegis faltering.

"Are you alright?" Liz called.

Amanda jumped up and strode towards Lucian.

"I'm fine," she said as she called on her Magic. Essentia lashed out from her, ripping at his Aegis. In the chaos and confusion, he fumbled his Magical Senses effect, leaving him blind once more.

Amanda knew this would be it. This would be her last chance. She pulled out all the stops. She threw everything she had at him, screaming in anger and rage at the monster who kneeled before her.

Tears fell down her cheeks as she blasted him. The surging energy rushed through her body like a hurricane whipping her red hair around her head like one of the mythical Furies borne to life. Magical energy, fire, and lightning flew out of her and slammed into the Nomad, his Aegis flaring black and blue from the attack until it finally fractured and fell with a pulse of blinding light, scattering to the four winds.

Lucian's body fell to the floor as her Essentia blast faded. He scrambled to get back to his feet, but Amanda didn't stop. Catching her breath, she called on her Essentia again, unravelling the other Magical effects he'd cast on himself. In his panic, he tried to resist, to push Amanda's Magic away, but his defences were confused and ineffectual. With one of her Multitasking minds, she delved into his head and took hold of his mind. All resistance stopped, as she took away his control over his Magic.

Amanda stood before the defeated Nomad where he knelt on the floor. He tilted his head back as if looking up at Amanda from his empty eye sockets, his face filled with hate.

She felt elated. Tired, but elated. She'd done it. She'd stopped him. She took a moment to just catch her breath and calm herself down.

She stood about six feet from Lucian with a few more rips in her jeans and her dirty top barely hanging on. Like Amanda, Lucian was covered in dust and dirt and slime, his body scratched and bleeding. He sat in a puddle amongst debris from the roof collapse an air of defeat hanging over him. He looked weak and pitiful. Not the powerful, competent Magus he once was.

"You're powerful," Lucian said. "Very powerful for a Knight. It's a shame you can't see the truth."

"What truth?"

"The truth that all Nomads realise. The knowledge that when the Archons return, only we will survive to rule by their side," he preached.

"Is that right?" she asked rhetorically, rolling her eyes.

"You would have made a sublime Nomad," he continued, ignoring her.

Amanda sighed. "You brought this on yourself, you realise? You had to know it would end this way one day."

"Just get on with it. Death would be a sweet release from your self-righteous whining," he answered, hanging his head. "I go to the dark embrace of my master in dread Tartarus."

Amanda sighed. "Very well, this is for all the lives ye've destroyed." She closed her eyes and pulled on the threads of Magical energy.

Lucian's body appeared to pull itself apart, ripping into shreds and splattering across the floor in front of Amanda.

She opened her eyes, and then looked away. She might have been the one to kill him, but it was still disgusting to look at.

She looked up at Liz who stood above her on the edge of the hole looking down. Xain, Orion, and Shaun had joined her.

"Eww, that's gross," Liz called out before disappearing, the sounds of vomiting coming from somewhere out of sight.

"You okay, Amanda?" Xain said.

Amanda nodded. "I am now." Her Magic flared, and she Ported up to stand beside her friends.

"Are you just going to leave him there like that?" Shaun asked.

Amanda looked down at the crimson stain on the dirty concrete below her.

She thought about it for a moment, before reaching out with her Magic and pulling down another section of floor. The rubble buried his remains, leaving nothing to find.

"That'll do," she said.

Xain raised his eyebrows. "I suppose it will," he said. "Rest in pieces, Lucian," he quipped.

She turned and saw Yoh, Maya, Raven, and Gentle Water all approaching from the tunnels looking a little battle-scarred, but otherwise relatively unharmed.

Amanda looked down at herself. She looked just as bad. She felt tired and really didn't want to be here any longer.

Liz ran over, wiping her mouth, and gave Amanda a hug.

"Are you alright?" Amanda asked her.

"I'm fine. I'm just glad we found you when we did," Liz said.

"I would have been grand, don't worry. It's over now."

Gentle Water walked up to her. "Lucian is finished?"

"Dead," Amanda confirmed with a nod of her head.

"Excellent. Then we done here. I believe we clear this place out."

"We should give it one last sweep before we leave," Xain said. "To be sure. Wouldn't want to leave a Nomad hidden here somewhere."

"Sounds good, let's go," Raven said. He walked over to Amanda and put his hand on her back. "Well done. Another Nomad gone for good."

"No bother," Amanda said and pulled him in for a brief hug.

She looked around for Yoh. He and Maya walked a few paces behind her. She let go of Liz's hand and moved in next to Yoh.

"You okay? You look like you're in shock," Amanda said.

"I'm alright. I just can't believe we did it. I've lived in New York for years and have seen first-hand Arcadians try and take out Lucian before and how badly that went. It just… it doesn't feel real yet. You know?"

"Kinda."

Yoh smiled at her. "You've not lived here as long as I have."

"What doesn't feel real to me is that it was me who killed him, and his lapdog, Raal. That doesn't feel at all real. I feel like there should be some big change in me."

"What you did, you did for all the right reasons, and you have undoubtedly saved lives because of it. There should be no stain on your conscience for this. We're Magi. We don't have a police force, we can't ask the mortal authorities to deal with the Nomads. They're our problem, so it's down to us to deal with them," Yoh said.

"Will the Magi council feel the same way?" she asked.

Gentle Water looked back at her. "I believe so. I feel sure they will be interested in events here. They will contact you, I have no doubt," he said.

"I suppose this changes everything here in New York, then, with Lucian gone," Amanda said.

"That's right," Yoh answered.

"It does," Gentle Water agreed.

"Victoria will want to know what happened as well, I bet," Amanda said.

"And the Legion. I have no idea how they're going to react," Yoh commented.

"Well, I ain't leaving," Amanda said. "This is my home. I'm staying, so I am."

- Mexico

Celest walked along the dusty desert highway. The relatively flat land gave way to mountains in the distance to her left, but Celest continued to walk north.

She carried little with her. Just a backpack with some essentials inside and the clothes she wore. She'd torn the legs off the jeans Amanda had created for her and wore them as shorts now.

She wiped the sweat from her forehead as a car passed by and pulled over a short distance ahead. She hadn't flagged it down, which gave her a moment's pause, but she couldn't smell anything untoward.

She walked to the door, bent down to look in, and saw a woman in her forties. "Can I help you?" Celest asked.

"You out here on your own?" the woman asked.

"Sure am."

"Where you headed?"

"North, into the States. Maybe L.A.," Celest said.

"Jump on in, I'll take you as far as I can. You shouldn't be out here all by your lonesome."

"I can take care of myself, lady," Celest stated.

"I can see that," the woman said, looking at her huge muscled arms. "All the same, jump in. Don't be a martyr."

Celest looked down the road at the journey ahead of her, before opening the door and jumping in, putting her bag into the footwell.

The car revved and wheelspun on the dry dirt before hitting the road and disappearing off north through Mexico.

Taking stock

Greenwich Village, New York

Sitting with her knees crossed and leaning back in her chair, Amanda soaked up the warm sunshine that beat down on her. City life buzzed around her with conversations in half a dozen different languages. People walked this way and that, going about their business, while the cars on the nearby road did the same, sounding their horns occasionally in frustration.

People were going about their day-to-day routines, unaware of the war all around them.

Amanda felt good today, really good. The coffee in her hand felt warm through the porcelain mug, its aroma mixing with others coming from the coffee shop she sat outside of. The smell of freshly ground coffee beans tingled in her nose as she sat enjoying the atmosphere.

The warm weather today had been a welcome surprise after a few days of cooler temperatures, so she'd splashed out and worn a light summer dress with knee-high brown boots.

Sat at the table with her, in a figure-hugging Maxi dress, Maria also took a moment to enjoy the sun. She wore sunglasses with large lenses to complete the sun worshiper look.

Amanda had just finished telling Maria about the assault on Lucian's stronghold. It had been a long story, but Maria has listened intently and asked questions as they went. Amanda felt emotionally drained after reliving the whole thing, so she was glad for a moment of silence to settle her mind.

When she'd moved here, she'd felt a strange mix of her usual optimism that all would work out in the end, but she also had a distinct lack of confidence in her ability to stand up to Lucian. She'd run with the boys on their missions numerous times before her trip, but she'd always followed their lead, and never took on their targets alone. They were their missions, she just happened to tag along.

But New York had been her choice, it had been her dream to move here. She'd brought her friends, and they would always be there for her, but this had been her choice. This had been her thing, her mission, and she didn't want it to fail. So many people had warned her about coming here and they'd all assumed she'd fail. They'd been convinced she'd made a mistake.

Deep down, she knew she was right. She knew this was her path, but *saying* she'd succeed, was very different to actually succeeding. When she'd first come here, she'd tried to hide. She'd heard the stories of Lucian and thought it best to slip under his radar and try to live here quietly and unnoticed.

That hadn't worked of course, and confrontation became inevitable. She'd been lucky though, and as it turned out, she felt reasonably sure she owed her life to a Nomad, of all things.

Thinking back to just before she'd moved here, she knew now that she'd just ignored the threat Lucian posed. She knew that she might have to stand up to him one day, but she hoped it would be somewhere off in the distant future and she'd deal with it then.

As it turned out, it had been the actions of others that had given her the drive and confidence to act, rather than react.

If she'd acted earlier with Lucian, she might have prevented Liz's kidnapping and maybe saved more of the kids in that hellhole in Columbia. If she'd acted earlier in Ireland, she might have prevented Alicia from being possessed. But, it went back further than that.

She remembered that after her Epiphany, when she'd had full use of Magic, she hadn't pursued it. She didn't embrace it or act on it, either which could have meant saving Georgina's life. It had been at that point, that she'd made a promise to herself and to Georgina to live life to the fullest, and now she could add to that, to always act and be proactive.

"So, there wasn't anyone else in Lucian's Sepulchre?" Maria asked.

"Not really. No Magi, anyway. There were a few Initiated mortals who we kicked out and told to leave New York, but that's all, really. We disposed of the Nomad's bodies. Well, Xain and Orion did, and we headed home."

"And the club has remained closed?"

"So far. I think it will get bought by someone one day, but we sealed up the entrances to the Nomad tunnels beneath it. It's far too dangerous for humans to go down there."

"So, how's Alicia now, then?"

Amanda raised her eyebrows at the question. "Well, that's a bit of a mystery," she replied. "When we got home, she'd gone. Disappeared. I have no idea what happened to her I've followed up with the orphanage, but they've not heard from her either. I'll keep looking, but even my Magic hasn't turned up anything."

"Well, I hope you find her."

"Thanks. Me too." Amanda smiled.

"So everything's calmed down now?"

"Pretty much. Gentle Water was right, the council turned out to be very interested in what happened and I even had a visit from one of their representatives. A guy by the name of Trevelyan. English bloke. He seemed nice."

"I know him. He's a friend to the Legacy, which is probably why they sent him."

"Well, he thanked us for what we did, but told us to keep things quiet. They need to see how the Nomads Lucian worked with would react. So far nothing, but maybe they don't know he's gone yet."

"They'll realise something's up pretty soon, and I doubt they'll let it go. Nymira isn't known to be terribly forgiving. Depends on Lucian's standing within the group, though, I suppose. If he wasn't liked, maybe they won't bother you."

"Yeah, well, we'll see. Time will tell, I guess," Amanda agreed.

"How's Liz after all that? She's been through a lot, by the sounds of things."

"I'm so proud of her," Amanda said, smiling as she spoke about her apprentice. "She's been amazing. She seems to have found a strength inside her that I never knew was there. None of this seems to have bothered her at all. She even took out one of the Scion wolves and an Initiated singlehandedly."

"Wow, that's impressive."

"I know. She asked Xain and Orion for some training too. She wants to go on some missions against the Nomads with them."

"Is she up to that?"

I'll let the boys decide on that. I think she needs more Magical training first, but in a few months, maybe."

"Best to leave it to them. Those boys will look after her and make sure she doesn't get in over her head."

"I know. They were invaluable on the raid."

Maria nodded. "On the topic of men, I've got to ask, Mandy, is there anything going on with you and Raven?"

"Ugh," Amanda answered, feeling a little deflated over that whole thing. "No, I think he's seeing someone. I went to speak with him one night and someone, a woman, I think, was in his room with him, and they weren't just having a chat."

"Any idea who?"

"None. I have no idea, and frankly, it's none of my business, really. I'd love to know, given it was in my house, but well, whatever."

"So, no one else then?"

"I had a one-night stand with Yoh," Amanda admitted. It came out before she'd really thought about what she was saying.

"Really? You little rascal."

"It didn't come to anything, though. That was just before he was attacked at the house. He's been distant ever since he changed into a Scion."

"Oh, shame."

"Yeah, well. He seems closer to Maya now."

"Is she nice?" Maria asked.

"I think so. She's a little aloof and doesn't say much, but she's always been friendly to me. I like her, actually. We seem to get on."

"You *like* her?"

"You really do have a one-track mind, Maria," Amanda smiled.

Maria laughed. "Why, I'm offended. I'd never stoop to such a low innuendo."

"Of course, you wouldn't," Amanda replied dryly. "So yeah, I'm signed off from men for a while, I think."

Maria smiled and looked at Amanda with mischievous eyes.

"Don't you get any funny ideas, though," Amanda said.

Maria raised her hands in supplication. "Did I say anything?"

"No."

"No… but if you ever want to try batting for the other team…"

"Jeez, Maria," Amanda said, putting her hand to her face.

Maria laughed. "I'm kidding. You're too easy."

Amanda raised her middle finger.

"Is that an offer?"

Amanda rolled her eyes, and they both laughed. "You're insatiable," Amanda said.

"I've been called worse," Maria mused.

Amanda smiled and admired her friend. Despite her protests, she was more interested in Maria that she let on. She was curious to see what it would be like. Maria was certainly interested in her, that was for sure. This was only the latest in a string of flirtations by her that had been going on for months.

But just because Maria was interested in her, didn't mean it was the right thing to do. Although she was curious, she also knew it would be crossing a line. A line that it was not easy to backtrack over once it had been crossed.

Maria was her friend, one of only a few who she really felt she could open up to, and she really didn't want to lose or jeopardise that. At least for now, anyway.

Tearing her eyes away from the pretty brunette, Amanda drank the last of her coffee and placed the mug back on the table. "Fancy a walk?"

"Sure," Maria answered, draining her own cup before standing and gathering her things. "Where do you want to go?"

"I've no idea. Let's see where this street takes us," Amanda said.

Epilogue 1

Niagara Falls

Kez stood behind Yasmin as they stood upon a rooftop, invisible to mortal eyes and watched.

The dark-haired girl wore all black and moved slowly, as if in a daze before she approached the railing and looked out at the wall of falling water that is Niagara Falls.

"You want me to watch her, my Baal?" Kez asked.

"Not in any great detail, just monitor her. I want to know where she is."

"May I ask who she is?"

"Her name's Alicia. She's a childhood friend of Amanda's."

It all started to make a little more sense to Kez now, as she looked down at the girl again. She hadn't moved from the railing.

"I have some ideas for her. Nothing concrete yet, but she might be useful," Yasmin finished.

"Of course, my Baal. I'll make sure she's watched."

Yasmin turned to Kez, and something approaching a smile crossed her face. She reached up and touched Kez's face gently with her hand "What would I do without you, Kez? Thank you." Yasmin leaned in and kissed Kez gently on her lips.

"It's my pleasure to serve you, my Baal," Kez answered.

Yasmin did smile then. "Good. I'll see you back home."

"Of course," Kez answered and watched as Yasmin disappeared. Kez looked back down at the lost-looking girl. A friend of Amanda's, Kez thought, she wouldn't want to be her when Yasmin put into action whatever plans she had for her.

Epilogue 2

The Vatican

"Come in," Mary called out upon hearing the faint knock on the door. She'd already okayed Augusto to come in, but he always knocked as well, just to be polite.

The door opened and in walked Augusto. One of her most competent knights, he also had a keen mind and a handsome face. He was tall and dressed in a suit with long, mousy hair down to his jawline with a well-kept goatee. He walked across the room, his long legs carrying him quickly to Mary's desk.

"Good morning, Grand Inquisitor," he greeted her.

"Morning, Augusto. What can I do for you today?" she asked, eyeing the folder he held in his hands.

"I have news of a witch you've been after for a while. Amanda. It seems she's turned up in New York."

Mary sat back, taking a keen interest in what Augusto had to say. "Go on."

"We've just found out that New York has been liberated from the control of Lucian, who has been declared dead. No word on who killed him, but it's the usual infighting amongst the witches and warlocks, we think. On looking into it, our source has discovered that Amanda has been living in New York for several months now. We're currently trying to ascertain if she had anything to do with Lucian's death."

"New York? Hmm, well, that fits with what we know about her past from the reports Vito brought in during his investigation."

"It does, and it looks like we were searching in the wrong location."

"Recently, maybe, but I have a folder full of evidence that placed her in Europe working with the Legacy Coven until she disappeared six months ago." Mary pulled out the folder from the filing cabinet behind her and placed it on the desk, a few photos of the young red-haired girl spilling out onto her desktop.

"So, what are your orders, ma'am?"

"Let's get some people in New York right away. Let's find out where she is, and who's with her. Then we can start to plan our next move," she said conspiratorially.

"Very good, ma'am. I'll get right on it."

"Thank you. You may go."

Mary watched Augusto leave, having left the folder on her desk for her to look through. She opened it up and looked at the photo of Amanda clipped to the front page. She pulled it off and held it up, recognising the scarlet haired girl in the image from the past two years of hunting for her. Every time they thought they were getting close, she disappeared again.

She thought back to the investigation she had sent Vito on over two years ago that had him jet-setting to America, Egypt, and Europe after a tip-off from someone who saw a demon in a New York alleyway with a certain redhead. That led to the discovery of a powerful Magical Artifact that Mary wanted to get her hands on, but which slipped through her fingers at the last moment because of Amanda and her friends. She'd lost a loyal and devout Inquisitor that day, and Vito had been tough to replace. She had a couple of capable and trusted Inquisitors now in Augusto and Assunta, but she still missed Vito.

It had served as a timely reminder of just how dangerous the Magi were. They could call themselves whatever they liked, Magi, Arcadian, Nomad, it didn't matter. As far as she was concerned, they were witches and warlocks in league with Satan and a very real threat to mankind.

She had pledged to hunt them down and purge the Earth of their kind, and Amanda was next on that list because she'd made it personal by killing Vito.

Mary placed the photo on the desk, whipped out her knife in a blur of movement, and stabbed the picture, burying the point of the dagger into the oak desktop, right through Amanda's head.

"I'm coming, Amanda."

Author Note

Thank you for reading Magi Rising. This version is the 2019 revised edition.

As one of my earliest novels in publication, the version that had been out there for the past few years was riddled with typos, errors, and clunky writing. I've come a long way as an author since then, and while I no doubt still have a long way to go, I knew I needed to go back to this series and clean it up.

So, that's what I've done, and this new version is much cleaner and easier to read.

One of the big reasons for this is that these novels form the main entry point for my Magi Saga universe and it was clear to me that they needed to be as good as I can make them.

The idea of making this a much bigger world was in part, influenced by two authors, both of whom I have worked for as a Cover Artist.

Michael Anderle and M D Cooper.

Anderle has his Kurtherian Gambit Universe, with the Vampire girl, Bethany Anne.

Cooper has her Aeon 14 Universe with her protagonist, Tanis Richards.

Both worlds start with a small series of books, before expanding out into other, separate series, all set in the same world. Both authors have also taken on collaborators to write in their worlds.

It was also not lost on me that both authors have a badass female main character who's out to save humanity. Which is exactly how you could describe the Magi Saga and Amanda.

Since making that choice, the Magi Saga world has grown, with a couple of side-series to expand the universe. I plan on growing it further down the line too.

So keep an eye out for the other books in the Magi Saga universe.

Other stuff:
I have a Facebook Group which you might like to join here;

www.facebook.com/groups/MagiSagaFans/

Check out my other books on the next page.
Many Thanks,
Andrew

Booklist

For full list of Andrew Dobell's Books, visit his website at;
www.andrewdobellauthor.co.uk/booklist

Printed in Great Britain
by Amazon